EMILY OWEN studied English Language and Literature at the University of Leeds, and completed her Masters by Research in 2018. She works as a copywriter and lives in Wakefield, West Yorkshire.

She self-published her debut novel *The Mechanical Maestro* in 2020, which is the first book in her series following the adventures of the Abernathy family and their clockwork creations.

G000135272

THE
COPPER
CHEVALIER

Emily Owen

SilverWood

Published in 2022 by SilverWood Books

SilverWood Books Ltd
14 Small Street, Bristol, BS1 1DE, United Kingdom
www.silverwoodbooks.co.uk

Copyright © Emily Owen 2022
Map © Mustard Ink Studios (mustardinkstudios.com) 2022

ISBN 978-1-80042-177-6 (paperback)
ISBN 978-1-80042-178-3 (ebook)

British Library Cataloguing in Publication Data
A CIP catalogue record for this book is available from the British Library

Page design and typesetting by SilverWood Books

For Marcus, to whom I'm indebted for his unwavering support and advice

Acknowledgements

I would like to thank the staff at the Bodleian Libraries, and Jasdeep Singh at the National Army Museum, for sharing material from their amazing collections to aid my research and helping me build pictures of places and people lost to time.

I must, of course, mention my proofreaders, who generously gave up their time to read earlier drafts: Teresa, who helped in the 'alpha test', and Lisa, Dave and my mum, Jayne, who volunteered for the 'beta test'.

I'd also like to thank my partner, Marcus, and brother, Nathan for answering my many questions on the technical side of things. Your knowledge of physics, electrics and vintage vehicles was invaluable.

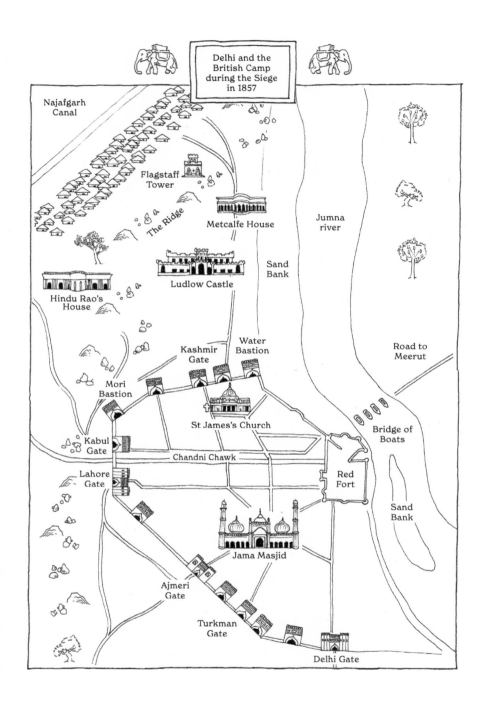

Delhi and the British Camp during the Siege in 1857

Najafgarh Canal

Flagstaff Tower

The Ridge

Metcalfe House

Jumna river

Sand Bank

Ludlow Castle

Hindu Rao's House

Kashmir Gate

Water Bastion

Road to Meerut

Mori Bastion

St James's Church

Kabul Gate

Chandni Chawk

Bridge of Boats

Lahore Gate

Red Fort

Sand Bank

Jama Masjid

Ajmeri Gate

Turkman Gate

Delhi Gate

Flagstaff Tower

A one-room, castellated tower built around 1828. Located at the highest point on the ridge, it formed part of the British cantonment and was used as a signal tower.

Metcalfe House

A mansion located near the Civil Lines, which suffered heavy damage during the siege. The house was built by Sir Thomas Metcalfe, who was the last Resident at the Mughal Court of Emperor Bahadur Shah Zafar II. Metcalfe held the position from 1835 until his death in 1853.

Ludlow Castle

Jokingly named after its original builder, Dr Samuel Ludlow, and its castellated Gothic battlements, the house later became the Residency office for Sir Thomas Metcalfe. Ludlow Castle sustained heavy damage during the siege, but was repaired by 1858.

Hindu Rao's House

A Palladian mansion built around 1820 for William Fraser, agent to the Governor General in Delhi. It was bought by Raja Hindu Rao, a Maratha nobleman, after Fraser's death. During the siege it was occupied by Major Reid and the Simur Battalion of Gurkhas.

St. James's Church

The first church in Delhi, which was built by Anglo-Indian solider Colonel James Skinner CB and consecrated in 1836. Skinner also built a mosque and Hindu temple in the city.

Jama Masjid

Delhi's principal mosque, which was constructed in the 1650s by Mughal emperor Shah Jahān – who also built the Red Fort and Taj Mahal. The mosque is constructed of red sandstone and white marble, and is a magnificent example of Mughal architecture.

That he was going to die was certain. The only question was how. Would the enemy or his own countrymen find him trapped beneath the rubble? Would he starve to death? Or would the stifling heat fry him first? He had given up on crying out for help. Every last drop of moisture had been sucked from his mouth – not that he was a stranger to the Indian heat. Nor was he usually given to morbid thoughts. It was simply that when one was trapped under a fallen building with little better to occupy the mind other than death, one's thoughts tended to gravitate towards such things. And then there was the pain in his left hand. He could move his right hand, but the left was caught underneath something. His fingers felt damp with gritty, sticky sweat. Or blood. He couldn't feel his legs at all, although he was sure they were trapped beneath something too. Perhaps the nerves had been severed. In which case, better to perish in this backwater corner of the world than return home, a source of shame to his family and no fit husband for his beloved.

The distant clamour of musket fire, shouting and screaming still reached him, along with what he fancied was the occasional explosive bang of a field gun. But there came a scuffling along the ground not so far away, like a boot kicking up stones. Somebody was approaching the spot where he was buried. He heard them disturbing the debris above his head – shouting something over and over again. Their words were so muffled that he wasn't entirely sure whether they were in English. They suddenly stopped. The next instant the harsh sunlight flooded him. He could just about prop himself up on his elbows and raise his head, shielding his eyes with his good hand. There was a figure standing before him, a gleaming, golden vision. They were holding the chunk of stone wall that had entombed him above their head – God knows how many tons it must have weighed.

'Private Peterson?' said a familiar, brassy voice. They tossed the stone aside as if it were nothing. 'Do not attempt to move.'

He saw the wink of a steel blade as the figure drew their sword from its scabbard.

'I'm forbidden to kill a human, but you may force me to do something I do not wish to do.'

A flash of silver crossed his vision. He felt the blade strike its target.

Chapter One

Four months earlier

'Are you sure you don't want to keep this?'

George stopped sorting through a pile of books on his bedroom floor and looked up at his brother. Douglas was holding a metal frog with chipped green paint.

'Yes,' he replied flatly.

'But it's one of the first automata we ever built!' Douglas protested. 'And it still works. Look!'

He turned the wind-up key sticking out of the frog's back and balanced the metal creature on his palm. A shiver ran along its body and it suddenly became animated, moving and croaking exactly like a real frog rather than a child's crude wind-up toy (even if they'd been children themselves, no older than five and three, when they'd built it). The frog sprang from his palm and began hopping about the room. George caught it mid-hop.

'I don't share your sentimentality.' He wound the frog down. 'If it serves no useful purpose, I see no need to take it with us.'

'But it's a sign of how far we've progressed since then.'

This was certainly true. George and Douglas Abernathy had once been clock and watchmakers by trade, but now they designed and built machines – primarily what might be termed 'androids' – on commission. In the short time they had been pioneering their new trade, they'd created an array of marvellous contraptions: acrobats and dancers of brass and bronze that were more graceful than any flesh and blood performer, 'mechanimals' of every species (and many mythical creatures), and even an android constructed of precious jewels, with bones of diamond and hair of ruby-red crystals.

The brothers' acclaim had originated from a wager with an eccentric earl, Lord Leyton, to create an android who could compose, as opposed to merely play, music. The resulting android, known as 'The Mechanical Maestro', became an unimaginable success and was the talk of the season. Lord Leyton had caused great upset amongst London's social elite when he had taken the android abroad with him a month ago, but Maestro was learning a great deal about the world as a result. He wrote letters to Douglas regularly.

George let the frog drop carelessly from his grasp onto the bare floorboards. 'What is the use in looking backwards? And it is a waste of space.'

'One mechanical frog is hardly going to take up much room!'

'I agree with Douglas. It's not like there won't be enough space in our new house,' said a female voice nearby.

Their seventeen-year-old sister, Molly, was standing in the doorway. She wore a floral dress, with her toolbelt around her narrow waist, and heavy leather gloves covered her thin forearms. Dainty in stature, although with masses of mousy, wild hair, she was like a wood elf in the guise of a chemist.

'How many floors does Ravenfeld Hall have again?' she asked.

'Three, along with towers, turrets, and stables in the grounds. Plus a chapel,' replied Douglas.

'So what are you worried about? All our possessions combined wouldn't even fill one floor, most likely. And you forgot to mention the surrounding two hundred and fifty acres of land.' She grinned. 'Plenty enough to create my dream garden in.'

'Be that as it may, might I remind you that there is still the matter of transporting all of our possessions to Ravenfeld Hall in the first place?' said George.

'I'm sure the airship can accommodate it all. Look here!' Douglas pulled a square metal device, with many tiny keys on its face, from a pile on the floor. 'It's that mechanical calculator we came up with five years or so ago, remember? We were all set to launch it when Thomas de Colmar's arithmometer pipped us to the post at the last minute. Do we keep this?'

Molly took it from him. 'Well, we've really no use for it. You and George are just as good. Let's test it.' She tapped a sum on the keys. 'What's...fifteen thousand two hundred and sixty divided by five?'

'Three thousand and fifty-two.' Her brothers answered in unison, George perhaps being a fraction of a second quicker. Something inside the machine crunched as the cylinder began to turn. The machine suddenly went *ping* and displayed the answer.

'It agrees with you,' declared Molly.

'Well, are you sure we should get rid of it?' said Douglas. 'After all it—'

But Molly had already tossed it over her shoulder into the scrap pile before he had finished speaking. An automaton with the large mallet then struck it repeatedly.

Douglas winced. 'I think we should be a bit less hasty about discarding some of these things.'

'Well, don't waste too much time deliberating over what to keep and what not to. It doesn't matter a great deal,' Molly sighed as she removed her gloves. 'I'm going to pay one last visit to the Royal Botanical Gardens. Can I take the airship?'

'Yes, but mind you take care with her. We'll need Spuggy to transport the bulk of our possessions when we eventually make the journey to Ravenfeld Hall.'

'Of course. It's not like I've flown her countless times before.'

'And have you started clearing your room?' Douglas called after her as she went.

'*Yes.* I'll finish packing later,' she said, somewhat nettled, before marching downstairs.

'She seems out of sorts today,' remarked Douglas, hearing the back door slam.

'You cannot chastise her for not having packed her things,' said George. 'You are no better, wasting your time showing me useless trinkets you've rediscovered when you could be sorting the rest of your things.'

'Fine. I'll do so now.' Douglas walked back along the second-floor landing. He paused for a moment to glance at the extension their father had built to be his workshop, which was now where they constructed their commissions. Perhaps they should tear it down. Then again, it had lasted twenty-five years, being as old as George was, despite looking as though it had been hastily cobbled together from scrap metal and wood. It might last twenty-five years more yet.

Douglas made his way down to the first floor, where his and Molly's rooms were. He sighed as he looked around his nearly empty room. It somehow seemed smaller rather than larger now he'd boxed most of his possessions. This had been their nursery, the nursemaid having occupied the small room next door, which was now Molly's. The largest bedroom, now George's, had been their parents' domain. Why had their mother so steadfastly refused to take in a lodger after their father died? They could have used the money.

'We are not that poor,' she'd say crisply whenever one of them raised the idea. 'I will not admit strangers into my house.' Most likely this was a consequence of her having been born to a duke and duchess. Their father was the clockmaker hired to fix a family heirloom. He'd fallen in love with the duke's beautiful daughter, whose vanity he flattered with his attention and the jewelled trinkets he made for her. The two lovers ran away together in the dead of night, eventually settling in London, where they remained until their deaths. While the family had never been destitute, it was not so comfortable a life as their mother had imagined it would be. There had been times when they'd struggled, especially after their father died three years ago. But George and Douglas had achieved what their father failed to: they'd made their fortune from their inventions. Then they'd experienced further good fortune. Shortly before their childless uncle, the Duke of Hereford, died, he'd named his estranged sister's elder son as his heir. George inherited the family's ancestral home, Ravenfeld Hall, which a distant cousin had previously wintered at. Their cousin was more than willing to exchange the Hall for the newer ducal estate near Shropshire, after George had renounced the new estate along with the dukedom (he'd agreed with his cousin to not make the Committee of Privileges aware of his existence, and did not challenge his cousin's petition to the House of Lords for the title).

A violent crash from downstairs ended Douglas's musings. George instantly appeared on the landing outside his door.

'It got out of its box again.'

The two of them raced downstairs to the parlour, where several wooden crates were stored, one of which was tipped on its side and spilling straw onto the rug. In the middle of the floor was Sweep, a small android about three feet high with a circular sweeping brush sticking out of the top of his head. He was sitting amongst the straw and tossing handfuls into the air. On seeing the two brothers, he froze. The next instant he skittered in the direction of the chimney, but George was faster. He grabbed the poker and swung it, sending the android sliding across the floor. George flicked a switch on the side of Sweep's head and he instantly became lifeless. Light slid along his glass lens-eyes.

'How does he keep waking himself up? I've never seen any of the other androids do that,' said Douglas.

'I suspect there's a fault with the switch. The slightest movement is all that's needed to cause it to slide into place.'

'Hm, we'll have to address that at some stage.'

'Why do you insist that we keep it? And all of those other rejected models?' George indicated the other crates with the poker.

'Well...' Douglas rubbed the back of his neck as he glanced at the crates and then at Sweep. The truth was he wasn't entirely sure. Sweep had been an experiment to create a mechanical chimney sweep, only he hadn't quite turned out as anticipated. (He would burrow up the chimney and stay there quite happily for hours, refusing to come down.) Usually when one of their androids was faulty, they would dismantle it and reuse the parts for their next commission. But occasionally Douglas would see something, like in this one: a kind of personality, which he couldn't bear to destroy. 'I suppose I have a certain fondness for this one – and them.'

'Utter foolishness. We should bind its limbs, so if it does wake again it won't run amok.'

'Good idea.'

'You find a length of rope. I'll make a pot of coffee.'

'No, I'll see to the coffee. You always make it too strong for me, and I think I'd rather have tea.'

'Suit yourself,' George shrugged before making his way upstairs. Of course, he knew the real reason Douglas had offered to make the coffee instead: he'd wanted to make sure George didn't sneak any spirits into his cup. He'd become even more irate about George's tendency to drink liquor than usual of late, so George had started trying to be more subtle about it. But on this occasion George had no such ideas. He merely wanted to distract his brother so that, while Douglas was otherwise occupied, he could investigate a matter that had caught his attention earlier in the day. As George had made his way downstairs to the kitchen at around eight o'clock that morning, earlier than usual, he had seen his sister snatch up a letter that had arrived in the morning post, tear it open and peruse it on the spot. She'd appeared utterly dejected for a moment and then she'd hastened to her room. She'd been unaware of his presence as he had concealed himself in the parlour.

Molly had left her bedroom door open, which made his task simpler. He didn't normally meddle in his sister's private affairs, but her crestfallen expression when she'd read that letter wouldn't leave his mind. Something wasn't right; Molly wasn't one to react so strongly over a trifle. George trod carefully about his sister's room as his keen eyes scanned its contents. She had packed most of her chemistry apparatus, but a number of plants and pickled specimens in jars remained in the room. Having found nothing beneath the bed, or by the window where her chemistry apparatus was formerly arranged, and having tested many of the floorboards before dismissing the idea as too obvious, his attention moved to the shelves on the back wall. He noticed what looked like fingermarks on a dusty shelf, showing the woodgrain beneath. The fingermarks were directly in front of a book clad in dark blue binding. Printed on its spine in gilt lettering was the word *Clarissa*, one of the novels that Molly had inherited from their mother. Hardly her first choice of reading material. Easing the book out, George flicked through its pages until, about a third of the way through, he found what he was searching for. It appeared Molly had cut into the pages, forming a rectangular cavity about an inch or so in depth – deep enough to conceal a number of plant seeds, scraps of paper and fragments of their mother's jewellery inside. Sitting on top of the pile was a folded letter. George lifted it from the pile and opened it. It was marked with the previous day's date and consisted of just half a page of script.

Dear Miss Abernathy,

I am afraid we must politely decline your request that you be allowed to 'observe' lectures concerning the Natural Sciences at the University of Oxford. This would be of no benefit to, and unsuitable for, a young lady such as yourself who has had no prior academic training on the subject, even if, as you say, you have studied several volumes on the subject, which in itself is a commendable accomplishment. I would recommend that you continue your private studies should you wish to expand your knowledge on the subject of Botany, although I would strongly advise you to consider what practical end this course of study may have. The study of the botanical sciences is a far more scholarly pursuit than ladies' botany, and there are undoubtedly alternative subjects that would be of far greater worth to one of your rank and sex.

Yours sincerely,

Professor Eldridge Penrose

George unconsciously tightened his grip on the letter as he read. Having read it through, he immediately replaced everything as he'd found it and made his way upstairs to his own room. He sat at his writing desk, took out a clean leaf of paper and rummaged through his desk drawer for writing materials. Dipping the pen in the ink, he briskly proceeded to write, completing the task in no more than a minute. He then sealed the letter, supplied the address, and swiftly retrieved his black frock coat before making his way back downstairs. He passed his brother, who held two steaming cups, on the second-floor landing.

'Where are you off to in such a hurry?' asked Douglas.

'To post a letter.'

'Can you not wait for the postbag?'

'I could use the walk. All these boxes are becoming unbearable.'

'Well, this is the first time I've known you to want to take the air.'

George paid him no mind, and continued on his course. Douglas pursued him into their clockmaker's shop on the ground floor, putting the cups down on the bare counter. 'Perhaps I'll join you.'

'I'd rather you didn't.'

'Why? Have you found a secret lair you don't wish anyone to know about?'

'If I say yes, will you desist?'

'Gladly.'

'Yes.'

'Oh, in that case I'm definitely coming.'

George turned on him fiercely. 'Perhaps it isn't the boxes but your persistent meddling in my affairs that I cannot tolerate. I am perfectly capable of handling myself without you needing to—'

A harsh knocking on the shop door silenced him.

'Does the sign not say we're closed?' George shouted.

The knocking came again, even harsher this time. Douglas unlocked the door, and the shop bell tinkled as he opened it.

'Can I help you, gentlemen?' Douglas asked the two men in grey greatcoats who were standing outside. Both were lean, with chiselled features and jawlines. They wore neat moustaches and leaden expressions.

George narrowed his eyes at the two men. He had eyes like pale sapphires that could send a chill down one's spine. He's noticed something about them, Douglas thought.

'We'd like you to come with us, Mr Abernathy – your brother as well,' said the taller of the two to Douglas, with no prior introduction.

'Might I ask why?' Douglas enquired, not even daring to correct the man that George had the right to that title as he was the elder brother.

'No,' replied the man.

'Might I ask who you are?'

'No.'

'And if we resist?'

The other man made a movement with his hand and the flaps of his greatcoat drew back like curtains. Beneath was a flash of brilliant scarlet red: a soldier's tunic. His hand was resting on the hilt of a sword. He drew the blade out of its scabbard an inch. It glistened and made a *sching* noise.

'Oh,' said Douglas.

The soldier retracted his blade.

'Oh, I am afraid you will have to be put under restraint,' said his less taciturn companion matter-of-factly. He held up ropes and cloth sacks. 'Strict orders.'

George looked from the soldier to his brother. 'Did you leave the stove on?'

'No.'

'Good. Let's hope this doesn't take too long,' he sighed.

The soldier looked offended by George's indifferent attitude. He put the sack over George's head before they were even inside the waiting carriage.

Chapter Two

Molly drifted through the sultry Palm House of the Royal Botanic Gardens. The air was like jelly. She felt as if she were melting. Fanning herself brought little relief and simply wafted the warm air around her face. It was easy to imagine that she was in a tropical forest, except for the neat, paved walkways, and cast-iron columns that supported the roof and confronted the tall palm trees like metal absurdities. The blue sky looked caged beyond the vaulted roof; the net of glass panes was like a spider's web. Molly paid little attention to her surroundings as she walked. How many times had she pestered her brothers to take her to the gardens when she was a girl? Sometimes, when they'd taken her with them on their scrap metal raids (and let her sit in their cart until it became too full), she'd be allowed to briefly visit the gardens. But she preferred it when Douglas took her, as then she could run around admiring the array of different plant species to her heart's content. Douglas always had to remind her to put her bonnet back on before they returned home, as he didn't want to give their mother another excuse to scold her. (Bonnets, like most forms of headwear, had always irritated Molly, and didn't even provide any real relief from sunlight. She had burned all her bonnets after her mother died two years ago.) When she was older, she went to the gardens alone to clear her head whenever her mother tried her patience too much. But often she simply went to enjoy the sights and fragrances – and to steal samples for her research.

Molly paused in front of a wilting palm with yellow leaves. It could be cured yet. She quickly glanced around to make sure no one was looking. She need not have feared. The young couple in front of her, half-screened by luscious green leaves, were too engrossed in each other to pay her any mind; and the fair-haired, dandified young man (probably a student) had his back to her as he busily sketched a handful of small white flowers that stood conspicuously against the green, leafy background of the bed, begging to be drawn. Molly took a small bag from her dress pocket and tipped what looked like a black sugar lump out of it. Crushing the lump in her palm, she sprinkled black dust around the palm's stem. She then dug deeper in her pocket for a small, corked vial of green liquid and added a single drop to the soil. The dead parts of the plant shrivelled away, while the rest of the palm became visibly greener and healthier. Seeing that the iron tablets worked cheered her a little, since she'd wanted a chance to test them for ages. (She'd found that plants grown using her growth serum were often deficient in certain nutrients, so she'd been developing various remedies to compensate for this – like plant medicine. If there was no great urgency, she let her plants grow at their own pace.)

The student behind her abruptly shut his sketchbook and hurried away. He cast a puzzled glance at Molly before he left. What was that for? She didn't think she looked that unrefined. She'd actually bothered to pin her hair up for once, since it was warm, and happened to be wearing one of her better dresses. Not that she cared what he thought of her.

Molly walked further down the rows of tropical plants, a sigh escaping her lips. The root of her depressed spirits was twofold. The first source was that obnoxious letter from Professor Penrose. She knew it had been a ridiculous thing to request, but there had been no harm in trying. She longed to know what knowledge on the natural sciences was being locked away inside universities. That said, she suspected it was nothing that she did not already know. She doubted that any Oxford professor (she'd written to Oxford due to its prestigious reputation and the fact that it wasn't ridiculously far away) could crossbreed two entirely different species of vegetable or develop a serum that could make an entire tree grow in the blink of an eye. How far she'd come from her first sweet pea experiments when she was three. What did she care for the opinion of Professor Penrose? What had he achieved that gave him the right to look down on her?

The second source of her melancholy was her imminent uprooting from her home. She couldn't think why, as she wasn't particularly fond of that old house above the clockmaker's shop. Perhaps it was simply fear of the unknown. One moment she was so impatient to be gone that she wished tomorrow was the day of departure. The next moment she'd be gripped by trepidation. She had seen their new home once and found nothing she disliked. She'd only conducted a preliminary survey of the grounds but was perfectly happy on that score, even if they were badly neglected and overgrown. Thinking about her garden made her smile as she stepped outside. People were strolling along the paths or chatting on the lawn. Everyone was enjoying the fine weather. Cashmere-shawled ladies carrying parasols remarked to one another how terribly hot it was, as impatient children tugged on their hands.

'Let's go, mama. I want to go home. I'm thirsty.' But their mamas were immovable.

Maybe the cooler air revived her, as Molly suddenly felt more like herself again. How ridiculous she was for moping. Bugger those stuffy academics. Her garden was all that she wanted. She felt for the airship keys next to the little bag in her pocket, supposing she had better return Douglas's airship before someone discovered which alley she'd hidden it down.

When the sacks were removed from the brothers' heads, they found themselves in a large room with dark, wooden panelling and drawn red curtains. Even so, they could still plainly see the armed soldiers stationed in each corner of the dim room, their eyes trained on the two of them. George and Douglas were seated at a long, rectangular table that stretched across almost the entire length of the room. Opposite them sat a bald-headed man with small, squinting eyes, a large, beaky nose and an iron-grey moustache. He was an army officer, judging by the silver crown and star embroidered on either end of his blue frock coat's velvet collar. The frock coat was decorated with two rows of eight gilt buttons and a gold and crimson sash, with a small gold cord and button on the left shoulder. The officer didn't pay the brothers any mind, but was engrossed by the letter in his white-gloved hand. Nothing happened for several minutes. From outside came the sound of horses' hooves clomping along a road.

Still without raising his head, the officer signalled to the fresh-faced soldier standing in the far left corner to approach him. The soldier promptly obeyed, and leant his head down to the old officer's level once he was beside him.

'Have they been offered tea, Corporal?' asked the officer.

'No, sir.'

'Then don't you suppose you had better ask?'

'Tea would be much appreciated,' interjected Douglas. 'It was rather stuffy inside that sack.'

The officer finally raised his head and fixed his eyes on Douglas, looking over the rim of his spectacles. 'And the other gentleman? How does he fare?'

'Rather parched,' answered George dryly.

The officer turned to his subordinate. 'Go and tell the servant girl to bring up a tray.'

The corporal promptly left the room. The officer seemed about to resume reading his letter, but then he removed his spectacles and cleared his throat. 'My apologies for the rough treatment, gentlemen, but it was deemed a necessary precaution. I've heard about how you escaped from Newgate, even if you were imprisoned under a false charge. And it would also be better if you remained unaware of our current location.'

'You mean to say we are not at the War Office?' asked Douglas.

The officer's eyes widened a fraction, then he let out a faint cough. 'As I said, it is better that you are not aware of that piece of information.'

'I take it we are not prisoners,' said George.

'Strictly speaking, no. Although, if you fail to cooperate, that may change.'

'In which case, would you please inform us why we are here?'

The officer rose. He was close to six feet in height, broad in the shoulders and chest but otherwise of a slender build. He held himself proudly as he walked around the table.

'I am General Brassington,' he said with an air of self-importance. 'I have commanded troops in Afghanistan, the Punjab and the Crimea – for my part in which I am to be one of the first to be awarded the Victoria Cross by Her Majesty in just under three weeks' time. In short, what I don't know about soldiering isn't worth knowing.' His tone of voice was rather precarious: hushed one moment, then booming the next. 'And I know all about you gentlemen. I have read about your achievements in the newspapers and I wish to offer you a commission.'

'What is the nature of the commission?'

'A soldier,' said George in response to Douglas's question. 'What else?'

General Brassington didn't seem to have heard this last remark, and strode towards the large map of the world pinned on the far wall with his hands behind his back.

'No doubt you've read in the papers about the situation in northern India?'

'The Indian soldiers have started rebelling against their British officers?' said Douglas.

General Brassington nodded. 'It started at Meerut, when the sepoys there – they're the natives the East India Company employs as soldiers for its private army – refused to obey their officers' orders and were punished accordingly. Only the troublemakers' allies broke them out of jail, murdered their officers – along with every civilian in the British cantonment – and then marched on Delhi. Granted, it should have come as no surprise, really – there had been warning signs that were ignored for far too long. Those sepoys in the Bengal Army had got far too big for their boots, made us think they were loyal to us and would die fighting for us – we even humoured them with that nonsense about not travelling overseas! Pooh! And that damn fool Canning did little to help matters either. The Crimean War was a warning call. The whole thing was a darn embarrassment, and if we don't act, this mutiny will result in a severe loss of faith in the British Army. However, it provides an opportunity to put a plan I have been devising into action. No doubt we'll suppress those mutinous brutes easily enough, but we have a chance to show them, as well as both our other colonies and British citizens, that we have the best manpower and the best military technology in the world.' He finally turned to face the brothers. 'That is why I sought you gentlemen. Your "androids" have caused quite the stir, and I at once recognised their potential. Which is why I wish you to create—' At this point a servant entered with a tray of tea things. Once the girl had set them down and meekly retreated from the room, the general cleared his throat again. 'Which is why I wish you to create a soldier...that is entirely mechanical.'

George groaned into his teacup.

General Brassington continued with his speech, undeterred. 'A soldier made of metal, twice as strong as any man, with first-rate reflexes and combat skills, and abilities no typical solider could ever possess. Capable of taking down entire battalions single-handedly. Who would dare challenge us? Any foreign army would tremble before such a thing. If it proved a success in the north of India, then we could produce hundreds and deploy them across our colonies to help defend the Empire. They would never question their loyalty, never perish from disease, and never disobey an order.' He took up his own teacup in his gloved hand, grimaced at it as he muttered 'Filthy', then put it aside. 'What say you, gentlemen? Do you think you are up to the task?'

George put down his cup and folded his arms across his chest. 'How long would we have to construct this soldier?'

'I want it ready as soon as possible, before this whole mutiny business blows over. Do you have any idea how long it will take?'

'No more than a month, depending on resources.'

'We will provide you with whatever you require. However, the android soldier will have to be constructed outside government premises, since this plan is not technically endorsed by the military or the East India Company. It is known only by myself and two other generals.'

'What of them?' George indicated the four other men in the room.

General Brassington followed George's gaze, appearing to have momentarily forgotten his subordinates' presence. 'Oh, they can be trusted – unless they wish to hamper their ascent through the ranks of the army.' The last part of his speech was blasted at the soldiers. Only one betrayed any show of emotion as his face twitched slightly.

'Um, pardon me, General Brassington,' ventured Douglas. 'Might my brother and I have a minute to discuss the matter alone?'

The general stared at him a moment, then signalled to his subordinates to exit the room. They promptly filed out of the door.

'You have five minutes,' warned the general before he followed the soldiers out and the door was closed behind him.

'So what do you think about this?' asked Douglas.

'Does it matter what I think?' George replied. 'This is not exactly up for negotiation.'

'George, they're asking us to make a machine that can *kill*. There's no telling what the repercussions might be.'

'I think what they're asking us to do is quite clear. Besides, it was only a matter of time before someone asked us to make mechanical soldiers, if you think about it. Our technology's potential as a weapon is obvious. I'm surprised no one has thought to build a fleet of your airships with guns attached to them.'

'Do you really want blood on your hands?'

'Do you really want to discuss morals with a general of the British Army?' his brother replied sternly. 'This is an order, not a request. If we refuse, they'll go to whatever lengths necessary until we comply. There's no telling what they'll do.'

'And there's no telling what they'd do with a mechanical soldier. How many Indians would they slaughter? Or people of other nations?'

'You cannot prevent that slaughter from happening. We can only determine the means. But it would also save lives. Think. If the mechanical soldier takes the place of a dozen human soldiers, how many men would be prevented from perishing needlessly on the battlefield? Some would also have families who would be affected by their loss.'

Douglas considered this for a moment. George was using his own moral stance against him.

'But the scale of the slaughter—'

'I know.' George cast him a cutting look. 'But how do you propose we get out of this? And if they have intelligence on us...'

'Then they'll have it on Molly as well.' Douglas let out a sigh.

'Time's up, gentlemen,' General Brassington barked as the troops re-entered the room. He promptly resumed his seat and folded his hands on the table. 'Have you come to a decision?'

Douglas and George looked at each other, the latter answering.

'Here is what we require...'

Chapter Three

The day had finally arrived. Molly stood on the threshold of her empty room, although it was no longer hers, of course. She attempted to impress the image before her onto her memory, but what she wished to remember was already gone. With a not so heavy heart, she turned to go. Her step faltered on the landing, and she walked in the opposite direction to peer at Douglas's former room. Only the bed remained. It was hard to believe that she and her brothers had shared this room when they were children; it seemed too small to have accommodated the three of them *and* all of her brothers' projects. There would always be half-finished automata and pieces of clockwork scattered across the floor. (Then their nursemaid would sweep the room, and the boys would be unable to finish a project as vital pieces for a machine were carried off in the dustpan.) As Molly grew older, a white sheet was hung across the room to allow her a space of her own. When their old nursemaid left the family, Molly was elated to finally have a whole room to herself – but not so elated that the bulk of the domestic work now fell to her.

It was not quite sadness or regret she felt on leaving the only home she'd ever known; most of the memories it contained weren't particularly happy ones. Nostalgia wasn't her strong point – she hit an emotional wall there. Why bemoan the loss of what could no longer be?

She saw something moving out of the corner of her eye. A small metal mouse had emerged out of its hole in the corner of the room and was scurrying across the floor. It stopped at Molly's feet and put its front paws on her boot. It looked up at her, as if to ask why all the furniture was gone. Molly scooped the mouse up and stroked its smooth tin skin with her finger.

'How did we forget you?' She slipped the mouse into her pocket, hoping it wouldn't nibble through her dress.

'Molly!' Douglas called from below.

'Coming!' she yelled back, hurrying downstairs.

She found her brothers in the hallway.

'Now, you're both clear on the plan?' asked Douglas.

'For the hundredth time, yes,' she sighed, leaning on the banister. 'Although I still think transporting everything by airship wasn't the best idea.'

'Well, we don't exactly have a coach at our disposal. Besides, this way is much faster.'

'As much as I think it a risky plan, it is too late to debate the point now. Let's be gone,' said George, taking the initiative by striding through the black door leading to the shop. Molly watched Douglas glance first at the parlour and then at the kitchen.

'You heard George. Let's get going,' she said as she made her way down the final three steps.

'Since when did you follow George's orders?'

'I don't. I just fail to see the point in dithering.'

'Eager to get to your new home?' he smiled as he followed her. 'Or do you fear you'll start weeping if you remain inside a minute longer?'

'Do you know me at all, brother?' she returned as she picked up her carpetbag and passed through the vacant shop, hearing her footsteps echo on the bare floorboards. She didn't look back as she stepped out into the street and Douglas closed the door behind him. Before her was an enormous bundle – about seven feet by seven feet – of their collective material possessions, wrapped in thick cord like a fisherman's net, with a hook at the end. The street was quiet at this time of day, so the bundle wasn't too much of an obstruction. This plan was mad, she suddenly decided. Utterly mad. It was too late now, though. The airship soon appeared in the sky above them. They could see George steering the enormous metal bird from inside its glass hood. A wind whipped up around them as he lowered it towards the ground. When it was a yard from touching the cobblestones, Douglas grabbed the net's hook and attached it to the ring on the ship's underside. A rope ladder unfolded from the ship's open side door like a tongue. Douglas climbed the ladder first and Molly followed, tossing her bag up to him so she had both hands free. If anyone in the street below was trying to look up her petticoat, she swore she'd send the bag back down on top of their head. The door closed behind her once she had boarded, and she took her seat in the rear of the ship. The red leather creaked as she leant back and made herself comfortable. George had shifted to the seat beside the pilot's, which Douglas was trying to slide into without much grace. Molly tried to push down on his foot, which was sticking up in the air.

'That's not exactly helping, Mol.'

She giggled and removed her hand as he finally took his place. She and George didn't mind leaving the driving to him on this occasion, given the length of their journey. It was thirty miles to Ravenfeld Hall. Douglas always preferred to drive the ship – Spuggy was his pride and joy, after all. (Molly felt rather smug that he'd eventually adopted her nickname for the ship, after his protests that it was 'undignified'). Still, sometimes she could drive the ship better, or at least more safely, than he could.

As the airship gently rose, Molly dared to have a last look at the bottle-green shop front. The gilt letters above the window that read *'ABERNATHY BROTHERS CLOCK AND WATCHMAKERS'* would soon be painted over by the next occupant.

The noise of the airship's engines grew fiercer until the ship shot off at full speed, although they went no higher. The ship was dangerously close to a row of houses. Each moment Molly expected them to lift upwards, but still they sped on.

'Is something wrong with—?'

They sharply bolted skyward, with the ship's nose pointing towards the heavens.

They ascended high enough to be well out of reach of chimneys and church spires. It wasn't long until they had cleared London and its smog, emerging into open countryside. George recited directions, which corresponded with the hand-drawn map on Molly's lap. There was a navigational device amongst the ship's controls, but it was too unreliable. There was not a great deal of variety in the landscape below. Occasionally an island of civilisation interrupted the sea of green, veined with rivers and hedgerows. About an hour into their journey her mind began to wander from her task, George's prodigious memory once again proving perfectly accurate. Another half hour passed. Molly had her head slumped against the window, with her shawl acting as a cushion.

'There it is! We're almost there!' cried Douglas.

Molly lifted her drowsy head and raised herself in her seat so she could see out of the front window. Although she had seen the house before, the impressiveness of the sight did not diminish. Ravenfeld Hall was predominantly Gothic in style, although there were a number of other competing schools of architecture in its design. The building's façade was grey stone adorned with elaborate carving, with mullioned windows and, in the centre, a rose window (although to Molly's mind it resembled a daisy), which gleamed in the low afternoon sun. The wings on either side of the building rose above the roofline of the main hall. Parapets with tall pinnacles bordered the roofline; weathervane-topped turrets pierced the sky, and battlements fortified the hall. A clock tower thrust upwards from the Hall's south side. To the Hall's left were acres of farmland, beyond which a river wound its way south, and to the right were open fields and the road leading to Holtbury, the nearest town. Molly glimpsed the vast woodland that formed part of the garden to the rear of the hall, before the airship steadily descended and hovered above the green lawn.

'This is the hard part,' said Douglas as he inched them towards the ground.

George opened the door and the wind rushed into the airship, whipping his black hair. 'The net is touching the ground!' He had to shout to be heard clearly.

'Right, I'll detach the hook.' Douglas wound a brass reel on the control panel, and Molly heard a clunk from underneath the airship. She watched the hook fall to the ground.

'Well, that went surprisingly smoothly,' said Douglas brightly as George pulled the door shut. 'Now it's our turn to land.'

They continued their descent until they bumped gently to the ground.

Molly wasted no time in climbing out of the airship, glad to move her stiff legs. She sprinted across the lawn to the front door, waiting for her brothers to follow. Douglas had the keys.

'Be patient a second, Mol,' he said, handing her the carpetbag she'd left in the airship in her haste. 'It's all ours now.'

He inserted the large black key into the lock. She expected the door to resist but it swung open fairly freely, letting out a small squeak rather than a groaning creak. The north hall was grey and dormant. The air was dusty and there were thick cobwebs in the corners of the lofty ceiling, but it did not spoil the impression of the place. A grand oak staircase led to the other floors; cobwebs were matted between the balustrades and tall, doglike creatures stood proudly on the newel posts, each holding a lamp in its paws. Molly stepped inside, hearing her footsteps on the marble tiles echo across the huge hall.

'Doesn't feel terribly welcoming, does it?' she said.

'Once the dust and cobwebs are cleared away, it'll seem much more homely,' replied Douglas. 'It's ours to do what we please with – Molly!' he called after his sister as she darted through a doorway to the right. 'Be careful where you go running off to! You could easily get lost in this place!'

'She isn't a child,' said George.

'And don't you go skulking off either,' Douglas warned. 'Although I wouldn't be as saddened if *you* were to disappear.'

'I don't doubt it.'

Molly came running back.

'The dining room is huge! It looks like the servants' hall and kitchen are down there too. I'll never have to cook dinner ever again! I'm off to put my bag in my room. I promise I won't lose my way.'

She shot up the staircase without waiting for a reply. Molly had already decided which room was to be hers. She climbed the stairs until she reached the second-floor landing, and flung open the door to a large room with white wainscotting and faded green wallpaper. It led to a balcony; from there she had a full view of the garden. Her garden. It was a mess of brambles, nettles and weeds at that moment, but the sturdy old oak and ash trees still towered above, their branches waving in the breeze to welcome their new mistress. The sparkling lake was just visible beyond the vast woodland.

Something nudged her from inside her pocket. Molly dipped her hand inside and retrieved the little mouse.

'I thought you'd have wound down by now. You're always full of energy, aren't you? Here, go find a new mousehole.' She knelt to the ground and the mouse alighted from her hand. Brushing her skirts as she rose, she watched it scuttle aimlessly across the floor before it found its way out of the room. Molly leant against the balcony as she savoured the sight of the garden and smiled to herself. She could see this as home.

Down below, her brothers were exploring the oak-panelled parlour on the ground floor. Austere, high-backed oak chairs and chests were in conversation with giltwood sofas and footstools upholstered in red or green silk. Uninspiring landscapes embellished the walls.

'Our cousin was certainly very generous, leaving us so many furnishings,' commented Douglas as he surveyed the room. He imagined the oak parlour would be most inviting on a winter's night with a roaring fire.

'Probably all of the things that he didn't care for. I'm sure the duke's new seat is amply and superiorly furnished.' George looked out of the window as he spoke, viewing the airship and its load parked on the front lawn. The gravel driveway and path led to tall, iron gates in the distance where visitors entered. He heard Douglas rummaging through the bookshelves behind him.

'He seems to have not been as generous with the family library. There are only two shelves' worth of books here. There doesn't seem to be anything to our taste.' His hand landed on a green-jacketed volume that refused to budge as he was shifting books along a shelf. He tugged at it. 'Oh, please be what I think this is.' He pushed down on the book and it stuck out of the shelf at a peculiar angle. Part of the shelving swung inwards: a hidden door. 'Aha! Brilliant!' He disappeared inside the hidden chamber. 'Come and take a look at this, George.'

George moved away from the window and joined his brother. The chamber seemed to be a storage space, but may once have been part of the original great hall before the building was remodelled a century ago. Above the fireplace was a fan of weapons: pikes, swords, crossbows and old guns. In one corner of the room, amongst the dusty trunks and faded furniture, was a knight's suit of armour.

'There's certainly a lot of history in this house.' Douglas removed a gauntlet from the suit of armour and slotted it over his left hand. He flexed his steel-clad fingers experimentally with a squeak.

George fixed him with a disapproving stare. 'When you've finished fooling around, you can help me unpack. We need to get to work as quickly as possible.'

Chapter Four

'Well, I think we're just about there, don't you?' Douglas drew his forearm across his damp brow and then stepped back to stand beside George. There was a satisfied smile on his face as the two of them contemplated their work. Their faces and clothes were smeared with dirt and grease, and both looked as though they'd rubbed charcoal rings around their eyes. They'd worked practically unceasingly on General Brassington's commission for a week. Once or twice, when Molly had taken a tray bearing supper or cups of tea to their new workshop, she'd found that they'd both fallen asleep while they were working. One would be slumped on the worktable and the other sprawled on the bare floor.

'Yes, I'd say it's finished,' replied George. The workshop was still empty enough that their voices carried a faint echo. It was located in a tower in the west wing of the Hall, where the noise and occasional explosions wouldn't disturb anyone. A lift conveyed their materials and equipment to them.

'I think we made a good choice with the finish, don't you?' Douglas asked.

'Definitely,' his brother replied with a thin smile. 'The resemblance is quite remarkable.'

'You think he'll recognise himself in it?'

'Physically, yes, although I wouldn't count on him seeing any of his mannerisms that we put into it.'

The android standing before them certainly did bear a striking physical resemblance to General Brassington, although its skin was gold, and it was somewhat taller at over six feet high. The smooth metal skin, free of creases, gave the soldier the appearance of a younger man too, as did the brown moustache. Its tunic was cobalt blue instead of a soldier's scarlet red. The enamelled white leather sword belt with a round, gilt clasp around the android's waist, and the white sash draped over its left shoulder, were replicas of a soldier's attire, although the belt's clasp bore no regimental number. The soldier's slender legs were clad in dark blue trousers, with a red stripe running down the outside of each leg.

'Do you wish to have the honour or shall I?' asked George.

'How about we toss a coin for it?'

'I call heads.'

Douglas flicked the coin into the air and then clapped it on the back of his hand. 'Tails. Looks like the honour falls to me then.' He twisted what looked like a silver medal on the android's chest but was in actual fact a dial. There came a bubbling and rumbling from inside it as Douglas swiftly retreated to George's side. They watched it expectantly. A few moments passed but it remained perfectly motionless. A spluttered hiss emitted from its knee joint.

'It should have moved by now,' said Douglas.

'I can't fathom it.' George circled the android and came back to his original standing position. 'The engine sounds as if it's working. Why hasn't it done anything yet?'

Douglas stared hard at the android as his fingers stroked his now bristly chin. Suddenly he snapped his fingers. 'I wonder...'

'What is it?'

'Let me try something.' Douglas strode up to the dormant metal soldier, inhaled deeply so his chest inflated, and bellowed a single word. 'Attention!'

He flinched away from the soldier as it jerked up its head and raised a hand to its temple in salute. The soldier stiffly marched forward, his body shuddering and jittering as hisses of steam spurted from between his joints. His head and limbs twitched involuntarily. Gradually he seemed to fall into a more regular rhythm, and his marching became less mechanical and more like that of a human soldier.

'At ease, soldier,' called Douglas, and the android abruptly came to a stop. He stared straight ahead blankly without blinking.

Douglas exchanged a look with his brother and then approached the soldier. He looked into his small black eyes with two flickering red dots at their centres. 'Can you speak, soldier?'

'Yes, sir!' bellowed the mechanical man in a deep, brassy voice that made Douglas's ears ring. Slapping a hand over his left ear, he turned to George. 'I think we ought to turn him down a little,' he said, before reaching up his hand and tweaking a dial on the side of the android's head.

'Now, soldier, in a moment we're going to do a few exercises. Is that understood?'

'Yes, sir!'

'And you don't have to shout,' Douglas winced, although this time the volume of the soldier's voice had not been quite as deafening.

'Sorry, sir,' said the android promptly.

'Now, first we're going to test your reflexes. George, the gun, if you please?'

George was already loading the revolver before Douglas finished speaking. He aimed it at the android.

Douglas addressed the soldier. 'Right, first of all—'

George fired the gun.

The soldier made a movement with his arm as if he had been struck in the chest. The force of the shot sent him staggering back.

'I didn't mean for you to shoot him now!' Douglas shouted as he drew his hands away from his ears.

'You said to test its reflexes. What would be the use in preparing it for an attack?'

'Well, it would have helped me. *My* nerves aren't made of steel. But I do see your point. Looks as though you hit him.'

George didn't look up as he cocked the revolver's hammer back to reload it. 'I wouldn't be so sure.'

The android slowly relaxed his curled arm and raised his hand. He held the bullet between his fingers.

'He caught it!' Douglas exclaimed.

The soldier examined the bullet then tossed it to the ground indifferently.

'Let's try it again.' This time George fired two shots in a burst of powder smoke. The android stepped aside so both bullets struck the far wall and sprayed flecks of stone onto the floor.

'Amazing!' cried Douglas.

'Somewhat impressive,' said George, lying the revolver aside on the worktable. 'But I'd like to see how it performs in combat. Where is the sword?'

'Here.' Douglas was carrying a sword sheathed inside a white leather scabbard lined with wood. He held it out to the soldier. 'Your weapon. I forged it myself especially for you.'

The android grasped the sword's hilt and slowly drew out the gleaming steel blade; it was exceptionally fine and slightly curved, with a gilded brass guard. He flexed it experimentally while Douglas brought out a stack of wooden blocks.

'Try cutting these.'

He severed the stack cleanly in two with one swoop of the blade.

'Very good! Are you ready to see how you perform in a duel?'

'Yes, sir.'

'George will be your opponent.' Douglas craned his head to see George approaching with one of the ceremonial swords that had originally hung on the north hall wall. 'His reflexes are rather sharp too. He's an experienced fighter.'

'I saved you dozens of times when we were young and the older children used to antagonise you,' George remarked, as he faced the soldier and examined his opponent's blade.

Douglas frowned. 'Not dozens of times.'

'Precisely fifty-eight times between you being the ages of three and eight,' returned George.

'I learnt to fight my own battles eventually.'

'After much encouragement. I was tired of forever coming to your aid.'

'I remember you taking down a boy ten years your senior and armed with a knife with nothing but your own self.'

'Hardly a trying fight. I didn't have to deal that much damage.'

'You dislocated his shoulder.'

'Enough. Let's get on with it.' George raised his sword.

The soldier mirrored his action. The air became palpably tense as the two opponents faced each other.

The soldier struck first. George easily dodged the blow, and the two blades clashed as he retaliated. There was something rather mesmerising in the way the two fought, Douglas thought as he watched the duel unfold. It was almost as if it had been rehearsed; one would strike and the other would seamlessly block or avoid their sword. But the soldier's strikes were becoming faster, his sword a flash of silver. He delivered a series of rapid strikes in succession; this time his blade sliced away a lock of George's black hair. Douglas saw him touch that side of his face. Had the sword nicked him there? He'd never seen anyone manage to leave a mark on George before – not without him allowing them to, anyway. His strikes were no longer so swift and clean, Douglas noted. Either he was tiring or the soldier was learning from him and predicting his movements. The next time the soldier lunged at him, however, George not only countered the blow but dealt one of his own, which came within a hair's width of the soldier's face. The soldier's returning blow was rather lacklustre. At first Douglas thought something was amiss with his hydraulics, but the android didn't seem to be fully concentrating any longer. He appeared to be listening to something.

'Someone is approaching the house, sir.'

Douglas peered out of the tower window. The soldier was correct. He saw a stout old woman dressed in widow's weeds hobbling up the drive.

'Is it an intruder, sir?' The soldier flexed his sword. 'Do you wish me to deal with them?'

'No, no, it's fine. It appears to be the woman who applied for the housekeeper job, but her interview with Molly is not until tomorrow.'

'She must have made a mistake about the date. We had better greet her, since Molly is out,' said George.

'Dressed like this? Although we cannot keep her waiting.'

'Cover your shirt with a frock coat and rinse your face. I will greet her.'

'No. *I'll* go. Then when you're presentable, I'll make an excuse to go wash.' He feared leaving George and the old woman alone together even for a short while.

'You can practise your swordsmanship,' he told the soldier. 'We'll return once our interview with this woman is concluded.'

Douglas raced down the winding flights of stairs to the south hall. The old woman was smiling when he pulled back the door.

'Good afternoon, Mrs Baxter,' he said somewhat breathlessly, although he was glad that he'd remembered her name at the last second. 'Please step inside.'

The woman shuffled into the hall. 'Are you the butler?' she asked.

'I'm afraid you're mistaken, Mrs Baxter. I am Mr Douglas Abernathy, one of the masters of the house. We are yet to hire any staff. Apologies for my appearance – my brother and I were just working on one of our machines. The mistress, our sister, is in town, you see. If you would like to make your way through to the drawing room, it is just through the door on the right there.'

'Oh, I'm aware, Mr Abernathy.' Mrs Baxter nodded and continued smiling as she shambled along the heavy, grey stone floor. 'I used to be the housekeeper when the old master lived here.'

'You did?' Douglas exclaimed.

She nodded slowly. 'Oh yes, although not for very long, of course. He was a very strange gentleman. Had some rather…peculiar interests.'

Douglas saw something moving out of the corner of his eye. Sweep emerged from one of the rooms and approached them, leaving a trail of black dust in his wake.

The old woman smiled fondly at the little android. 'Is this your boy, Mr Abernathy?'

Douglas looked down at the two of them. He was seriously beginning to doubt this woman's faculties. He felt it would be too complicated to explain to her about Sweep. 'I suppose you might say that.'

Mrs Baxter began rifling through her purse. 'I am sure I have a mint humbug in here somewhere. Ah! Here you go, my dear.'

She placed something into the android's hand. Sweep walked over to Douglas and held it up to him. It was a thimble.

'Pardon him for not saying thank you, Mrs Baxter. He is rather shy. *Go back to your room,*' he hissed at the android. Sweep shot off.

'Would you care for tea, Mrs Baxter?' asked Douglas as they entered the drawing room.

'Oh, that is most kind, sir, but I must decline, thank you.'

She sank into the sofa that had its back to the window. Douglas sat on the sofa opposite.

'So you said that you were previously housekeeper here, Mrs Baxter?'

'Oh yes, for two years, until I married my late husband. God rest his soul.' She shook her head sadly. 'He was knocked down by a carthorse not three months since.'

'I am sorry to hear that, Mrs Baxter.'

'He did not leave me a great deal of money, and I don't wish to be a burden on my daughter's family, so I thought I would search for a situation.'

'Are you sure the position won't be too…taxing? It will be quite different to how things were in your old master's day.'

'Oh, it should be no trouble. I might not be as sprightly as I once was, but I am hearty and know a thing or two about running a house. I was always very particular about the accounts and made sure that we didn't spend above our means. After I married, Mr Baxter always complained that the joints of meat I bought were too small, but I told him that the extra expense wouldn't justify buying a larger joint.'

'I see. It never hurts to be prudent,' Douglas smiled. 'Well, as the advertisement said, we are only a small family and don't intend to be too demanding on our staff. We are not ones for entertaining, so you shouldn't expect to have to prepare the house for large parties.'

'The old master was very fond of entertaining. The balls he gave were some of the best in the county! It seemed that as soon as one party had left, we were preparing fresh bed linen for another.'

'I gathered that my cousin had a fondness for company.' And for the occult, he thought. An examination of the wine cellar had produced some rather interesting finds. It had taken a while to scrub all of the chalk markings off the floor. They were still unsure what to do with the animal skulls. Douglas wondered what sort of people his cousin's guests had been, but was not entirely sure that he wished to know the answer.

'I would offer to give you a brief tour of the house and explain your duties, but I suspect it would be covering old ground for you. That said, we do intend to change the house significantly.'

'Oh, I assure you I remember it all quite well, Mr Abernathy,' Mrs Baxter smiled. At that moment Douglas happened to glance out of the window behind her. He saw the soldier outside, stalking along the overgrown hedgerows. He also saw the soldier's target: his sister, who was making her way towards the house.

'Uh, please excuse me a moment, Mrs Baxter. I just recalled that I neglected to inform my brother of your arrival.' Douglas hastily rose and retreated from the room into the south hall. He ran down the passage that connected the north and south halls, then darted into the oak parlour and thrust the window open.

'Soldier!' he hissed sharply. 'What are you doing out here?'

'Master Douglas!' the soldier hissed back. 'There is a female approaching the premises. Is she an enemy?'

'No, that is Miss Molly. She is my sister and mistress of this house.'

'Miss Molly?' He glanced in her direction. 'My apologies, master. I did not know her likeness.'

'No harm done. Now, return to the workshop and remain there unless otherwise instructed. Is that clear?'

The soldier saluted. 'Yes, sir!'

'You can sneak in through this window so no one will see you.'

'That won't be necessary, Master Douglas. I think I can reach the workshop. I had little trouble descending.'

Before Douglas could say a word, the soldier extended his legs until he could reach a protruding stone in the wall, and then swung himself through the tower window. Closing the parlour window, Douglas caught Molly flitting past the half-closed door that opened onto the north hall. She was too absorbed by one of the letters in her hand to notice him as she went upstairs. Returning to the drawing room, Douglas saw George sitting opposite Mrs Baxter. He had been speaking to her but stopped as Douglas entered, looking at him questioningly. His face was clean but a little red, and his eyes were just as tired. Then again, they always seemed to be recently, even before they'd started working on the soldier. He could have sworn that George was looking thinner too.

'My apologies for that interruption. Don't feel that you need stop for me.'

George folded his arms across his chest. 'I think I am satisfied. I have explained about the wages and duties.'

'Well then, perhaps, Mrs Baxter, you would at least care to see the servants' hall and housekeeper's quarters?'

'Oh, I will spare you the trouble, Mr Abernathy.' Mrs Baxter rose. 'I would be sorry to take up any more of your time.'

'We shall inform you of our decision shortly. There are still one or two other applicants to be interviewed.' Douglas showed her out. When he enquired about the length of her journey home, she assured him that she lived only a short distance away and that the walk did her good. Mr Bates – her son-in-law and one of the labourers at Darkwater Farm – had been kind enough to bring her in his cart on his way to town. As soon as she paused to draw breath long enough so that Douglas could politely wish her 'Good day', he shut the front door, relieved to be spared a narrative about all of her relations, which she had been on the verge of giving. He returned to the drawing room to find George pouring himself a drink from the decanter on the little table.

'Perhaps we should reconsider building our own servants.'

'George, we discussed this—'

'That woman is unfit for the position.'

'But she is a poor widow.'

'Many women are poor and widows. That does not make them competent housekeepers.'

'She has experience. She was formerly housekeeper here, after all, and she was completely unfazed by anything around her. How many interviews have we conducted now?'

'Eleven.'

'How many of those ended with them running from the house screaming?'

'Seven.'

'Well? Won't you at least consider her?'

George stared hard at Douglas for a moment, then sighed. He sat in his chair and picked up a newspaper. 'Very well, if only to put an end to the matter.'

'I'll write to her to inform her of our decision. I must remember to wire General Brassington about the soldier, too.' Douglas suddenly felt rather tired and in need of a drink himself. He poured a small measure of brandy into

44

a tumbler and then sank onto the sofa. 'At least that ordeal is over.'

They heard the unmistakable stomping of Molly's footsteps coming towards them.

Douglas sighed. 'And here comes the next.'

Seconds later Molly burst into the room. She was shaking the letter that was bunched in her fist. 'You sneak!' She smacked the letter down on the table, causing everything that was placed on it to give a little leap into the air. 'How much did you offer the university? They offered me a *place on the course!*' She fixed her eyes on Douglas, and on seeing his perplexed expression turned her gaze on George. The green fire in her eyes seemed intense enough to burn though the newspaper. 'You found my letter, didn't you?'

George slowly lowered the paper. 'I offered to make a modest donation to the Natural Science School in return for them granting your request. I never asked them to give you a place at the university.'

'Well, they have.'

'That sounds like an excellent opportunity, Mol,' ventured Douglas. 'After all, I should imagine you would be the first woman to—'

She held up a finger to silence him. 'Shut it. I don't want to be made to feel grateful.' Her voice was gradually growing steadier. 'Of course you thought nothing of going behind my back,' she said to George.

'I fail to see the problem,' he replied. 'They denied your request and I attempted to get them to reconsider so that you might have your wish granted.'

'By bribery.'

'If you choose to see it as such. The ends justify the means.'

'You're assuming I'll accept the place?'

'I think it would be incredibly foolish of you not to.'

'The only woman? I'd be a laughing stock. No one would take me seriously.'

'If that's how you choose to see the matter, then so be it.' George resumed reading his newspaper. 'You can write to the university yourself to inform them of the fact if you would prefer.'

'George has a point, Mol,' Douglas hazarded to speak. 'He was acting out of your best interests as far as he could see. And they'll take you seriously once they see what you're capable of. Do you think any other student could crossbreed a Venus flytrap and a carrot, or grow tomatoes the size of pumpkins?'

Molly stared at him and then sighed. 'I'll consider it.'

'We've also hired a landscape gardener to assist in the construction of your garden,' George informed her from behind the newspaper.

She shot him a bleak, thunderous look. 'What for? I don't want some pompous snob meddling with my garden. I know their type. They've read every book on the subject of good garden design, but never planted a seed in their life, most likely.'

Douglas put a finger on his brother's newspaper and pulled the paper down. 'See, George? I told you we'd get such a response.'

'For your information, I was well aware of how she would take it.' George put the newspaper down and looked Molly straight in the eye. 'But I knew it would be near impossible for you to single-handedly undertake a project of this scale. And this man is not what you imagine him to be. He is a young landscape gardener by the name of Greenwood, who was recommended by a member of the Royal Botanic Society. I had Professor Penrose make enquiries. Mr Greenwood is recently established and has never had a commission such as this before.'

'So you thought a second-rate landscape gardener would be sufficient?' she said disdainfully.

'We hired a relatively unknown landscape gardener because we were well aware of your contempt for his older, "pompous" contemporaries,' returned George.

'Oh, I understand your reasoning perfectly well, and I appreciate your good intentions, but mark my words, I will not let my garden suffer if he turns out to be not up to the task.'

'So you admit you need help?'

She smacked her hands down on the table and looked Douglas hard in the face. 'I don't need help, thank you very much, Douglas. But he could be of some use, and I don't intend to give him an easy time.'

Douglas smiled behind his tumbler. 'No, I don't expect you to, Mol.'

'The next time you consider going behind my back, don't. I'd rather my failure be my own than my success be bought by my brothers.' She swiftly exited the room, shutting the door behind her.

Douglas turned to George. 'If this goes badly, you have to take responsibility for it, since hiring this landscape gardener was solely your doing as well.'

'So be it.'

Chapter Five

General Brassington arrived at Ravenfeld Hall to inspect the mechanical soldier the following week, after he'd received Douglas's wire informing him that the android was complete. There had been something of a mad scramble inside the dining room as the General's Clarence was trundling up the gravel drive. George and Douglas had pushed the long dining table against the far wall and placed the now unwound mechanical soldier in the middle of the room.

'They're already at the door,' said Douglas as he hastily shut the dining room window. 'That was rather close.'

'Don't fret,' replied George coolly. 'It sounds as if Molly is performing her role.'

They'd asked Molly to act as parlourmaid and admit their visitors. They really needed to hire a butler, but their advertisement had produced no response yet.

Molly ushered the general into the dining room, giving her brothers a meaningful look before she departed that said, 'I don't envy your position. Good luck handling this old boy.' General Brassington was flanked by three of his men as he entered, whereupon he gave a perfunctory nod and salutation to George and Douglas. Upon seeing the mechanical soldier, the general's brows furrowed and he removed his pipe from his mouth. He strode to the android and glared at him. Then he glared at him some more. Douglas was starting to become apprehensive when the general barked a laugh. The sound bounced off the white-wainscotted walls.

'A spitting image!' he declared. 'Very impressive indeed. Is it made of gold?'

'No, sir. The gold is merely a veneer. The android is actually made of a very strong compound of various metals, including steel and titanium. As well as being economical and durable, it is light enough to allow him to achieve great speed and strength. His casing can withstand a bullet quite easily too. We thought gold would be a tasteful finish, with the added benefit that it won't corrode easily,' explained Douglas.

The general grunted and tapped the android's torso with his knuckles. The metal answered with a clank. 'Why blue rather than red for the tunic?'

'We thought it better to create a contrast so it's clear that the android is not considered to be a true soldier,' answered George.

'Hm. Probably a good idea.' The general sucked his pipe for a moment. 'How do you wake it up?'

'I'll show you, General.' Douglas twisted the dial on the android's chest. The soldier's limbs jittered, and there was that familiar hiss of steam before he opened his eyes. On seeing General Brassington, he saluted.

'At ease, soldier,' said the general.

The soldier swiftly lowered his arm.

'What is your duty, soldier?'

'To defend the Empire and her interests, sir.' He answered in the general's own voice.

The general nodded. 'Good.' He turned to George and Douglas. 'It is perfectly stupid!' He barked another laugh. 'An ideal soldier indeed. So it runs on steam, does it? Like a locomotive?'

'Essentially, yes. A clockwork mechanism inside him generates friction to ignite his boiler.'

'How is the fuel inserted to feed the boiler?'

'The same way you or I consume "fuel". It's inserted through his mouth. I'm sure things like twigs and dry grasses will be readily available in India. Coal would burn for longer, of course, but it'll be hard to obtain. Allowing him fuel rations might be advisable.'

'Yes, perhaps,' said the general vaguely. 'But what can the soldier do, exactly? Did you equip it with everything that I asked you to?'

'Everything and more.' Douglas smiled. 'Including strength…'

The soldier lifted the dining room table above his head effortlessly, setting it down gently again.

'Superb reflexes' —Douglas tossed a glass across the room and the soldier's arm shot out and grabbed it, the limb having now stretched to about a yard long— 'with arms and legs capable of extending up to three yards.'

The soldier's arm retracted and he placed the glass on the table.

'His eyes can magnify images and see into the distance for miles, while his hearing is as good as any hound's. He'll hear the enemy approaching from a mile away.'

'That all sounds very fine, but how do you mean to prove that it can really do all this?' challenged the general.

'You shall see, General Brassington,' Douglas grinned. 'First of all, however, I must ask you a question. How many medals do you have on your person?'

'Three.'

'Are you sure?'

Frowning deeply, the man looked down at his breast and felt at the gap in his decorations between the two circular medals proudly displayed on his red tunic.

'You see, we had him perform a little exercise upon your arrival. As soon as he caught sight of your carriage, he stalked you as it made its way towards the house. His task was to take one of your medals without you noticing.'

The soldier held up a silver, cross-shaped medal, dangling it by its purple ribbon. 'I confess I took it as your carriage was approaching the house, sir. I leapt onto the carriage roof and extended my arm to pluck the medal from your person when your head was turned in the other direction. I sincerely apologise, sir.' He bowed and stretched his hand out to the general. General Brassington gingerly took the medal from between the android's gloved fingers.

The soldier had narrowly managed this feat, Douglas thought. He had retreated to the house and vaulted through the dining room window only moments before the Clarence stopped outside the front door and George had temporarily wound him down.

'His combat skills are also exceptional,' continued Douglas. 'He's proficient in shooting, boxing and, of course, swordsmanship.' At that moment the android felt it necessary to show off his sword to his audience and demonstrate its sharpness by taking a piece of fruit from a bowl on the sideboard, tossing it above his head and slicing it in two. Douglas felt drops of juice spray his cheek. 'He's also a good tactician. He is equipped with a comprehensive knowledge of the most effective military campaigns throughout history, stretching back to the Greeks and the Romans. He can also learn from personal experience.'

'But it cannot learn to disobey orders, can it?' demanded General Brassington.

'No. He cannot disobey a direct order from an officer.'

The general eyed the android. 'Dance the hornpipe,' he commanded.

The android promptly crossed his arms and began to jig on the spot.

The general roared merrily.

'He won't stop until you tell him to,' said Douglas.

'Very well. Stop dancing.'

The soldier stopped.

General Brassington nodded approvingly. 'I am satisfied with your efforts, gentlemen. This soldier of yours might do the job very nicely indeed.' He turned to the android. 'Now look here. You are to accompany me to India to help put down the mutiny that has broken out there amongst the sepoys. It has spread across the garrisons and cities of northern India. As we speak, the rebel sepoys are marching from town to town, murdering their own officers *and* British civilians – they'll slaughter anyone who is not of their race. They have even killed loyal sepoys and the native servants in the cantonments and cities that are now in their clutches. They're little more than savages. We have tried to civilise them. Missionaries have been arriving in India by the dozen, but so far it has done little good.' The general shook his head sadly. 'It is time to take a harder line with them. They must be made to pay for their crimes. We must put down this rebellion as swiftly as possible. The leaders will be dealt with and made examples of, and any sepoy guilty of murder shall face justice. They will taste the full might and wrath of the British Army. Do you understand?'

'Yes, sir!'

'We shall be setting sail for India at the earliest opportunity. If we make good time, we should reach Bombay by early August. From there, we shall make our way north.' The general craned his head over his shoulder to face one of his subordinates. 'Fetch the crate, will you, Private?'

'Aye, sir.'

The private and another soldier swiftly exited the room. When they had gone, the general looked sternly at George and Douglas. 'I thank you, gentlemen, for your services. I'm most satisfied with what you've produced. However, I must caution you not to speak to anyone about this once we leave here today, or there could be severe consequences – both for the security of our nation and for yourselves.' Without removing his beady eyes from the two brothers, General Brassington placed a swollen envelope on the mantle. The banknotes were visible inside the open flap. 'Good day.' He marched out of the room, his boots clomping loudly after him.

The soldier was looking somewhat perplexed.

'You will be dormant for the journey to India, so it will seem as though no time has passed for you,' said Douglas as he approached him. 'But remember this.' He tapped the gold medal on the soldier's chest beside the disguised dial. 'Discretion is your greatest ally. Don't let them know all of your secrets. It will give you the greater advantage. You understand?'

'I believe I do, Master,' the soldier replied as the general's men re-entered the room with a large wooden crate. They set it down on the floor and removed the lid, causing fragments of straw to spill onto the dining room's polished wooden floor.

'Tell it to step inside and then put it to sleep,' ordered one of the men, but the soldier marched inside the box and lay down without further instruction.

'Good luck, soldier.' Douglas twisted the dial anticlockwise once more, and the android's eyes closed. The lid was placed over the crate and the three soldiers hammered nails into it. Douglas couldn't help thinking of a coffin. The soldiers carried the crate between them out of the front door and loaded it onto the carriage's roof. Douglas watched from the oak parlour window as the Clarence clattered back down the drive. He heard the clink of glass and the trickle of liquid behind him. Could George not last an hour without a drink? The general had been wrong on one point, though: the android wasn't a mindless fighting machine, he was a fully conscious being. George and Douglas had refrained from creating another such android as Maestro was, since it was not necessary to make any of their subsequent models so advanced and the technology was still so experimental. They had attempted it once more, not long after Maestro was created, but the poor subject had soon been driven mad and had to be taken apart. But in this case they'd felt it necessary to try again. Neither of them wanted to risk unleashing a mindless machine, armed with swords and guns, on northern India.

They'd constructed the soldier's mind differently to Maestro's, giving him different traits and abilities. His skill with a sword was 'instinctive', as was Maestro's prowess as a musician, although George and Douglas had fought with the soldier to hone his combat skills. They'd also had him study *The Art of War* and similar works for a fortnight. But perhaps he might surprise them, as Maestro had done, by displaying characteristics or skills they'd assumed to be beyond him. Some of the soldier's features would certainly come as a surprise to the army.

Douglas watched the gates at the end of the drive close behind the carriage. 'There'll be hell to pay when they find out what we've done.'

George looked into his nearly empty glass. 'Undoubtedly.'

Chapter Six

When the soldier was next awoken, he found himself in a parlour with bright turquoise wallpaper. Three gentlemen were staring at him. One he recognised as General Brassington, who was standing nearest to him. Sitting in a high-backed green chair was a younger man, with dark, neat mutton chops and a short moustache, who was wearing a smoking cap and gown. The third man, whose hair and complexion were fairer, was seated on a sofa that was also upholstered in green. Like General Brassington he was in mess dress, wearing an open scarlet shell jacket with white edging. His gold braid-trimmed red mess vest was visible underneath.

This wasn't what the soldier had anticipated. He'd been told that he was to wake up in India. They still seemed to be in England, although his internal thermometer acknowledged that the temperature was higher than it should be.

'Well, gentlemen, what do you think?' General Brassington asked his companions.

'The resemblance is striking,' remarked the officer in the cap and gown as he sucked on his cigar, exhaling deeply and slowly through his nose. The soldier watched the two tails of smoke dissolve into the air. 'And it's quite a splendid sight. It'll give the rebels a shock, that's for certain.'

'A bit scrawny-looking, isn't it? It's a wonder it can stand on those legs,' the fair gentleman smiled.

'Oh, he is no weakling, I assure you. Here.' General Brassington handed the soldier a bronze ornament that had stood on the mantle. 'Show them how strong you are.'

There came a peculiar creaking sound, then the soldier stretched out his hand and uncurled his fingers; the metal figurine had been crushed as if it were clay.

'Not bad.' The dark-haired gentleman stubbed out his cigar and rose. There was dignity in his bearing and his face was calmly composed, betraying no sign of amazement at the android's feat of strength.

'Soldier, this is Brigadier-General Fowler. He commands the brigade that you are to accompany,' explained General Brassington.

The soldier saluted him, but General Fowler did not look directly at him.

'That over there is Major-General Quincy.'

The man in question nodded.

General Fowler briefly stared at the android and then addressed General Brassington. 'So it really runs on clockwork?'

'He is powered by steam,' General Brassington grinned.

'Isn't that going to present some difficulty? Water is scarce enough out here as it is.'

'I can run solely on clockwork if required, sir,' said the soldier. 'Although it would be rather like if you were dehydrated. I could function, but my abilities would be impaired.'

'I see.' General Fowler took up a cup of coffee from a small table.

'Pardon me, General Brassington,' said the soldier, daring a second time to speak without being asked to, 'but I am somewhat confused as to where I am. I understood that we were to be in India by now.'

The general frowned. 'But we *are* in India. See for yourself.'

The soldier looked to the window with the blinds down that General Brassington was pointing at. When he drew the blinds up, he was surprised by the scene that greeted him. It was a military station, half-hidden in the dusk, but he could clearly make out the white bungalows with tiled, gabled roofs, and the palms sticking out amongst the border of trees on the edges of the station. What little grass there was appeared dry and pale. He heard men's voices and horses' hooves.

'You see? We are in the cantonment town of Ambala. It's not so different from England. It is far more sanitary than the natives' dwellings.' General Brassington grimaced. 'We lose perhaps a dozen men a day to heat and disease – not that that should be a problem for you, soldier. *Hassan! Hassan! Come in here this minute. There is a lizard on the wall.*' There was indeed a small reptile on the far wall. The soldier had thought it was a trophy nailed to the spot, since it hadn't moved at all.

A smiling Indian man presently entered the room. He wore a white shirt and breeches, with a white cap on his head.

'Get that disgusting creature out of here, Hassan!'

The man bowed, then he plucked the tiny creature from the wall and carried it from the room.

'This foul land is full of such vermin. Did I tell you, Horatio, that only yesterday I found a *cockroach* on my bedroom floor?'

'You did, sir,' replied General Quincy. Was there a smile hovering on his lips?

'I had the servants clean the house with chloride of lime following that unwelcome little discovery. I'd quite forgotten about such things while I was on furlough in England. One takes it for granted at home that one's bed will not be infested with insects. Now, why don't we have a little demonstration of what the automaton can do? Let us see how good a shot he is.' General Brassington took up a teaspoon between his fingers. 'See if you can shoot this in flight, soldier.'

He handed the soldier a pistol and held the spoon aloft. After making a motion as if to tap something with it three times, the general tossed the teaspoon into the air. No sooner had he let go of it than the soldier fired the pistol. The teaspoon landed on the carpet and the three officers craned their necks in its direction. There was a hole through the middle of the spoon.

'Impressive,' said General Fowler. 'I'll still have to see it perform in the field, though.'

'In good time.'

'Are you certain we shouldn't send any soldiers with it, Brassington?'

'Of course. The whole point is to show what he is capable of in order to convince Colonel Kirk to accept him amongst his men.'

'Kirk won't take to it, even if it does succeed.'

'I'd lay a guinea that he will.'

The soldier wanted to ask what was being spoken about, but knew better than to speak out of turn again. He had been insolent enough questioning whether they were in India or not.

The two younger officers inspected the soldier and asked General Brassington about his abilities, the soldier answering any question that General Brassington was unable to.

'And what does this medal here do?' asked General Quincy, pointing at the smaller, plain gold medal that the soldier wore to the right of his dial. It was marked with the letters *AB.s.*

'It is merely my maker's mark, sir.'

'Oh, I see.' He sounded somewhat disappointed. There was something boyish about his countenance, although his nose and jaw were finely chiselled.

General Fowler put down his coffee cup and stood beside General Brassington. 'Shall we put it to the test, then? We cannot afford to waste much more time.'

General Brassington nodded to him, then looked directly at the soldier. 'Your first task is to capture a band of men who we believe are acting as spies for the rebels. They once belonged to a Native Infantry regiment that formed part of the Delhi Field Force when General Anson was still in command, but they went to join the enemy in Delhi instead. Their camp was spotted a few miles from here. You are to bring the traitors back here, where they will face justice. Is that clear?'

'Yes, sir.'

The soldier crouched amongst the undergrowth and observed his target. Even in the dark of night, he faced no difficulty grasping his surroundings. His ears alerted him just fine to what was going on around him. He heard the chirping of insects and the gurgling of his boiler from within him, accompanied by the ticking of clockwork. From across the plain there came the sound of the enemy camp several yards away: distant voices and clattering metal. Their camp was situated in the remains of a temple, which was without a roof and half-devoured by greenery. He increased the magnification of his vision until he could see the men sitting around a smoking fire through a window hole – nine in all. At least two, he thought, were villagers or escaped criminals. Some of the men wore red coats and white breeches like any other sepoy, others wore native dress. The soldier calculated his plan and was sure that he could take them all. Retracting his vision, he sprinted across the dusty plain on light feet. He leapt into a tree that overlooked the camp. Since there was scarcely any of the temple roof remaining, he could observe his targets clearly. Cooking pots and weapons were scattered about the camp. Some of the men looked to be asleep. He couldn't comprehend their language, but it sounded as if four of them were discussing something confidential. They talked gravely. The man with the grey-streaked beard commanded the most attention, and looked to be the leader; perhaps he'd formerly been a native officer. All four were unaware of the android's presence. He raised the rifle that General Brassington had issued him with, took aim, and shot the grey-bearded man in the shoulder. His target cried out in pain and pressed his hand against where he had been struck. A deep red patch bloomed on his shirt.

The next instant a volley of bullets was directed at the soldier. Most of them missed or rebounded off him. He leapt down from the tree and landed in the midst of the camp. The men closest to him retreated, and all emitted gasps or unintelligible cries at seeing such an unusual being, as the campfire's flames gave his gold skin a fiery shine. But the men soon recovered from their shock. One resumed shooting him at close range, but the soldier grabbed hold of the musket's barrel and thrust it upwards towards his attacker, hitting him in the chin with his own weapon. The soldier swiftly followed this with a second blow to the back of the neck with his elbow that put his attacker out of his senses, and the man fell to the ground. Almost simultaneously another target came at him from behind, but the soldier's other arm shot out and, dropping the rifle, grasped hold of the pistol in the man's hand. He crushed it in his hand, possibly along with a fingerbone or two. A strike to the side of the head immobilised the target. Retrieving both his rifle and the enemy's musket, he sharply twisted around and shot two men in succession; one was struck in the shoulder and the other in the leg. Another man gave out a fierce cry and charged at him with a curved sword, his blade clashing with the soldier's sabre. With his next strike the soldier severed his assailant's blade cleanly in two. A sharp kick then sent the man hurtling into a wall. He slumped to the ground and did not move. His turban prevented his skull smashing.

The remaining three men attempted to flee, but the soldier stretched out his leg and tripped them up, dragging them back by the scruff of their shirts. He dealt with them easily enough. The soldier then surveyed the camp and the fallen men. All of the targets had been eliminated – no fatalities. He quickly rounded them up and bound their wrists and ankles with rope before they regained consciousness – the two men he'd shot were groaning weakly on the ground, but he bound their limbs also in case they attempted to escape. He then retrieved the horse and cart that was tethered to a tree nearby, loading all nine men into the back. Mounting the horse, he rode in the direction of Ambala. When the horse grew tired, he pulled the cart himself (the cart's load was not much of a struggle for the soldier) while gripping the animal's reins so that it could trot alongside him. Out of the corner of his eye he observed the beast bop its head as it walked, its bit jingling and its strong heart thumping in its chest. It was a magnificent specimen of its species, but evidently was in need of refuelling. As the fiery dawn broke, they reached Ambala. This was the first sight of the mechanical man for many of the soldiers positioned there, and they stared at him as he entered the barracks. General Brassington and General Fowler came to meet him.

'Well done, soldier,' General Brassington's voice boomed. 'You made short work of the task. Come and see, Fowler.'

The other officer examined the cart's load, being met with nine pairs of hostile eyes set in glowering faces. 'My men will see to them. You have done your part. Let us see what Kirk makes of this. You might be able to convince him after all, General Brassington.'

Since the soldier was no longer needed for the present moment, and was proving a distraction for most of the troops, he was ordered indoors and wound down.

Chapter Seven

Molly sighed as she finished making her bed. (Even though they'd hired a first housemaid, Martha, Molly still preferred to do some things herself, true to old habits.) Her bedroom was rather changed from how it had been when she arrived at Ravenfeld Hall. She'd wanted to give the room a bright, cheerful air and felt she'd succeeded, especially on a day like today when the sunlight was pouring in. The faded green wallpaper had been replaced by primrose-coloured paper with a mint-green, leafy print. She still had some of her chemistry apparatus on her desk, but most of it was in a separate apartment dedicated to the purpose of conducting experiments. She wasn't used to having so much space. The bookshelf on the far wall was proving useful, however, given the reading she was having to do in preparation for the start of the Michaelmas term in a few months' time. To think that she was really going to study at *Oxford*. She wanted to push it to the back of her mind sometimes. Another concern occupied the chief of her thoughts at the present moment: Mr Greenwood was arriving that afternoon. She wanted to escape into the garden alone for a few hours that morning before she had to meet him. Retrieving her straw hat and leather gloves, she stepped out of her room.

Poor Martha really had her work cut out for her, Molly thought, as she descended the staircase. She was more like a maid-of-all-work than a housemaid. They were yet to hire a second housemaid, kitchen maid and butler. Mrs Baxter had supplied Martha and the cook from her circle of acquaintances. The housekeeper herself was proving nowhere near as competent as her subordinates. Molly was still having to help in the kitchen and provide Martha with some relief after cleaning the enormous house all day long. So much for never having to clean or cook dinner again. When Molly was on the first-floor staircase, she noticed a steel rope dangling beside her. It trailed all the way down to the hallway.

'What on—?'

'Up here, Mol!' She heard Douglas's voice echo from high above. Seconds later he came whizzing down on the rope, which was attached to a belt around his waist.

'What are you doing?'

'Fixing the clock in the tower,' he said breezily, hanging upside down from the rope.

'Shouldn't you be working?'

'George banished me from the workshop, and since we don't have any other outstanding commissions at present, I thought I'd see about the clock.'

'Why did George banish you?'

'He said he could do a better job of it alone, and he was in such a foul temper that I thought I'd better leave him to it.' The playfulness gradually faded from his voice as he gave this brief explanation. Molly sometimes felt as though there were two versions of Douglas: one that was pragmatic and serious, and one that was exuberant and rather childish.

'He has been very short-tempered lately. Something isn't right,' she admitted, picking at the soil that was still lodged under one of her fingernails.

'I know. He keeps making frequent trips into town for God knows what reason. Probably to visit some alehouse he has become a regular at. I have been meaning to confront him about it but you know how he'll just evade the question.'

'Unfortunately so,' she sighed. 'Don't stay like that too long or you'll faint.'

He flipped himself upright, and was now red in the face.

'I'm going to the garden for a while,' said Molly.

'You've remembered about Mr Greenwood, haven't you?'

'Of course,' she said over her shoulder as she continued on her way downstairs. All the cobwebs had been removed from the north hall, so while it was still imposing it wasn't nearly as eerie. Martha was dusting the drawing room as Molly passed the open doorway on the right. She was a thin, dark-haired girl of fourteen, with a sallow complexion and freckles. She could be somewhat curt, but she was pleasant enough and careful in her work. Molly had noticed a strange, sweet, strong smell coming from the servants' hall the previous day, which she'd thought to be a herb-heavy dish cooking or a new metal polish. She had an idea what it actually was but she wouldn't mention it to anyone unless she was certain, nor could she assume that Martha was the one responsible. Then again, it would explain how she coped with the strain of the job.

Molly exited the house through the south hall and made her way down the dirt path, past the grimy water fountain and through the shrubbery archway that led to the woodland on the other side. Removing her shoes so that she could feel the grass against her feet, she ventured deeper into the woods. Sunlight dripped between the leaves of the trees, and a calm breeze blew. Birds twittered from their branches, the only other sounds being leaves rustling and her feet disturbing the undergrowth. Brambles ran amok in huge tangles so she had to mind her step. She still had plenty of weeding left to do. The path split into two ahead; the left path led to the lake and kitchen garden, the right path to an overgrown meadow. Neither of these was her objective today. She had come to the woodland for a specific purpose, although she had a little time to wander and admire. She loved those grand, sturdy old trees. Many of their trunks were robed in thick ivy. Molly approached the largest oak and began to climb it. From the top of the tree she had a splendid panorama of her surroundings. Beyond the hall's front lawn and iron gates was Darkwater Farm on the right and the road to Holtbury on the left. A fly was pulling up outside the front gates. Perhaps it was one of her brothers' clients, although Douglas hadn't said they were expecting anyone today. Not that they told her everything. She watched a man get out of the cab and stare perplexedly at the gates. Molly could practically see his bemusement as they opened of their own accord. Clearly she wasn't the only one who had perceived his arrival. There was a sign on the right-hand gatepost informing visitors that they needed to press a button and speak into the brass tube, which was connected to another tube in the servants' hall, along with the mechanism for opening the gates. They were having to answer callers themselves as Martha was never around to hear the receiver buzz and Mrs Baxter claimed that she was unable to hear it, repeating the same line that she must start remembering to bring her hearing trumpet. Maybe they should make hiring a butler a priority.

The man said something to the cab driver before the fly turned back down the road, and he made his way down the gravel path on foot. Molly scurried back down the tree almost as quickly as she had gone up it, and leapt from the third-highest branch to the ground. There were still many more trees to treat and she was running out of time. She had only managed one batch, however, before she heard approaching footsteps from behind her. Did Douglas need her for something? But when she turned around, she saw it was the man who had got out of the fly. He wore a moss-green sack coat and trousers, with an olive-green bowler hat. He was smiling broadly at her as he approached with cautious steps. She immediately realised who he was.

Molly fixed her eyes squarely on the young man. The moment he felt the sting of her gaze, his smiling and possibly somewhat unnaturally cheerful demeanour faltered. He raised one hand slightly, as if to shield himself from the wild-haired girl walking down the overgrown path towards him.

He held out his hand. 'You must be Miss Abernathy. I am glad to—'

She stopped just short of him, planting her feet with a firm step on the grassy walk, and, unsmiling, cut him off. 'I suppose you are the landscape gardener my brother sent to tamper with my garden?'

'Tamper!' he exclaimed. 'Why, I believe there has been some misunderstanding, Miss Abernathy. I—'

'Let me make this clear to you, Mr Greenwood,' she snapped, pointing her finger at his blinking eyes. 'I did not request, nor do I require, your presence here. If it weren't for the fact that my brother has paid your first lot of wages in advance, I would have you cleared off my land this very minute.'

He stared, struck dumb with awe and transfixed by her flashing green eyes. This spirited, wild-haired girl was nothing like what he had expected. She was a Celtic queen shrunk into the body of a nymph!

'However...' She drew herself up, raising her chin slightly. 'I will listen to what it is you propose to do with my garden. But if I find fault with the slightest detail, don't think I'll hold back.'

Mr Greenwood adjusted his hat. 'Miss Abernathy,' he said in a much less jolly manner, 'I wouldn't ask you to hold back in the slightest. Let me explain. Your brother hired me to assist you in executing your vision for what your garden should be. I don't wish to tamper with it in the slightest, although I will make suggestions where I feel they are appropriate. I also have my skilled team of gardeners at your disposal to assist with the labour.'

'While you're correct in your impression that you're here to assist me in creating my vision – not that I need assistance – I want to make it clear to you that, while my brother is the one paying your wages, you are answerable to me on all matters concerning this garden and my word is final. Is that clear?'

'Of course.' He nodded firmly, reaffirming his hold on the pocketbook tucked underneath his left arm.

'Good. Then we understand one another.'

'In that case, would you be willing to conduct me around the garden? I must begin by acquainting myself with it.'

'At this moment in time it is little more than a giant thicket,' she said flatly. 'But I shall humour your request. We shall cover every inch of it today.'

'Today?'

'That's what I said.'

'Oh, but that may take a great deal of time. I wouldn't wish to impose—'

'The sooner you have a complete picture of it, the sooner you can get to work.'

She retrieved a pair of boots that were dangling from a tree branch, their laces knotted together. He hadn't realised she was barefoot until now. She caught him watching her unknotting the laces and scowled at him. Mr Greenwood quickly averted his gaze and his eyes landed on something of interest. A nearby tree's trunk was covered with deep, dark lesions and its leaves were black, with powdery white spots.

'I have never seen a disease like this before,' he said as he knelt down and examined the tree more closely.

'It's caused by fungus spores.' Molly laced her second boot.

'Hm. Is it only this portion of the woodland that is affected?' He perceived that this tree was not the only one with blackened leaves. A cluster of perhaps a dozen or more were similarly afflicted. He rose to his feet and shook his head. 'This will all need cutting down.'

'No it won't.'

Mr Greenwood looked at Molly incredulously. She returned his stare with one hand on her hip.

'But the infection has spread too much, Miss Abernathy. There is no hope of them recovering.'

'There is every hope. Watch.' With her other hand, she pulled out a bottle of purple liquid from the belt fastened around her narrow waist and flipped back the cap. Eyeing him all the while, she tipped the bottle upside down onto the ground near the tree's roots. There was a delay of five seconds, then something miraculous happened.

It was as if time was in reverse. The lesions on the trunk knitted themselves together until there was not a trace of the damage left. Black leaves became green and healthy once more. The whole tree was radiant with health and life.

Mr Greenwood stared open-mouthed at it, then cleared his throat. 'Astonishing as that was, Miss Abernathy, I fear you will need a great deal more to cure every single tree—'

'*Uh.*' She held up her finger. Behind her, each infected tree was undergoing the same transformation, until all were healthy once more.

Mr Greenwood could only gaze at the sight with wonder.

'I've been curing the entire woodland at a steady rate. On average a dosage of that size can treat a dozen trees. I have plenty more of the mixture,' she explained. She was about to propose beginning their survey of the garden when she narrowed her eyes at him. 'How old are you?'

'Twenty.'

He didn't look it. Perhaps if he weren't so clean-shaven it might add the additional couple of years that his face was lacking. His hair was the colour of barley, on the cusp of brown and blonde.

'Come, let's get started, Mr Greenwood. There's much to get round.'

'Of course. Lead the way, Miss Abernathy.'

If he annoyed her too much, she could push him in the lake, she thought as she moved down the path.

*

Shortly after Douglas had pointed Mr Greenwood in Molly's direction, he decided he'd try to find the courage to interrupt George and deliver his post. He saw a little rotund automaton at the foot of the oak staircase, nudging the bottom step repeatedly. Douglas picked it up and tucked it under his arm before staggering upstairs. It was heavier than it looked. He set it down on the first floor and it rolled away down the landing. Passing through an unassuming wooden door, Douglas climbed the secret staircase that led to the tower where their workshop was, feeling the air around him grow colder. They had been at Ravenfeld Hall just over two months now and each of them had found their own spaces. Douglas's bedroom and study were on the second floor, as was Molly's bedroom. George's room was on the third floor and he had his study in one of the turrets.

The heavy oak door to the workshop was before him. He tried to listen to what was going on inside but he couldn't hear a great deal.

'I know you're there,' came George's voice from inside. 'Either state your business or go away.'

'Post for you.'

'Bring it in.'

Douglas hesitantly inched the door inwards. George was slumped in a wooden chair with his arms resting on the worktable. He didn't seem to have made much progress on the android since early that morning when he'd kicked Douglas out. It had all of its limbs now, at least.

'There's three letters addressed to you. Four commissions also came in the postbag that I want to run past you.'

He held three of the seven letters in his hand out to his brother. George took them and held them listlessly.

'Mr Greenwood has just arrived. He and Molly are out in the garden now.' This didn't seem to have produced any reaction from George. 'I'm not sure what she'll make of him, although he did seem very polite. I hope she isn't too stern with him.'

Still George did nothing other than stare at his work. He had placed the letters on the table unopened.

'Are you not listening, or deliberately trying to ignore me?'

No response.

Douglas whacked him around the back of the head with the fan of remaining letters. 'You're still drunk, aren't you?'

At last George slowly lifted his head and regarded his brother with impassive, red eyes.

'No, for your information.' Even his voice sounded lethargic.

'You expect me to believe that?'

'I do, however, have quite a severe headache, which you are only serving to aggravate.' He placed a palm on his temple.

'Then why don't you go to bed and rest if it's that severe?'

'I've been having trouble sleeping lately.'

'Well, you don't seem to be able to concentrate on working, so it might be worth a try. And Molly claims cowslip tea is good for headaches and insomnia.'

'Will you please just shut up?' George exclaimed, clawing his black hair with both hands.

Douglas had long been undaunted by his brother's outbursts by this point, and sat in the chair opposite him. He waited a few moments to allow George's temper to cool before he attempted to speak again. He tried to manage his voice so it was steady and gentle.

'It's only because I'm concerned about you. I'm starting to be greatly troubled by your drinking.'

'Well, you needn't be.'

'Really? George, I can see there's been a change in you over the last few weeks. Both Molly and I have noticed it. What is it you're hiding?'

'Nothing.'

'So you haven't been getting through even more of the brandy than usual? I've been watching the bottle steadily empty.'

'No,' he said defensively.

'What have all these late night or early morning trips to town been about, then?'

'That is my own private business. It need not concern you. It hasn't been interfering with my work, so there is no problem.'

'*No problem?* Do you think the business is all I care about? You believe that I don't care for my own brother's well-being? And as for it not affecting your work, it seems to be doing so today.'

'As I said, it is just a headache, most likely brought on by lack of sleep.'

Douglas could tell that George was attempting to keep his composure, although his voice was strained. However, he was finding it difficult to conceal his own frustration.

'Fine, keep it to yourself then. I have enough concerns without having to nanny you.'

'Who said you must? I am perfectly capable of being responsible for myself.'

'Responsible? What about all the times you've gone and done something reckless and I've had to step in? Like your drunken wager with Lord Leyton.'

'If it wasn't for that drunken wager, we wouldn't have all of this.' He gestured to the room around them. 'It was a calculated risk.'

'Oh, stop pretending, George. You're not always in control of everything, least of all yourself.'

'You're the one who feels the need to be in control. You like to think you can control *me*, for a start.'

'Oh, nobody can control you. You're far above everyone else,' retorted Douglas sarcastically.

'Well, I'll save you the trouble of being concerned about me from now on. You can stay out of my affairs and I will stay out of yours. The next time you have been rejected by some woman you've become infatuated with, or you decide to attempt a fatal flight off the roof—'

'I was six years old—'

'—I won't be there to help you.'

'I am not a child any more. I can fend for myself.' Douglas hated how his tone was bordering on that of a child in a fit of passion.

George observed him coolly. 'I suppose we'll see.' He quit the room without another word. Douglas resisted the urge to shout an insult at him.

Molly and Mr Greenwood started their tour on the meadow side of the garden, where they had their first major disagreement. Mr Greenwood thought the meadow would be better 'cultivated' but Molly wished to leave it as it was.

'Well, I agree about keeping the wild flowers, but surely it would be better if we were to bring the meadow in line a bit? It could do with trimming and a bit more colour introducing into it. Maybe create some walks with seating?' he'd said.

'I think you'll find that there's plenty of colour already,' she replied as she strode through the tall, dry grasses. 'There's poppies, daisies, cornflowers, cowslips… I think anything else would simply result in overpopulation.'

'But it looks simply…wild.'

'And that's how I intend it to stay. The farmer has already asked if he can use some of the grass as feed for his cattle once most of the blooms have died back, and I obliged him.'

Mr Greenwood remained silent until they returned to the gate.

They retraced their steps to the woodland and took the opposite path. The temperature was starting to climb and Molly felt herself sweating at the roots of her hair beneath her straw hat. She couldn't believe he'd caught her in her faded, sprigged gardening dress, without a petticoat or stockings. She had intended to change into something more respectable before meeting him, if only he hadn't arrived so ridiculously early. Well, perhaps it was better that he see her for what she was. Maybe it would drive him away sooner. They came to a circular clearing in the trees that looked like something from a fairy story. Molly had stumbled across it several days ago. It was carpeted in emerald-green grass and fenced by a perfect ring of trees, which shielded it from most of the sun's light. All manner of wild flowers grew at the bases of the tree trunks. Pink and purple foxgloves rose elegantly above the other flowers with their columns of bell-shaped petals, and little daisies were sprinkled across the grass. Down the centre of the clearing ran a trickling stream, which eventually fed into the lake. The water was so clear that the mossy pebbles lining the bed were visible beneath.

'I'm planning to build a little cottage or something of that nature here,' she said. As soon as she had seen this place she felt almost as if it had been intended as a retreat for her, although she wasn't much given to superstition.

'What would this cottage look like?' Mr Greenwood scribbled something in his pocketbook. He seemed as enchanted as she was by the place, entering the clearing before her. 'Not like a summer house? Although something like a little chalet would look rather fine.'

'I was thinking maybe stone or wood with a thatched roof – nothing too modern. Something in keeping with the landscape.'

'And what would you intend it to be? A place to bring visitors in the pleasant weather?'

'A laboratory.'

'Oh.' His pencil ceased scratching.

'And something of a place to escape to as well.' She sat down on a fallen log covered with moss. She could expect to find spiders in her hair and clothes later on.

'I see. Well, perhaps I might do some sketches for you?'

'I don't see why not,' she shrugged, watching him make more notes in his pocketbook. 'Have you actually done any large projects before, Mr Greenwood?'

'I confess that I haven't. I have designed an Italianate summer house for a baron, Lord Colton, and a kitchen garden for an acquaintance of mine. But I won't always be content with small projects. I crave something more significant.'

On hearing this, Molly rose. 'In that case, I have something to show you that you might appreciate. Follow me.' They left the clearing and continued down the path until the trees began to thin and they reached the red brick walls of the kitchen garden.

'How good are you at climbing?'

'I beg your pardon, Miss Abernathy?'

'There's no key for the door, and the lock is too rusty anyway. I've asked my brothers to fit a new lock but they haven't got round to it yet. So I've been having to scale the walls to get in.'

'I see. I should be able to manage.'

'I'll go first.' She placed her hands and feet in the deepest grooves she could find and began to climb. The day before, her foot had slipped and she'd fallen to the ground. Her hands still bore the thin red scratches from where they'd scraped against the rough brick. She hoped she wouldn't repeat her mistake in front of Mr Greenwood; the embarrassment would be more painful than the fall. When she reached the top, she pulled herself over the wall and leapt down, landing with her knees bent. Her feet tingled with red-hot pinpricks for a moment, but she had managed her descent with some grace. She heard Mr Greenwood beginning his ascent. Shortly afterwards, a hand appeared. He dragged himself onto the top of the wall and remained sitting there.

'Are you all right, Mr Greenwood?' She smiled at him.

'Quite all right. I'm just debating how best to start the journey down.'

'Jump.'

His grip on the wall tightened.

'If I can manage it, I'm sure you can. Be sure to land with your knees bent.'

He looked uncertainly at the ground. A couple of moments passed before he swallowed, braced himself, and let go of the wall. He landed in a crouched position and raised himself with surprising dignity.

'My word!' His eyebrows shot up as he took in the sight of the kitchen garden. 'This is splendid, Miss Abernathy. Did you do all this?'

'I did.' She put her hands on her hips and followed his gaze. 'Although there is much work still to be done.'

In a few short weeks, the barren beds had been transformed. They were filled with sprouting vegetables and vibrant flowers. The sweet smell of flora and onion filled the air. Butterflies fluttered amongst the beds. Mr Greenwood examined her tomatoes, still green but of more than a modest size, before something else caught his eye.

'What are these? I know what they look like but surely they cannot be what I think they are.'

'They're a hybrid between a moss rose and a lily.'

'So they're "mollies"?' He smiled proudly at that.

'Yes.' She rolled her eyes. (Had Douglas told him her nickname for some unknown reason, or was he just proud to have compounded the plants into a woman's name?) 'A lot of these specimens were uprooted from my previous home, but they seem to have taken well. Others are more recent experiments.'

'And you really did all of this yourself?'

'Yes.' She plucked a deadhead from a flower and walked further along the brick path. 'As hard as that may be for you to believe.'

'I do believe it. Well, as much as I can, given the nature of your achievements. Healing those trees, crossbreeding two distinct species – it's incredible.'

'Well, not all of the plants in here are crossbreeds.' She picked two pods of peas from a plant and offered him one. He accepted it. 'So this kitchen garden is a fixed feature. That's not up for negotiation,' she said, stuffing a pea into her mouth.

'I promise I wouldn't dream of uprooting a thing, Miss Abernathy.' She heard a pea crunch in his mouth. 'Although I assume you will want a greenhouse. A large one.'

'Several large ones. I have already designed what they are to look like.'

'You have? Then I should like to see the designs. It seems you will leave me little to do,' he grinned.

'Like I told you, I don't need assistance. My brother is convinced that the scale of the task is too great, but I've had long enough to think about what it is I intend to do.'

'Well, allow me to phrase it a different way. You know the character of this garden and how you envision it – this will go here, that will go there, and so on. But there is a risk of not being able to see the greater picture – not being able to see the wood for the trees, if you will. An outside party can provide a fresh perspective. I can be the one to draw it all together.'

'Hm, you're not bad with metaphors, I'll give you that. But you're implying that my plan lacks cohesion.' She tossed her empty pod over the garden wall. He did likewise.

'Well, from what you've said as we've been discussing the matter, it seems as though you have an awful lot of conflicting ideas.'

'There is an awful lot to consider.' She drew away a strand of hair that was dangling between her eyes.

'Take these greenhouses, for example. Do you know exactly where they are to go?'

'Yes. On the south side of the garden near the lake.'

'And do you know how long these will take to build? And at what cost?'

'That would have been my next step. Although that might be one area where you can assist me. I assume you'll be able to give me estimates as to how much things cost?'

'Yes, but I'm not a clerk. I want to be involved in actually putting the garden together.'

She met his hazel eyes and felt a pang of guilt. It wasn't his fault really; it was George who she should be cross with. It would be unfair not to let Mr Greenwood do something; she could only imagine how frustrated she would be in his situation.

'Well, if you do have any alternative ideas, perhaps I will listen to them.'

He seemed shocked for a moment, then brightened. 'I appreciate that, Miss Abernathy.'

Molly turned away from him and brushed her hands on her skirts. 'Are you ready for some more climbing? There's still lots more ground to cover.'

'I suppose,' he grinned. Something caught his attention and he peered down at the bed where green stalks were just starting to emerge. A sign sticking out of the ground next to it read '*DANGER*'.

'What is in that bed there?'

'Carrots. Don't get too close.'

Chapter Eight

Lieutenant-Colonel Kirk had not taken to the soldier. At first he refused to even let him into his battalion.

'What does General Brassington mean by pushing this oversized toy soldier on me?' he asked General Fowler. 'What the hell are the two of you playing at? We're about to send reinforcements to the Field Force to help recapture Delhi, and you think now is an appropriate time to test this so-called new weapon of yours?'

What disrespectful words to speak to a superior officer, thought the soldier. Outrageous.

Colonel Kirk was the brigadier-general's senior in years, if not in rank. The lieutenant-colonel had light orange hair and a pale, pink face that was badly sunburned around the nose. He was far paler than General Fowler, whose tan skin showed him to be accustomed to India's climate.

'I could not think of a better time, Colonel,' replied General Fowler calmly.

'This is no time for larking about, man. I don't have time to waste keeping an eye on that boiler on legs. What if it mistakes one of my men for the enemy and sticks a bullet in his head? I can't afford to lose any more.'

'It won't. And I told you how it captured those rebel spies.'

'So you say.'

'Every soldier in the cantonment witnessed it.'

'That is the only reason I permitted you to entertain me with this foolish scheme, since you had me curious to see the mechanical soldier. Having seen it, however, I do not wish to have it amongst my men. It will unnerve them, for one thing. It certainly unnerves me.'

'I am giving you an order, Colonel. I don't require your approval. I only wished that you might be taken by it to make proceedings easier.'

Colonel Kirk had no response to that.

'Do you understand me, Colonel?' prompted the brigadier-general.

'Yes, sir.'

General Fowler nodded stiffly and departed from the colonel's office. Colonel Kirk rested his fists on a table spread with maps.

'That foolish lad,' he chuntered under his breath, probably thinking that the soldier could not hear him. 'Thinks so highly of himself. If it weren't for this whole mutiny business, he'd never have been made a brigadier-general. All the old officers are dropping like flies and being replaced by these inexperienced young boys.'

He wiped his sweating brow with a lightly freckled hand and looked at the soldier from beneath bushy eyebrows. 'You understand English?' he demanded.

'Yes, sir.'

'And you have to do whatever you're told, don't you?'

'Correct, sir.'

'Then listen well – don't cause me any trouble or I'll have you melted down into bullets, and I don't care what Fowler or Brassington might think. Am I clear?'

'Yes, sir.'

'Do you understand our objective?'

'We are to form part of General Nicholson's movable column and provide assistance to the British force on the Ridge outside Delhi, sir.' General Brassington had explained all of this already. The Delhi Field Force entrenched on the Ridge overlooking the city of Delhi were in urgent need of men and guns if they had any hope of retaking the city, which had fallen to the rebels some months ago. General Nicholson was the man to do it, General Brassington had said. The man's reputation was legendary. He was

said to have once ridden into a village of robbers and decapitated the chief –
in front of the chief's own men. Having secured the Punjab, he could now
direct his attention to Delhi.

The column set off down the Grand Trunk Road at once. On either
side of them were clumps of trees that shielded their view, eventually giving
way to an endless stretch of dry plain overlooked by the majestically mighty
Himalayas in the far distance. The soldier could see what he believed to
be snow on the peaks of the mountain range. Further along the road they
passed the occasional hamlet or stone structure. Colonel Kirk had the
soldier wear a makeshift cowl made of sacking, to 'not attract attention'.
But it did not stop the men noticing him, or him noticing them. There must
have been 2,000 men in the column, mostly infantry, with some artillery
and cavalry. The soldier reckoned that he saw two Indian soldiers for every
British one. He caught the eye of one British infantryman who smiled
easily at him – unlike the rest, who looked suspicious or alarmed on seeing
his face. He also caught the occasional glimpse of General Nicholson: a
tall, powerful-looking man with a black beard. When they arrived at the
British camp, the soldier saw that General Brassington's faith in General
Nicholson was well placed. Spirits visibly lifted when the men on the Ridge
saw him and the reinforcements, with people erupting into cheers. A fresh
wave of hope swept through the camp, and men emerged from their tents
to greet them, their faces illuminating at once. Hardly anyone seemed to
notice the shrouded metal soldier. The camp was truly in a sorry state.
Everywhere there were wounded men – prey for the hordes of blackflies
that had infested the place.

The camp was positioned near the top of a slope. From the rocky Ridge
that crested the front of the camp, the soldier had a splendid view of the
city of Delhi, which hovered in the heat like a mirage in the distance. From
his vantage point on the Ridge, he could just make out the minarets of the
Jama Masjid on the hazy horizon. The slope below the Ridge gave way to a
green plain, dense with walled gardens and trees, which ran to the city walls.
In the Civil Lines, to the west of where the soldier was standing, was the
gutted shell of a sprawling English mansion, Metcalfe House, which was the
easternmost picket of the British position. To the north was Ludlow Castle,
which was relatively close to the city walls. (The soldier could see some of

the rebels skulking about near the enemy batteries.) The mighty Jumna river ran to the west of the soldier's position; the Bridge of Boats stretched across the river, allowing travellers from the direction of Meerut to reach the city from the opposite side of the riverbank. That must have been the direction the mutineers arrived from back in May, when they rode from Meerut to Delhi and invaded the city. The Ridge was recaptured by the Delhi Field Force nearly a month later. Delhi was two miles south of the camp, beyond the Civil Lines. The city was enclosed in red, sandstone walls, with gates and bastions positioned along the walls at intervals. The Red Fort, home of the Great Mughals, was of the same red stone and was located near the riverbank. To the south of Delhi was the Jama Masjid, a magnificent mosque with three white marble domes, and a tall red minaret on either side. The soldier magnified his vision to examine the city, although he knew he would gather little useful intelligence from such a distance.

The soldier expected to be on duty guarding the Ridge, but Colonel Kirk issued him no orders and was cooped up in a tent with the other officers for the best part of the day. Instead the soldier hovered around the camp, trying to avoid attracting attention where possible, until he could find an opportunity to consult with Colonel Kirk.

The men had supper as night fell. The soldier remained outside on watch while most of the officers were in the mess, since a bottle of water was all the refreshment he required. He heard the men's talk and laughter without really listening to it. There were complaints from some – the officers, he believed – about them having had the same thing for supper two nights in a row. His attention was captured by the sight of the stars. He had heard that some men could read the night sky like a celestial map to navigate. Master George and Master Douglas had at least fitted him with a compass. He pulled back the glove covering his left wrist and opened the panel in his casing that concealed it. The needle was pointing northward. Closing the panel, he gazed up at the moon. The soldier exhausted the magnification of his vision to examine its craters. The image remained strikingly clear until a certain point, when the celestial body became blurred. He tried to locate the precise point so he knew for future reference. Since he had no other duties, he decided now would be a good opportunity to polish his sword, and took out the necessary apparatus from the leather pouch bag by his side. He heard the sound of footsteps approaching him, but did not turn around to look until the man was directly behind him. It was the young infantryman who had bestowed a smile on him earlier. He was lean, with ashy blonde hair and a wispy beard, and without a forage cap on his head. His loose, dirty, white shirt was tucked into his light grey trousers.

'Stargazing?' he asked.

'I was merely testing my magnification.'

'So you *can* talk to us. We had bets on whether you could or not. I lost.' He sat down beside the soldier and took a swig from the glass bottle in his hand. His poor excuse of a moustache was darkened by sweat or the bottle's contents, like a dog with a damp muzzle. 'They're frightened by you, some of the lads here. They don't know what to make of you.'

'That is to be expected.' The soldier crumbled part of his bath brick to powder in his palm. He concentrated on mixing the pulverised brick with oil in a small dish before him, until he formed a paste. 'And what do you make of me?'

The infantryman shrugged. 'I'm not entirely sure. That's why I came to talk to you.'

'I see.' The soldier drew his weapon from its scabbard.

'Nice sword.'

'Thank you. One of my makers made it for me.'

'Might I handle it?'

'If you please.' He watched the infantryman flex it experimentally before returning it.

'It's slightly heavier than it looks. Little on the long side, too.'

'To a human, yes. It feels feather-light to me. It was crafted especially for me, like an extension of my own body. I've wielded other swords adequately, but none feel like this does.'

'Must have cost a pretty penny.'

'I'm unaware of its monetary value.' The soldier paused from polishing his sword's blade with a paste-covered cloth. He opened his water bottle and poured a small amount of water down his throat.

'You drink?'

'In a sense. I run out of steam otherwise. I can only carry out basic functions without it, and I'd be in no fit state to fight.'

'I see. They say you're faster and stronger than any man.'

'I am indeed faster and stronger than the common man, although there may be exceptions. I have heard stories of such individuals in places called circuses.'

'I think even they'd struggle to compete with you.'

'I would not know. I have only heard stories from some of the men.'

'So I am not the first to talk to you?'

'You are, as a matter of fact. I confess I overheard a great deal of their talk. My hearing is very sharp.'

A pause ensued. The soldier finished polishing his sword.

'So you're modelled after Brash Brass, then?' ventured the infantryman.

'I beg your pardon?'

'General Brassington. "Brash Brass", we call him. Thinks very highly of himself and loves to give out orders, just to hear the sound of his own voice. He's terrified of diseases, though – that's why he hardly ever ventures beyond headquarters.'

'That seems a rather disrespectful thing to say about an officer.'

'You'll see for yourself the longer you're out here.'

'But to answer your question, I was indeed modelled on his appearance.'

'You sound like him too.'

'My makers might have made me so as a mark of respect.'

'Respect, eh?' the infantryman chuckled. 'So what do they call you?'

'I'm afraid I don't catch your meaning.'

'What's your name? Did they name you after General Brassington as well?'

'Why, no, I was not given a name at all.'

'Well, that won't do.' He put down the bottle and took out a silver cigarette case. 'We'll have to think of one for you.'

'Neither do I have an official rank.'

'You're a weapon. That's how they view you – like a bayonet on legs.' He chuckled as he took out a cigarette. 'I'm Private Simon Peterson, 1st Bengal Fusiliers, in case I didn't say so earlier.'

'You didn't.'

He chuckled again.

Two men wearing khaki tunics and trousers approached them. Brown leather pouch belts were worn over their tunics, while a leather strap hung from their left shoulders. One was a young, burly-looking sepoy of the 2nd Regiment of Infantry, Punjab Irregular Force (judging by the regimental buttons on his tunic), with a neat moustache and mutton chops. A light turban, which the soldier believed was called a pugree, was wound around his head. The other man also appeared to be a native infantryman of the same regiment, although his dark head was bare, without a turban or cap, and his skin was a shade or two lighter than that of the man beside him. There was something else about his countenance that the soldier could not put his finger on. A trim beard covered the lower half of his face, although it did not disguise his angular jaw structure.

'Might I borrow a cigarette? I'm out,' the second man said to Private Peterson.

'Here.' He tossed the cigarette case to him. 'Come and join us if you like. I was just keeping our friend here company since nobody else will pay him any mind.'

The two newcomers sat facing Peterson and the soldier. Peterson lit his cigarette and leant back, with his elbows resting on the ground behind him. 'So what do they call you two?' he asked the two men.

'Jatin Singh,' replied the burlier man. He had bright, dark eyes and an animated countenance.

His companion extracted a cigarette from the case before answering. 'Henry Powell.'

'I beg your pardon?' the soldier could not help saying.

'Rather unusual name for a native, isn't it?' Peterson voiced the soldier's thought, although in a far more disinterested manner.

The man regarded Peterson with calm eyes and adjusted his sitting position. 'My father was a European officer. My mother was a dancing girl from a village near Meerut.'

'Your father was English?' said the soldier. Now he could see traces of the Englishman amongst his features. Nor did he speak with the pronounced accent of someone whose mother tongue was not English like his companion did, although there was a slight variation in how he uttered certain sounds.

'Oh, it is not that surprising, soldier,' remarked Peterson. 'In fact, it was quite the thing fifty years or so ago. British men from the Company often

80

took Indian wives and went native, adopting Indian dress and such. But it is practically unheard of now.'

'What is the Company?' asked the soldier. He had heard it mentioned by several other men.

'The East India Company: our employers. They rule two-thirds of India as an agent of the British government, and we protect their territories.'

'So why do the British officers no longer take Indian women for wives?'

'Their attitude changed,' explained Powell, rolling his unlit cigarette between his fingers. 'British officers no longer took the trouble to learn the language of their sepoys, and increasingly sought to have as little to do with them as possible. My father was something of an exception. He was deeply interested in Mughal customs, and was ridiculed by his fellow officers for it. He was a patron of many local artists, and our house was filled with paintings and sculptures. I remember a very fine ivory chess set that my older brother and I used the pieces from to add to our toy soldiers' armies. But when my father was set to return to England, after my mother died, he was faced with the problem of what to do with my brother and me. My father was in debt, and our house was sold along with its contents to go towards the loan repayments. His relations, who'd disapproved of his marriage from the beginning, proposed that my brother, the fairer son, should be sent to live with his sister and her husband, who were very wealthy, while I was to be raised by my mother's relations. Perhaps my father had enough of the Englishman's pride to feel ashamed of returning home with such a dark-skinned son, as he agreed to the scheme. My mother's family were never very accepting of me. They owned a farm and I found life there extremely dull. I joined the army as soon as I was old enough.'

Singh had evidently heard this tale before, and shook his head sadly.

Poor fellow, thought the soldier. He had a claim to both worlds but did not feel entirely at home in either of them.

'That seems rather unfair,' Peterson reflected. 'That one son should be rich and favoured while the other is poor and neglected, all because of the hue of their skin.'

'My aunt had no children, so my brother was made her husband's heir. I believe he took his uncle's name upon turning eighteen.'

'I bet he's a spoilt fool who doesn't know the value of money,' said Peterson.

All four were silent for a moment. Singh seemed entranced by the soldier. 'Are you solid gold?' he asked eventually. He had a way of speaking that was eager yet gentle, with a full and rich voice.

The soldier shook his head. 'The gold is merely a veneer. The rest of me is steel, titanium, iron, brass and copper.'

'Copper,' Peterson echoed, tapping ash from his cigarette. 'Copperton. Like Brassington. That could be a fitting name for you.'

'Private Copperton?' suggested Singh.

'Hmm, I think just Copperton sounds better. But it's for him to judge.'

'Copperton,' the soldier mused as he stroked the end of his moustache. 'Yes, I believe that will suffice for a name.'

Chapter Nine

The next few days were rather uneventful, with hardly any cannons being fired by the enemy. They sometimes launched sorties on the British position, senselessly attacking from the front and being beaten back. They had not learnt from their previous failures, and repeated this strategy again and again out of sheer stupidity, desperation or foolhardy courage. Colonel Kirk placed Copperton on the Ridge during the night to provide relief to some of the men on duty. The android remained erect and motionless, observing and listening keenly, until sunrise – driving off any mutineers who dared to attack. On other occasions the colonel would set him to work retrieving used cannonballs, since ammunition was running low. But Copperton frequently found himself without orders, and took to patrolling the camp until he had the opportunity of speaking to Colonel Kirk. The camp consisted of neat rows of tents just below the top of the Ridge, the bungalows having been burned by the rebelling sepoys some months ago, before the Ridge was reclaimed by the Delhi Field Force. Copperton had taken to residing in Peterson's tent instead of his crate, after Peterson invited him to do so and Colonel Kirk made no objection. (The man Peterson formerly shared his tent with had been killed, and his possessions auctioned off.) The only other structures in the Field Force's territory were the Flagstaff Tower, a short, rotund structure in the middle of the Ridge, and Hindu Rao's house, a Palladian mansion near the tip of the Ridge's spine, which was strongly fortified. Copperton would walk from the infantry lines to the siege park and burial grounds, and back again. He made this patrol at least twice daily. Colonel Kirk had ordered Copperton not to go too close to the outlying pickets and make a nuisance of himself by distracting the men.

The other soldiers gradually grew accustomed to the sight of Copperton, and no longer lifted their heads when he passed them. There was a sense of languor about some of the men. He saw one trying to tempt a fly with some sugar on a bed of gunpowder, only to blow up the little blighter the moment it blundered into his trap. Copperton was surprised to see that there were two ladies at the camp, one of whom had two children and a baby with her. He had also not realised that General Quincy had been amongst the column's numbers, until he saw him the evening after their arrival, when Colonel Kirk presented Copperton to those present in the officers' mess tent. After Colonel Kirk explained to them what Copperton was, one senior officer declared, 'Absolutely ridiculous, Kirk,' and his brother officers laughed – General Quincy amongst them. The joke was lost on Copperton. Since the men were eager for their soup, Copperton was dismissed from the tent.

Peterson, Powell and Singh remained his most frequent companions, and he would talk with them often. Peterson was not confined to his society, however, and mixed freely with everyone. He seemed able to charm anyone, although he went about doing so in the most unusual fashion: he would insult and jokingly mock the man on their first meeting, and gradually grow friendlier. After that, even his most blatantly insulting comments were met with roars of laughter. This breach of manners baffled Copperton. Half the camp – those not in the newly arrived column included – seemed to know of 'Petey'.

The weather had stayed relatively dry until the third day of their being in camp. The heavy rain did not show any sign of stopping once the heavens opened. It was leaking into the tents. Copperton had his arm thrust out of Peterson's tent to catch as much of it in a pan as he could, although it was still only a quarter full.

'What are you doing?' asked Peterson.

'Why waste drinking water to replenish my boiler when I can use the rainwater? My lungs act as filters to purify the water before it reaches the boiler.'

'I see your point.'

Why did Peterson keep looking up at him every few seconds? Copperton heard a scraping from his side of the tent, where he was sitting on the edge of his charpoy. Powell and Singh were also present on this occasion, sitting at either end of Copperton's charpoy (all that remained of the dead man's belongings, although the sheets and pillow had been sold). They'd brought a report that there could be a siege on Delhi as soon as the siege-train containing howitzers, mortars and much-needed ammunition arrived.

'I doubt it'll be that soon,' said Powell. 'General Wilson is reluctant to do so, I have heard. Surely there is a more competent man to lead the Field Force than him?' General Wilson was head of the Delhi Field Force and the ultimate authority in the camp.

'But why wait?' asked Singh. 'The longer we wait, the more men are lost to the cholera.'

'Tell that to the generals.'

Copperton found Powell's attitude towards his superiors most disrespectful. Sun Tzu warned that the worst military policy to adopt was to besiege a walled city, it was true, but the Field Force had found themselves in an unfortunate situation, and there was simply no better alternative.

'What do you know of Brigadier-General Fowler and Major-General Quincy?' Copperton asked, as he was curious about General Brassington's associates.

Singh was the one to answer. 'General Fowler is much respected by his sepoys. He speaks Hindi to them like it is his mother tongue. The English officers admire him also for his... What is the word, Powell, that starts with "r" and means "to be determined to achieve one's purpose"?'

'Resolute?'

'That is the one. They admire his resolve.'

'But that word is a poor fit for General Fowler. He's a sententious fool,' his friend continued.

'Do you have a good word to say about any of the generals in camp?' asked Peterson.

'Not many.'

Peterson still didn't look up from what he was doing. The charpoy's frame creaked as he shifted his sitting position. 'What do you think of

General Nicholson, Powell?'

'I think he is the most competent of the lot of them, even if he has a reputation for vicious hatred towards Indians. He hanged any rebels he came across without trial as he marched along the Grand Trunk Road, didn't he? Although if he had his way they'd be flayed, impaled and burned alive as punishment for mutiny.'

'Hm. I heard he once whipped his own servant to death.'

'It wouldn't surprise me if that were true.'

Peterson ceased his scraping and put down his knife. 'Look here, Copperton. What do you think?' He held up a small, wooden figurine. Copperton saw it was a miniature version of himself.

'Not a bad likeness,' he declared.

'You've got something of a talent there,' remarked Powell.

'My family are carpenters from Liverpool but I didn't find it too exciting a trade, and always wanted to go to sea. I used to make models of famous ships as a boy from cast-off pieces of wood. But I ended up in the army instead.'

'For what reason?'

'My friend persuaded me to enlist for the Indian Service. He made it out to be a grand adventure. Said it'd be like a treasure hunt and that there was gold and jewels all over the place in India. We'd sell whatever treasure we found and be rich as kings. It seemed like a good idea, especially after a few pints. We enlisted together, although poor old Robert died from disease not long after we arrived.' He sighed, but then smiled. 'I soon found out that it wasn't as easy to make a fortune in the army as I'd expected.' He caught Singh giving a nod of assent and turned his attention to him. 'What about you, Singh? What's your story?'

Singh shrugged. 'Nothing original. My family are landowners. My mother's relations owned much land in Oudh, before the British took it away from them. As a boy I heard my great-uncle's stories about his time serving the Company. He spoke of the time he spent with his brother soldiers and of their sahib, a man called Johnson, who regarded them as his sons. My uncle would proudly show me the string of gold beads and red coat he wore. "You should become a soldier, Jatin," he said. "You have the build of a soldier and could become a jemadar." So I joined a year ago. Only it was not quite like it

86

had been in my uncle's day. The pay was still the same as it had been in his time, though, and seven rupees a month does not go as far now.' Copperton thought that the young man certainly had an orator's voice, as Singh added, 'But I don't regret my choice.'

'For what reason?' enquired Peterson.

'Many reasons. I did make good friends amongst my fellow sepoys, for one thing.'

'And how did you become acquainted with Powell?'

'I asked him to teach me English when I heard him address an officer in his own tongue. I thought it would help my progress. That was before I realised that becoming a jemadar is based on the number of years of service a sepoy has and not on merit.'

'His English was not terribly bad when he approached me – it only wanted polishing,' said Powell.

Singh laughed. 'My *munshi* does me too great justice. I keep notes of words in my little book.' He brandished the notebook in question. 'And I note differences in how men talk. How they say words.'

'Accents, you mean?' asked Peterson.

Singh nodded enthusiastically. 'Yes. Indian *and* British. I am not as good with English accents, but I notice your accent is very distinct, Peterson.'

He grinned. 'I'm afraid I don't talk terribly nicely, but you're welcome to make a study of me if you wish.'

'It interests me. Can I ask you questions if I need more informations?'

'More *information*,' corrected Peterson gently. 'And feel free.'

'You're wasted as a soldier, Jat,' said Powell. 'You are a scholar and a poet at heart. You shouldn't have listened to that damn fool uncle of yours. Haven't you always wanted to be a poet since you were young?'

'Ever since I read that book of Urdu poems when I was twelve. I'd never read anything like it before, and it opened my eyes to a new style of writing. But my own poetry isn't very good.'

'Your poem about our metal friend here was rather fine. What were those lines that caught my attention yesterday? "Skinned in the sun's golden rays, with eyes of ruby fire" – something like that. And I must say that you raised a valid point earlier about promotion in the native army being based on length of service. It discourages young men such as yourself who are full of energy and vigour – yet another oversight of the English officers.'

Copperton could abide his contemptuous tone no longer. 'Forgive me, Powell, but I think that you forget yourself. You are far too liberal in your criticism of your employers and superiors. I am sure the wages they pay are fair and that they are more than willing to reward good service with promotion in due course. I am certain of their good judgement, and so should you be.'

Powell briefly met Copperton's eyes. The man's eyes were light brown, almost topaz, and made Copperton think of a tiger. He lit a cigarette, and smoke snaked out of the end as he contemplated Copperton. 'So if you were ordered to kill any of us here, you would do it? With no good reason?'

'It is not for me to question orders, only obey them. As it is for all of you.'

'Well, that's not terribly reassuring, seeing as you evaded the question,' muttered Peterson as he began whittling something new.

Powell regarded Copperton with his usual sedate, tranquil stare. 'Let me ask you, Copperton, why did the mutiny start?'

'Because of the matter with the greased cartridges.' Copperton had heard of this matter from General Brassington shortly before the column's departure. A rumour had spread from a magazine at Dum-Dum, near Calcutta, that the cartridges for the new Enfield rifle were greased with a mixture containing cow and pig fat, which was objectionable to both Hindus and Muslims. 'The sepoys believed it was a plot by the British to rob them of their caste, when they bit the paper to open the cartridge, and to then force them to be Christians – utter hogwash, of course. We would not force them to abandon their paganistic ways by such underhand methods. The whole thing is ridiculous. They made a tremendous fuss over nothing.' General Brassington's voice had been a whisper throughout this speech, but his last statement had boomed across the parlour and caused his servant to jump as he poured tea.

Powell seemed amused by this explanation. 'It takes more than greased cartridges to ignite a rebellion – that was merely the spark which lit the tinder.'

'I don't quite follow, Powell.'

'It's like a pot of water left to simmer until it boils. There has long been resentment at British interference in India. All that was needed was an excuse to rebel, which the cartridges provided.'

'But the British were trying to civilise the natives, maybe in the hope that one day they could rule themselves,' protested Copperton.

'There'll be little hope of that now,' said Peterson. 'I can see why they resent us coming here and changing things, but you must admit some of their customs were barbaric – like widows flinging themselves on their husband's funeral pyre.'

Powell drew on his cigarette. 'It's not simply about religion or customs. No doubt there will be those who genuinely believe that the British were trying to rob them of their caste by having them bite cartridges smothered in pig and cow fat, but most of the mutineers used it as an excuse. I doubt the British were really grinding cow bones into our flour either, but the Hindu sepoys were more than willing to give credit to the rumour. India has been invaded by foreign powers throughout its history. The grievances of most of the mutineers could be seen as more professional – they had to contend with poor pay and prospects. Increasingly strict regulations also threatened to undermine the advantageous status of the high-caste Hindu sepoys who dominated the Bengal Army. There was an outcry over the Enlistment Act, but I doubt any sepoy would ever need to serve overseas and lose their caste in doing so. It discouraged Brahman and Rajput Hindus from enlisting in the Bengal Army – as their fore-fathers had done, at any rate. They felt threatened that a job that was rightfully theirs was being taken away from them, and that the British were trying to supersede them with a Sikh army. Not to mention that the terms of enlistment were changed, so newly recruited sepoys were to be enlisted for general service only, and thus not receive a pension after being discharged. Others feel resentment at the changing of boundaries. The Company's unjustified annexation of Oudh caused much anger.' Powell glanced at Singh, but the latter made no remark; he only sighed.

'All right, Mr Powell. You remind me of my old Sunday school teacher. No need to preach to us,' said Peterson.

Powell discarded the cigarette butt and crushed it underfoot. 'I'm simply explaining to our mechanical friend the ways of the world. It's obvious he is as naive as a child.'

Copperton was quite confounded. Up until that point he had never considered the mutiny in such a light. To his mind, the rebels were bloodthirsty savages who would jump at the first excuse to commit murder and destruction. Could it possibly be that there was more to the matter than he had been led to believe? Looking at Singh, he could see how a man of a less stable temperament might react to such unfair treatment. But it was merely the shadow of a thought, and it slid from his grasp as he was on the verge of glimpsing this new vision. Just attempting to contemplate the enemy's view appeared traitorous to him.

Outside, the rain continued to pour, relieving the silence within the tent. Copperton thoughtfully chewed a piece of leftover wood from Peterson's whittling.

'Question, Copperton: if you eat coal or wood to fuel your boiler, it must produce charcoal and ash. So where does all of that go?'

'I regularly clean out my firebox with the aid of a small shovel and a brush, Peterson. I believe you were imagining something different. Am I wrong?'

'Yes, but it stands to reason – if things go in one end, they usually come out the other.'

Copperton was about to reply when his head jerked up sharply. 'Do you hear something outside?'

The other three exchanged enquiring looks.

'No. What are we meant to be hearing?' asked Peterson.

'It sounds like someone's creeping around outside.' Copperton was certain of it. Beneath the dull fire of raindrops on the tent was an undertone of rustling and shuffling. But no shadow, not even a faint one, could be seen on the other side of the tent.

Powell knelt on the ground and lifted the canvas to peer outside, armed with an Adams revolver. 'There is no one there,' he declared, and replaced his weapon.

'Perhaps it was a dog,' said Singh.

'It didn't sound like a dog to me,' replied Copperton.

'But who would go creeping around in the rain?' asked Peterson. 'It's unlikely it was an enemy. If they did break into the camp, they couldn't expect to get far picking us off one tent at a time – someone would hear gunfire or screams. How could they even have entered the camp undetected?'

'I couldn't say,' Copperton admitted. But he was certain there had been someone about, whom he'd unknowingly driven off when he asked if the others heard the noises outside. Was he their target? Maybe the rebels had sent a spy to gather information on the Field Force's new weapon. Whoever it was would return, and Copperton would uncover their identity.

Chapter Ten

Molly was planting a row of trees along the drive when Mr Greenwood arrived with a pocketful of ideas. He discussed them with her as she planted young trees from the barrow beside her, like a pram full of infants, and moved steadily down the drive. The row of trees on the opposite side of the drive had already been completed.

'You know, I was thinking that perhaps we could have a little Italian-style summer house overlooking the lake—'

'No.'

'I promise it wouldn't intrude upon the scene.'

'No. I told you, I don't like any of that ornate rubbish.'

He sighed and took out his pocketbook, scribbling furiously at something. Maybe he was obliterating a sketch of the summer house. Molly paused in her digging. It wasn't ideal to be carrying out this task in the August heat, and his presence was only stoking her temper. Her arms were on fire and her dress clung to her damp back. A band of sweat formed under her straw hat. She'd already been annoyed at discovering muddy gashes streaked across the lawn that morning – Douglas's doing. Nevertheless she tried to maintain her composure.

She smiled lightly. 'I am providing you with a challenge, Mr Greenwood. I'm encouraging you not to merely copy what everyone else is doing.'

'You certainly are providing me with a challenge, Miss Abernathy,' he muttered.

Molly was unsure whether she was meant to have heard that. Insolent swine. She wrestled the spade out of the ground. 'If you insist on being involved, here.' The spade landed at his feet. 'Roll up your sleeves and get digging, Mr Greenwood.'

She wanted him to look shocked or outraged, but instead he simply regarded her with raised eyebrows before placing his pocketbook and coat on the lawn. Rolling back his shirtsleeves over his brown arms, he picked up the spade and plunged it into the earth. She watched the easy rhythm with which he worked; he'd held a shovel before. Taut muscles stood out along his forearms.

'Are you just going to stand there and watch me, Miss Abernathy?'

'I was merely checking that you were taking your work seriously, Mr Greenwood. That should be deep enough to plant the next one.'

Molly knelt beside the newly dug hole and placed the young tree into it. She packed soil around it as Mr Greenwood knocked in some of the earth from his pile into the space around the root ball. After gently patting down the top soil, Molly rose to her feet.

'I see you're not afraid to get your hands dirty after all,' she remarked.

'When I was younger, I informally served as an apprentice to the head gardener of Lord Colton's estate. I enjoyed it, despite my father's disapproval.'

'Why did he object?'

'Because he thought becoming a gardener was too lowly for me, even if he is of quite humble antecedents.' He rested his elbows on the spade's handle while its head was burrowed in the ground. 'He is an estate surveyor and worked for Lord Colton for many years until the old baron's death. He now works for his son, the new Lord Colton, who I suspect regards my father as a creaking old fossil. My father has always wanted me to succeed him, and I have no brothers to take my place. His line of work has never quite interested me. I always wanted to do something more creative. I suppose being a gardener would have contented me to a degree, but it was not meant to be.'

'So what happened after your apprenticeship ended?'

'I went to study agriculture and botany at the University of Edinburgh.

While I was there, I read books on garden design and decided that was what I wished to do. I didn't finish my degree, not feeling the need to, but I made good friends while I was at Edinburgh, and that led to my first commission to design a kitchen garden. I am also helping one of my university friends put together an illustrated encyclopaedia on British ferns.'

'And what does your father think of all this?'

'He was furious that I had abandoned my studies and tried to walk my own path.' He smiled, his eyes cast down on the ground. 'He said, why would I dream of perusing such a risky profession with no guarantee of regular work, when he had secured a steady position for me? I think he accepts it a little more now, although I'm hoping that my first true commission will help win him over completely. But for now I am tethered. He insists I help him manage Lord Colton's affairs, as my father is growing infirm, and he still believes that I shall succeed him. And I am still reliant on the allowance he gives me to supplement my income, something he doesn't let me forget.'

'Pretentious old fool,' Molly concluded. 'I know the troubles of having a stubborn parent who decides your destiny for you. My mother tried to force me to marry an undertaker's son when I was fifteen, although the actual wedding would probably have taken place around now.'

'And you refused?'

'Yes, although I confess my brothers stepped in on my behalf.'

'Rightly so. If I had a sister, I would have done likewise.'

'Even if she was poor?'

'Even then.'

Molly was unsure whether she entirely believed that, but she looked at him with greater respect. He'd had to struggle to be where he was. Fair enough, his father could afford to send him to university, but he'd chosen to fight for what he wanted and make a name for himself. And he actually knew about botany. But it seemed his prospects depended on her and her garden, unless another opportunity arose. Surely his friends could secure him a commission elsewhere?

She noticed something had fallen on the ground, and stooped to retrieve it.

'Oh, that is my card. It must have fallen out of my coat pocket,' he said.

'Mr Arthur Greenwood,' she read before returning it to him.

'I'm not used to being addressed as Mr Greenwood – that's my father. I've always been Mr Arthur.'

'In that case I'll address you as such.'

'Thank you, Miss Abernathy, or would you prefer Miss Mary?'

'Molly. Only my mother and my nurse called me Mary.'

'In that case, if you wouldn't mind stopping for a moment, Miss Molly, I would like to show you my larger sketches for the laboratory.'

'I suppose I wouldn't. Come through to the drawing room and I'll bring us some lemonade.'

'Do you not have servants?'

'Our only maid is occupied with the laundry today. I'm not above serving myself.'

His puzzled expression showed that he was unsure what to make of this latest breach of propriety.

Around mid-afternoon, George set off for Holtbury on foot. The unrelenting heat seemed to be giving way, the blue sky blotted by swathes of white and grey cloud. They could expect a storm that night. He'd anticipated that Douglas would enquire about his errand, but to his surprise he merely asked what time he was likely to return, affecting to sound less interested than he probably was.

Even the sun's retreat behind the clouds did little to ease his sore eyes as he walked along the dry, dusty road that led to Holtbury, a mile and a half away. Holtbury was a prosperous market town, boasting a post office, a railway station, and a record for the most public houses per square mile in Hertfordshire (twelve on average). The road to the town was fringed with hedgerows, beyond which stretched patchworks of green and pale gold fields. Occasionally there would be a break in the hedgerows where a narrow path led to a dilapidated cottage. The tenant farmers' dwellings and the labourers' cottages needed renovating, the responsibility for which now fell to George as custodian of the Ravenfeld estate. Darkwater Farm was rented from him, as was a neighbouring farm a quarter of a mile away. The farms were more of a burden than a source of income, but at least he did not need to interfere in their day-to-day business, since the farmers were accustomed to not having the owner of the Hall around to advise them about buying livestock and such matters. Their cousin certainly never troubled himself about them when he resided here.

Not too far ahead of George was a female figure, and he soon closed the distance between them. The woman was walking in the same direction as he was, but at a much slower pace. George watched as she staggered and slouched. Was she intoxicated? Then she swooned. George instantly flew forward and caught her in his arms before she fell to the ground. She was a young woman, with fair hair showing from beneath her bonnet. For a moment she seemed insensible, then she opened her eyes. Shock registered in her countenance. Her lips appeared dry and there was a wet sheen on her face.

'Do not fear. You were about to faint and I was walking not far behind you.' George lifted her into a more upright position. 'Are you able to stand?'

'I – I think so,' she said shakily. 'Although I confess to feeling dizzy still. Oh, I felt so faint a moment ago. Thank you for your assistance, sir.'

Certainly not intoxicated. More likely she was suffering from the effects of the heat.

'Do you live nearby?' he asked.

'At the vicarage. My father is the reverend there.'

'I'll accompany you back to your home. It's doubtful whether you can make it there without fainting in the middle of the road. Take my arm.'

She hesitantly leant her weight on his left arm and he was careful to walk slowly so he did not overexert her. They continued down the road for several minutes before she spoke. 'I thank you for your kindness, sir.'

'You needn't thank me. It is no trouble.'

'I have been rushed off my feet all day visiting the poor and have had no time to stop for refreshment.'

'That was foolish of you. Even if your intentions were good, you must take care of yourself.'

'Yes, I suppose you are correct.' He felt her gazing at him. 'Are you the gentleman who lives at Ravenfeld Hall?'

'I am, along with my brother and sister. My name is Abernathy.'

'Yes, I recall hearing that name mentioned in town. You have just recently come here?'

'Not three months since.'

'Not long then. I have not seen you in church, but I suspect that you use your family's own chapel.'

'No, the chapel is in a state of disrepair.' He was not in the frame of mind for a remonstration at not having entered a church since his mother's funeral.

'Oh, what a pity. I always think it a shame to let such old places go to ruin.'

For one who had been on the verge of fainting minutes ago, she showed no intention of saving her breath. He suspected that she was a very simpleminded girl whose thoughts were filled with charitable works.

'I am Miss Fairweather,' she announced. 'My family moved here when my father took over the vicarage three years ago. Holtbury is a charming town with good, honest folk. I suspect that there are places in greater need of my father's gifts, but it is as worthy as anywhere else.' George heard the smile in her voice. 'I have four little brothers and sisters at home who I care for, now my poor mother is no longer here. It is testing at times but I do not think it a burden. They are such dear little souls.'

Why was she telling him all of this? Perhaps the heat was making her delirious. Fortunately they were within sight of their destination. A startled maid answered the vicarage door, with a small child clinging to her skirts. More children could be heard screaming from within.

'She is in need of fluids and rest. She almost fainted in the road,' said George as he delivered Miss Fairweather to the woman.

'Really, miss, you will make yourself ill one of these days!' tutted the maid. 'But thank you, sir. You are a true Christian.'

He tipped his hat to the woman and returned down the path, taking out his pocket watch. That affair had only cost him three-quarters of an hour. No matter; he was not far from his journey's end now, unless a similar episode should greet him further down the road.

Douglas had been driven from his study by the sweltering heat gathering at the top of the house. It was even too hot to work on his latest project: a steam-powered carriage. He knew the stories of steam-powered stagecoaches exploding as they were conveying passengers, but he thought he could improve on their design. That, at least, had been the initial idea. Gradually he'd become frustrated with the limitations of steam and how sluggish and ugly the thing was, with the boiler sticking out of its rear. Suddenly reminded of Robert Anderson's work, he turned towards electricity and constructed an electric motor, which relied on rechargeable batteries. The resulting 'auto-carriage' was still heavy and difficult to control, but he'd driven it around the grounds of the estate without incident (apart from marring the lawn). The speed gauge peaked at fifty-eight miles per hour. Douglas reckoned he could beat that, once he improved the batteries and built a new motor. For now he had to be content with staring at the stables from the oak parlour window as he tried to answer letters from the tolerable coolness of the ground floor. (The disused stables were the perfect place to store his projects – Spuggy was quite snug there.) He was pleased with the auto-carriage's red finish, although the courtyard of the stables now resembled a slaughterhouse from where the paint had dripped.

The breeze from the open window teased the paper as he tried to write, but it was too weak to send everything flying off the writing desk. His brother and sister had both ventured into the sun. He, however, had to remain indoors or in the recesses of the shade, since he burned easily. This was the only reason he'd ever resented having red hair and pale skin. The fact it made him a target for bullying had never really upset him, even when he was still a boy. Those ruffians had plenty of other reasons to make him their victim: that he used to be short for his age, that he had an unusual lineage, that he was frightfully clever.

When his task was done, he wandered about the house without any clear objective. Then he ventured onto the lawn on the south side of the house, and settled in a chair under a large tree, with a book for company, remaining there for the rest of the afternoon. The drawing room windows were open, and he overheard Molly and Mr Greenwood having an intense discussion. He'd heard the front door shut when Mr Greenwood finally left. Hopefully the cook, Martha and Mrs Baxter had taken refuge from the heat, although it was approaching seven o'clock when he returned indoors, and an agreeable coolness had descended over the house. Douglas found Mrs Baxter knitting by the fireplace in the dining room. Sweep was holding her ball of yarn.

'Sir!' she exclaimed. 'I did not hear you come in.'

'Forgive me if I startled you, Mrs Baxter.'

'It is quite all right, sir. It's rather hot in the servants' hall, so I thought I would seek refuge here. I have just spent a rather idle hour knitting new stockings for my eldest granddaughter, Betsey. She is a stout girl, and my knitting needles have struggled to keep up with her ever since she was a baby.'

'How old is your granddaughter, Mrs Baxter?'

'Fifteen next week.' She wore the gratified smile of a grandmother when discussing her descendants. 'She's in want of a situation.'

The old lady had more cunning about her than Douglas expected.

'Well, perhaps there might be a place for her here, since there is only Martha and the cook at present. We would benefit from having a kitchen maid or under-housemaid.'

'Oh, that is so kind of you to offer, sir. I assure you she is a good worker, although she can be saucy on occasion – but very rarely.' She had momentarily damaged her cause in letting this blemish on the girl's character slip.

'Well, you may bring her here for an introduction with my sister and we'll see what we can do for her.'

The old lady thanked him profusely and laid her knitting aside. 'I suppose I had better do the accounts and make sure we are not in want of anything,' she sighed as she rose unsteadily from her chair.

Douglas was touched by the attention she devoted to the household accounts, which she addressed punctually at the same time every evening, just as she had done when the old master had lived at the house. However, apparently her aptitude for numbers was not what it once had been. In reality the responsibility for the accounts fell to Molly, who would check the old lady's work and correct any errors. The accounts relating to the business were George's duty.

Mrs Baxter pulled back the drapes and shook her head. 'There'll be a thunderstorm tonight, sir. I hope Master George returns home before it starts.'

'You mean he hasn't returned yet?'

'Well, I've been in here all afternoon, sir, and I haven't seen or heard him come in.'

Douglas did not have a great deal of faith in the old woman's eyes and ears (did she realise she'd betrayed her lie that she'd only been sitting here an hour?), but he feared that she might be correct on this occasion. He turned to Sweep, who was rummaging through Mrs Baxter's work bag while her back was turned, and addressed him in a low whisper.

'Did you see my brother return?'

He shook his head.

That wasn't right. George had said he would be back by this hour. Douglas had a peculiar premonition that something was amiss. He pushed it out of his mind and told himself that his brother would come home soon and it was none of his business how George chose to spend his time. He returned to his study and attempted to absorb himself in his work until dinner. Two more hours passed and still George hadn't returned, having failed to attend the meal. Molly found Douglas pacing the drawing room when she came downstairs to retrieve the book she'd left there after her meeting with Mr Green—Mr Arthur.

'What's the matter?' she asked.

'George still isn't home yet.'

'It is getting rather late,' she observed, glancing at the clock on the mantle. It had just gone ten o'clock. 'But he's returned home at all sorts of ungodly hours before. How many times did he wake us in the early hours of the morning back in Soho?'

'But surely he'd have thought to come home in this weather? He could drink himself into a stupor beside a warm fire,' he replied dryly, trying to mask his anxiety.

The patter of rain from outside filled their ears. No one had closed the windows or curtains. The rows of newly planted saplings on the drive glowed green in the dark outside; the particles Molly had injected into their leaves were doing their job. Hopefully they would dim their phosphorescent light as the sunlight returned, just as she'd intended.

Douglas suddenly stopped in the middle of the room. 'I'm going to retrieve him.'

'You're not planning on walking the mile and a half to town in a storm, are you?'

'I'll take the auto-carriage.'

'This isn't the first time he's been out this late, you know,' she reminded him as she followed him into the south hall.

'True, but I've been concerned by his behaviour lately. He's getting worse.'

'I wish I could say that I disagreed with you,' she sighed as her brother swept out of the door.

Douglas brought the auto-carriage to a screeching halt, knocking over several barrels in the process. He hardly registered that fact as he climbed down from the driver's seat and surveyed the street. He sprinted towards the inn on the corner, feeling the pinpricks of rain on his face. The rain had started to teem down as he reached the inn door. His enquiries produced little result, other than a list of other inns to try and an umbrella which a sympathetic man gave him. At the next inn he tried, someone claimed to have seen a man matching George's description, although he had left a while ago. Douglas pressed the old gentleman for the exact time but he couldn't remember – possibly two or three hours since. In this manner Douglas followed his brother's trail, but after striking lucky at three places, the trail ended. George seemed to have not visited either of the two subsequent inns Douglas investigated. He retraced his steps to the last place where George had been sighted only an hour ago. He heard the rumble of thunder in his left ear. The diagonal rain hissed like sand and cast a ghostly, pale yellow halo around the gaslights. Douglas stood on the corner of the street outside the apothecary, watching the water drip off his umbrella. The thunder rolled across the dark sky, crashing like waves. Where else might George have thought to go? Perhaps he hadn't been travelling with any particular destination in mind by that point. Suppose he had been attacked? George was a capable fighter, even while intoxicated, but there was no telling what might have happened. Determining to follow every possible path that his brother might have taken, Douglas followed the road, which led him around the back of the inn. A store of barrels crowded the building's rear side; the gaslight caught a boot sticking out from between them. Douglas cautiously drew closer towards the horizontal figure concealed in the shadows. Peering over them, he saw that it was George.

He was lying on his right-hand side, his left arm across his chest. Not far away from his right hand was a small glass bottle. Douglas picked it up. The damp label was just about legible. '*LAUDANUM*' was written in bold red letters, with '*Opium tincture*' in smaller, discreet black print beneath. Casting the bottle and umbrella aside, Douglas crouched on the ground beside his brother.

'What did you do? You fool, *what the hell did you do?*'

He tried to raise George off the ground. He was soaked to the skin and ice-cold, more like a statue than human. Douglas tried to tell if he was breathing. He was, but very hoarsely and erratically. Douglas's relief was tainted with fear. He wished Molly was with him; she would have known what to do. It was all he could do to get George home. With some difficulty, he managed to haul his insensible brother over his shoulder. Douglas heard something splatter onto the cobblestones. George started to cough and splutter violently. At least it was a sign of life. Douglas struggled to carry him back through the streets. When he reached the Horse and Coaches, the first inn he had enquired at, the man who'd given him his umbrella earlier offered his assistance. They carried George between them back to the auto-carriage.

'I'd offer to fetch Dr Brown but he's attending to a woman in labour, at the village two miles away from here,' said the man.

'Are there no other doctors?'

'Not since old Dr Richardson closed his practice. I can send someone for Dr Brown as soon as he returns.'

'Please do. I'm sorry to ask so much of you.'

'There is no need, sir. You gave our Martha a situation when no one else would employ her because of her bouts of ill health.'

Douglas suddenly registered the man's striking resemblance to their housemaid, with the same heavy eyes. He'd been in too much of a blind panic to notice earlier.

They laid George down in the back of the auto-carriage and, after thanking Martha's father once more, Douglas drove home as fast as he dared to. Dr Brown would certainly struggle to make it back to town in such treacherous weather. Molly was waiting at the door. They got George to his room and Molly immediately oversaw his care, dry clothes being her first objective. She waved away Douglas's remarks that maybe he should undress their brother.

'It's fine. I'll put his nightshirt on first then yank his trousers and drawers off from the ends, so I'll see nothing. Just let me see to him. You go and change out of your own wet clothes.'

Douglas left her to work and sat in his bedroom, finding he could do nothing but wait.

Chapter Eleven

Dr Brown arrived early the following morning and officially diagnosed that George was suffering from a fever. On perceiving the good effects of Molly's remedies, he, in his superior wisdom, immediately forbade her to administer any more of them to the patient, and instructed her to give George the tonics that he provided. Molly bore the doctor's scorn with patience. As soon as he had gone, she poured all of his medicines away and continued to use her own. Two days later the doctor returned and, satisfied that the fever had broken, attributed the change to his own doing. Douglas put his hand on Molly's stiff shoulder while the doctor examined the patient.

'It doesn't matter who has the credit. The important thing is the outcome,' he whispered to her. He felt her shoulder relax.

Shortly after the doctor had been dismissed, George awoke. He was met with the angry stares of his brother and sister at the foot of the bed.

'What?'

'You know what.' Molly leant against the wall with her arms behind her back.

George realised that something was attached to his wrists. When he looked at his hands, he saw manacles and chains. The other ends of the manacles were attached to the bedposts. 'What is the meaning of this?'

'Well, since you were recovering, we took the opportunity to restrain you while you were still subdued enough,' said Douglas.

'Unbind me right now.'

'Not until we're certain that we can stop you attempting to destroy yourself.'

'I wasn't trying to destroy myself.'

'Maybe not deliberately, but you did a decent job of it all the same,' said Molly.

'You're going to tell us exactly what led to me finding you lying on the ground scarcely alive outside that inn,' demanded Douglas.

George looked away from them. 'I simply miscalculated the effects produced by a particular substance.'

'Laudanum, you mean,' said Molly dryly.

'It was not a great amount.'

'Did you have a deal to drink beforehand?'

'A considerable amount, or else I wouldn't have considered taking it.'

'You know that combination could easily have killed you?'

'In a rational state of mind, I would have.'

'But what is it that drove you to do it?' asked Douglas.

George didn't reply immediately. 'The effects of the spirits were diminishing. It was requiring greater quantities to produce the desired effect. So I tried other means.'

'But why?' Douglas demanded. 'Why do you do this to yourself?'

'To quieten my mind,' he answered simply. 'At any given time my mind is at work on several things at once. Without something to exercise my faculties, all of these other thoughts collide with one another. Likewise, if there is a problem my mind struggles to solve, it will not rest until it arrives at the solution. Stopping the clamour is most easily obtained by chemical means.'

'At the expense of your health?'

'Irrelevant.'

'And the risk of damaging your mind for good?'

George said nothing, training his eyes on the medicine bottles on the bedside table.

'Not to mention the concern it causes Molly and me.'

George still wouldn't meet Douglas's eye. 'So what do you intend to do with me?' he asked.

'Well, we're going to keep you like that until we're sure you won't go reaching for the brandy or visit the apothecary at the first opportunity.'

'The fever was actually beneficial in that respect,' Molly added. 'But it might take a few more days for you to adjust to not having any alcohol inside you. Thankfully, I have a remedy to help ease that process, which I intend to start work on right away.' She then left the room with a purposeful stride.

Douglas casually picked up a chair by the back and placed it by George's bedside. 'You gave her quite a fright, you know,' he said calmly as he sat down. 'And me.'

George pulled himself to a sitting position. 'You shouldn't concern yourselves with my affairs as much as you do.'

'But we do. We care about what becomes of you.'

'You should be more concerned about the business since I am currently indisposed.'

'Fear not. I can manage things for now. We're not behind with any of our orders.'

Douglas looked his brother in the eye. His eyes were the same sharp, pale blue as always, but they somehow seemed duller. Something was lost from them. It had been a frightful experience seeing George in that state over the last three days. He'd always seemed impenetrable and in control of everything around him, but there he'd lain in his bed, vulnerable and weak. Of course, George didn't care if he damaged his health through his reckless behaviour. Douglas knew what drove his brother: the need to solve the next puzzle, to satisfy his curiosity, to understand why something worked. He didn't care for much else, he just needed a challenge. Except...he did care about some things. His family, for one. Like when Douglas had scarlet fever at the age of four, and George maintained a vigil by his bedside when no one else was around to care for him. Many people assumed George was formed of pure reason and without feeling. They were wrong. And when he was roused to extreme feeling, a torrent of anger could be unleashed that was frightening to witness. Shortly after their father's death, one way the two of them supplemented the family's income was with a little scheme involving boxing. The essence of it was this: George fought in the ring while Douglas, in disguise, placed a bet on him. But this was not professional boxing. In these establishments, the London Prize Ring rules were scarcely adhered to;

low blows and gouging might pass unremarked. The men George fought were usually larger and stockier than him. George would purposefully let his opponent land a number of blows and he'd seem as though he was on the brink of collapsing – before knocking out his opponent with hardly any effort, much to the crowd's astonishment and disappointment. Since the odds were never in George's favour, the payout was always high. Unfortunately, one night Mr Sprecher, a friend of George's latest defeated opponent, recognised them. Sprecher had also been one of the bullying ruffians who preyed on Douglas, and thereby unluckily crossed George's path years ago. His face still bore the scars. Sprecher and his friend waited for Douglas outside, with the intention of beating and robbing him by way of revenge. Douglas was able to fend off Sprecher without much difficulty, but the other man caught him off guard and managed to hit him in the eye and dash him to the ground. Then George appeared, saw what was happening and flew at his brother's assailant. He almost beat the man to death; he might have done had Douglas not persuaded him to stop.

'He's not worth you being hanged for!' he'd shouted, trying to haul George off his victim. When Douglas caught sight of his brother's face, twisted by rage and streaked with blood, even he was a little unnerved. But George soon calmed down, and Molly was waiting for them with a bottle of iodine solution when they returned home. They put an end to their scheme after that.

Thinking about it now, Douglas realised it was around this time that George started drinking excessively and his temper became even more volatile – once responsibility for the clockmaker's shop was handed to them. They were no longer free to pursue their own interests. Every day was the same. The two of them were without mental stimulation – making nothing but pocket watches and clocks. They still had to support their ailing mother too, which meant they had no disposable income. Money was still tight even after she died, as it had cost a small fortune to bury her in a manner befitting a duke's daughter. Their future had looked bleak. If only they'd known what fate had in store for them.

George turned his head towards the ceiling and rubbed his eyes. His chains clinked. 'At least tell me you won't bring that damn doctor in here again.'

'Oh no, don't concern yourself about that.'

A brief silence ensued. The sunlight in the room ebbed and flowed. Compared to the sumptuous and opulent rooms that populated the rest of the house, George's chambers were severely plain. No paintings crowded the dark blue walls and no trinkets cluttered the shelves. According to the original plans for the house, this was intended as a guest bedroom, with an adjoining dressing room that was then left unfinished.

Douglas resumed speaking. 'You know, I saw the vicar's daughter in town, and she seemed very concerned for your health when I told her that you were ill. She said you came to her rescue when she was close to fainting in the road. I think she likes you.'

'I hope you said or did nothing to encourage her.'

'Well, no. But I did nothing to discourage her either. She is not an unpleasant girl.'

'That is of no consequence to me.'

'Do you really have no interest in the fairer sex?' Douglas asked half-jokingly.

'None. Most women, by man's design or nature's, are empty-headed and foolish.'

'Don't let Molly hear you say that – and *she* is certainly not empty-headed or foolish.'

'Our sister is a rare exception. Incredibly rare, I should say.'

'And how many other young ladies have you encountered in your lifetime who were exceptional?'

'Personally, none.'

'Not even Mademoiselle Roux-Voclain?'

'I suppose I discounted her on the grounds that her morality was questionable, and it was because of our sister's efforts that she was apprehended for her crimes.'

'But she was a genius, albeit a deceptive one.' Douglas still felt his cheeks burn slightly when he thought of Claudette.

'I'll allow that. But that still only leaves us with two exceptions out of the entire population of females.'

'I disagree with your method of assessing females,' Douglas smiled. 'I have met plenty of girls who were good-natured and kind-hearted. There's more to a person besides their intelligence.'

'There you are pronouncing your own preferences in a companion. That is no less one-sided an assessment.'

'So let us imagine for a minute, theoretically, that there was an exceptionally rare woman who was to your liking in existence. What qualities would she possess?'

George raised his eyes and actually seemed to devote some serious consideration to the question. 'It is nearly impossible for me to say.'

'This is pure speculation.'

George sighed. 'A quickness of mind and understanding. She would not be trivial or too talkative, but would offer sensible, stimulating conversation. She'd be self-possessed and not easily influenced by the views of others.'

'Well, I'd say that those are not as unlikely qualities to be found in most women as you make them out to be.'

'One or two of those qualities may surface in most women, but they are undone by a multitude of faults.' George's head sank back on the pillow. Douglas thought his brother had probably had enough of talking for the present, and quietly got up to take his leave. He hurried downstairs to the kitchen, where Molly was at work, having established a home-made pharmacy.

'How is he?' she asked while juicing half a lemon.

'Sitting up and talking,'

'What were you talking about?'

'George's ideal bride.'

Molly let out a laugh. 'Does he have someone in mind? Poor woman.'

'Nobody at all. I think there's more chance of the British government granting India independence than of George finding a wife.'

'Perhaps you could build him one?' Molly grinned at him as she strained the juice.

Douglas laughed.

Molly put the dishevelled half-lemon aside and began juicing the other half. 'I don't think I'll ever marry.'

'You think marriage is worthless too?'

'No, not necessarily. I just don't see myself as somebody's wife,' Molly shrugged, her eyes on a pan of water that was starting to bubble. Bruised crescents rimmed her eyes. She had nursed George for the last three days and nights, administering medicine, changing the moist rag on his forehead and making sure he wasn't too warm or cold. She'd slept in an armchair beside his bed until the fever had broken the previous night.

'Well, I still stand by my views on the subject. I think there is something to be said for the marital state. I'd rather like to think that one day I might have a family of my own.'

'Are George and I not sufficient?' She raised her head and fixed her green eyes on his. (They'd both inherited their mother's eyes.)

'It's not the same as that. You know what I meant.'

'I know. I didn't mean to sound harsh, but you know what *I* meant.'

'Molly, you and George are as much a part of me as my own heart or arm. No matter what happens to us, we'll always be a constant in one another's lives.'

'Good. I'd rather lose an arm than have it a different way.' Molly added roots to the pan of boiling water, along with the lemon juice and peel. 'I think I've managed to get the last bits of sediment from the juice. Now I just need to wait for the mixture to boil.'

'You're sure this'll work?'

'Positive.' She nodded firmly, causing wisps of her hair to bob. 'Remember Mrs Neville's husband?'

'I do. I recall he was fond of his gin.'

'But he was cured of his fondness, correct?'

'Yes, miraculously.'

'There was nothing miraculous about it. His wife locked him in their bedroom and kept him away from alcohol of any kind. She said the first week was the worst. He hardly slept, was constantly irritable, swore at her something rotten, and it was a trial getting him to eat, but after that he improved. She asked me if there was anything I could give him, and I came up with this.' She indicated the boiling pan. 'It's to help curb the cravings. But I'd wait before giving George that just yet. I'll try him with this first.' She poured yellow liquid from a crystal jug into a glass.

'What is that?'

'Juice from my fruits. It'll benefit him after the fever. I've asked cook to make him some broth later this afternoon. You know,' she added, 'we can't keep him shackled to the bed forever. How are we to ensure that he doesn't slide back into old habits once he's freed?'

'I'll think of a solution.'

'Miss Molly?' The housemaid was hovering in the doorway, with a salver in her hands. 'There is a gentleman here to see you, miss. He sent his card.'

'Pass it to me, Martha.'

The girl gingerly offered her mistress the salver, and Molly lifted the card from it. She struck the table with her other hand as she read it. 'Mr Greenwood is here.'

'I can tell him that you are out if you wish, miss?'

'No, I'll go and greet him. If not it will only delay the meeting to another day, and I'd rather get it over with. Please send this up to Master George. Oh, and Martha?'

'Yes, Miss Molly?' The girl paused as she was about to take the glass of juice from Molly.

'Do you have any complaint that you take laudanum for?'

The girl stared at her in confusion. 'Why, yes. Doctor Brown gave me some for my back pain when I saw him a few weeks ago. Only a couple of drops, though.' She sounded slightly affronted at this personal enquiry, but Molly was too exhausted from worry to mind a great deal.

'Are you dependent on it?'

'Dependent? I wouldn't say so, but it certainly helps, miss.'

'I must ask that you stop taking it and dispose of any that you have left. You'd do better not to listen to that foolish Dr Brown. If the pain continues, you can come to me and I'll give you something for it. Do you understand?'

'Yes, miss.'

'Good.'

Molly marched swiftly out of the kitchen.

Chapter Twelve

Another uneventful week passed before Copperton and the newly arrived soldiers received word that they were to pursue a force of mutineers, possibly as many as 6,000, who were planning to intercept the siege-train on its way to Delhi. The rebels were reported to be heading towards the canal bridge at Najafgarh, twenty miles west of Delhi, and Nicholson's column were to follow them. The column left the camp before daybreak. Heavy rain had reduced the ground to a bog, and they waded rather than marched along. Copperton proved himself useful in dragging the heavy guns that were mounted on wheels, as they often became stuck in the mud. The other men were visibly suffering and they made slow progress towards their destination. Many, he knew, had a hankering – a lust – for vengeance. News from the faraway city of Cawnpore had reached them two days previously. The mutineers there had offered safe passage down the Ganges to their captive Europeans, only to turn on them once they were escorted to the riverbank and had begun to board the boats. Almost every single one of the men had been killed, and the women and children were not entirely spared. The surviving civilians were taken back to the city and held in the Bibigarh, or 'lady's house', which a British officer had built for his Indian mistress. Several weeks later, the women and children were slaughtered by their captors. Their butchered bodies had been discovered down a well by General

Havelock's force. That anyone could do such a thing was inconceivable, and yet there was no mistake in the report. It was clear the mutineers would stop at nothing until they'd eradicated every last European on the continent. What further evidence was needed of their barbarity? Powell's argument about professional grievances was drowned beneath this fresh evidence in Copperton's mind. These butchers of innocent women and children would be brought to account. The righteous would prevail over the evil. It was as simple as that.

Copperton was in no danger of running out of steam as he marched through swamps and flooded countryside, but mud and weeds somehow entered through his joints and clogged his gears. It took two flushes of water to clear the mess away. Sunset was creeping in by the time the column approached the enemy position. Even in the failing light, Copperton could see where the rebels were, on the opposite side of the drainage cut, or *nullah*. At the heart of the enemy's position was a serai, an old stone enclosure, guarded by high stone walls. With his magnified vision, he saw four guns on sandbags before the serai, and enemy riflemen positioned along the walls above. There were two villages to the left and rear of the enclosure that the enemy also occupied. But to reach the enemy position, the column first had to cross the ford of the swollen drainage cut which ran across their path. The water reached the men's chests, but Copperton simply extended his legs and crossed the ford in two strides. The men were deployed to the south of the serai. General Nicholson advised them to hold their fire until they were within twenty or thirty yards of the enemy. As Nicholson gave an inspiring speech, Copperton looked around at the half-drenched men, searching for a glimpse of his friends. He failed to spot them. He did see General Fowler's grave face, however.

The horse artillery moved first, then the rest of the lines followed. With a cry of 'Charge!', the fighting commenced. Copperton charged into battle and shielded the troops from the enemies' blows and bullets. He was thrown into a tumult of battery fire, shouting men and screeching horses. One or two unfortunate fellows were shot or became trapped under their horses, but the damage inflicted on the enemy was far greater. Copperton saw one British soldier slip on the muddy ground and fall. A rebel saw it too, and advanced to bayonet him. Copperton quickly extended one arm and hauled the man back by the collar, and the lucky fellow narrowly missed the rebel's blade. He set the dumbfounded man on his feet and, once satisfied that he had regained his senses enough to continue fighting, concentrated on the matter at hand once more. Scaling the serai walls presented no great difficulty – Copperton practically leapt over them. When he arrived in the courtyard, the rebels seemed to lose all heart for a fight at the sight of him. It was as if they were staring at death itself; they turned and ran as fast as their legs could carry them, some even dropping their weapons in their desperate haste. Copperton could not believe the sight before his eyes. The cowards were actually attempting to flee! Few were given the opportunity, and were swiftly dealt with by bayonets. With the serai cleared and the four guns captured, the column turned their attention to the surrounding villages. Copperton left it to the men to clear the villages of the rebels, for Colonel Kirk had entrusted him with another mission. To the rear of the entrenchment, running adjacent to the ford they had crossed earlier, was a bridge, around eighty feet long and twenty feet wide. It led towards Delhi, and was the only bridge that would allow the rebels to reach the British rear. It was essential that it was captured and destroyed. Copperton was to set the explosive charges.

The noise and smoke of the battle faded away, replaced by the sound of rushing water as he drew closer to the bridge. Copperton slowed his pace as he reached it, trying to comprehend what he was seeing. Before him was a wall of thick grey mist. Even in the darkness of night, he could still see it. It was isolated to the bridge and seemed to be rapidly dispersing. As the mist faded, he could distinguish a man standing in the middle of the bridge. Not an enemy, but a European officer in a red uniform coat and white helmet. Copperton magnified his vision and realised it was someone he knew: General Quincy. Around his feet, sprawled on the ground, were a dozen rebel soldiers. Copperton thought he heard the general say, 'Not strong enough.'

'General Quincy, sir!' Copperton called. The officer whipped around instantly and fixed his gaze on Copperton. He covered his mouth as if struck with horror, and then ran into the thick of the mist. As the last of the mist cleared, he was nowhere to be seen. Copperton ran onto the bridge and gazed down into the raging black water below. It was the only place the general could have gone, but he would surely have been swept away. He then turned his attention to the fallen rebels. They were still breathing, some even rousing from whatever stupor they'd fallen into. Copperton heard the sound of the horse artillery's approach and promptly went to meet them. Colonel Kirk accompanied them.

'Excellent work, soldier!' said the colonel. Both he and his horse were cut, but not severely. 'You needn't have spared those rebel sepoys, but perhaps they might know something useful to us.'

'Sir, you are mistaken. I did not—'

'Clear them off the bridge, unless you'd rather send them to a watery grave. It makes little difference really. Then finish setting the charges.'

'Yes, sir.' The urgency of the command swept away the matter of the mysterious mist. Copperton dragged the half-conscious rebels off the bridge and began setting the explosive charges. He then stood and watched as they were lit, producing a mighty explosion. The bridge's collapse was a spectacular sight to behold. It broke apart like brittle biscuit, with chunks of stone falling into the water with huge splashes. The debris was swept away downstream. When the job was done, Copperton extended his vision to the opposite side of the riverbank. He thought he could distinguish a man on horseback fleeing the scene.

The battle was over in no more than an hour. Despite the column's efforts, many of the rebels had fled, abandoning all of their artillery on the battlefield. Copperton found Petey, Powell and Singh on the return march. They said little, far too fatigued for conversation, although the rain attempted to revive them by pouring down in torrents. The men rested only briefly, sleeping on the cold, damp ground. But there was no despondency of morale, especially on their return to camp with the news that they had thirteen captured guns and more spoils besides. The band played merrily to welcome them and they were met with cheers from everyone in the camp. As they were sitting in Powell's tent the following day, Copperton, Petey, Powell and Singh discussed their experiences of the fighting, since they had played different roles in the battle. Powell and Singh had assisted in clearing the villages of rebels.

'There was one village to the rear that held out longer,' said Singh while eating a mango. 'We surrounded them but they fought fiercely and a lot of our men were killed, including Lieutenant Lumsden. Many of the enemy managed to escape in the end.'

'Nevertheless, I think we can safely say that we were victorious,' said Petey. 'I reckon Copperton scared them off. Wasn't it your job to blow up the bridge, Cop?'

'I only set the charges. The honour of lighting them fell to someone else.'

'It was still an important part to play.'

'I hear General Fowler tried to save one of his sepoys from being stabbed by a rebel armed with a tulwar, and was shot in the back,' said Singh. 'They don't know how bad.'

Copperton watched Powell's face contort, as if he'd tasted something sour. Perhaps he was imagining himself in the unfortunate officer's place. It was a most unpleasant thing indeed to befall a man.

'I only wonder what General Quincy was doing on the bridge,' remarked Copperton.

Petey's brow pinched. 'Quincy? He was never amongst us.'

'What do you mean?'

'He was here at camp, bedridden with fever. He wasn't one of the officers involved in the battle.'

'But I saw him. I swear it.'

'Could you have been mistaken? It must have been hard to see through all that rain and dark, not mentioning the confusion of the battle,' said Singh.

'I am certain that it was him. I even heard his voice.'

'But how could it possibly have been him if he was meant to be in a tent twenty miles away? And what could he possibly be doing there, away from the main fighting?' demanded Powell.

'I haven't the faintest idea,' confessed Copperton.

'Do you really suspect a superior officer of foul conduct, Copperton?'

'Of course not! That is inconceivable. Perhaps he was sent on a secret mission.'

'That is incredibly hard to believe,' said Powell flatly.

Petey got to his feet. 'Well, I could have a word with Quincy's aide-de-camp, Harford, and see if I can get anything out of him. He might at least be able to vouch for his master being in the tent all day, to put your suspicions to an end, Copperton.'

'I do not have any suspicions. I simply wished to understand what he was doing there, although if it is something I am not meant not to know, I'd rather simply think of the affair no more.'

'I see. You tell yourself that while I go find Quincy's aide.' Petey strolled off before Copperton had time to protest.

'He'd talk the mutineers into giving up the city, that one could,' muttered Powell.

Powell taught Singh and Copperton how to play cards. They were joined by a couple of other sepoys, who seemed uneasy around Copperton and did not stay long into the game of brag. Petey returned when the remaining three players had just begun a fresh game.

'Well?' asked Powell. 'Judging by that smug air of yours, you have something to tell us.'

'I got talking to Harford. I made it look as if I was completely indifferent about what I wanted to ask, but I soon got what I wanted out of him. Quincy wasn't in his tent all day yesterday. Harford was given strict orders not to bother him, but concern – or curiosity, rather – got the better of him. He stuck his head inside the tent around twelve o'clock to ask the general an urgent question, only to find him absent.'

'Strange.' Powell put down his cards. 'It seems you might be right then, Copperton.'

'If so, what does that mean?' asked Singh. 'All that tells us is that he wasn't where his aide-de-camp believed him to be.'

'But that's not all,' added Petey. 'Harford mentioned that Quincy received a message three days ago that greatly discomposed him.'

'So much so that it brought on his illness?' said Powell.

'Apparently so.'

They all looked at Copperton.

'This is absurd,' Copperton declared, rising as high as the tent would allow him. 'There is nothing to suggest that General Quincy is involved in anything…illicit. Who's to say that he did not receive distressing news that discomposed him so greatly that it brought on his illness? Perhaps a relation or valued friend has been killed. So many of the officers here have had their nerves badly shaken. It is hardly any wonder that General Wilson struggles to act. We must not entertain these suspicions. I shall dwell upon the matter no more.'

None of the three men inside the tent spoke, but their questioning expressions remained unchanged.

Chapter Thirteen

On the fourth day after the doctor was sent away, Douglas was bringing his brother a letter, along with a cup of Molly's passionflower and skullcap tea, which she was administering to their brother three times a day as it relaxed the nerves (it seemed she had a tea for everything), when he realised that George was not in his shackles. Molly denied having freed him, and a thorough questioning of every single one of the servants and androids produced no evidence to suggest that any were guilty of having done so. In the end, they had to believe George's claim that he'd freed himself and chosen to remain where he was. It seemed he'd decided to cooperate, and wanted to prove his willingness by remaining a prisoner in his own room. After that, they stopped locking his bedroom door (although he could easily have picked the lock all along if he'd wanted to).

On the sixth day, Douglas was at the breakfast table reading a letter when George appeared in his burgundy dressing gown, looking pale, haggard and like he hadn't slept in days – which he probably hadn't.

'How do you feel?' Douglas asked.

'Like death,' George answered as he sank into the chair opposite and rubbed his left eye. He reached for the coffee pot on the table.

Douglas moved it away with the dining room poker.

George reached for it again.

Douglas moved it further out of his reach. 'Molly said no coffee for another few days.'

George scowled as Douglas pushed the teapot towards him. He poured himself a cup nonetheless. He'd been in a foul mood throughout the last few days, but seemed comparatively calmer today.

'When she came to check on me this morning, she said that I was over the worst.'

'Yes, but you could slide back at the first opportunity.'

George drained his tea and poured himself another cup. There was still a slight tremor in his hands; yesterday it had been so bad that he couldn't lift a cup to his lips without spilling some of its contents.

'You could do with eating something as well,' Douglas remarked.

'I intend to, so you can stop fretting. Any news?'

'Not a great deal. I'm managing fine with the orders for now. Oh, a letter came from Maestro. He and Lord Leyton have arrived in Venice. Maestro says he's ridden in a gondola and seen an opera at the famous Teatro La Fenice opera house. It seems Lord Leyton is suffering from the effects of prolonged exposure to the sun. "*He was unable to leave the hotel yesterday and refused to let anyone see him other than Bellamy and me. A bath of icy water seemed to revive him, although he still complains of headaches. I do what I can to soothe his mind with my music. He fears that the redness of his skin won't fade before the masquerade ball next week. I'm unsure why this troubles him so, if it is to be a masked ball, but he believes it to be an issue. I am to perform at the ball and do hope that Master Josephus can attend. It would be a shame for him to miss it as he has talked of it greatly, and I am very much looking forward to it.*" That sounds very typical of Lord Leyton, but I doubt he'd miss such a grand party as that.'

George grunted. Nothing further was said as Douglas took up a newspaper and George piled his plate. Douglas hadn't glanced at a newspaper for over a week as he'd been so busy trying to handle the business on his own. He was attempting to work his way through some of them, in case their soldier made an appearance on any of their pages. There was not a whisper about him, it seemed – not even in any of the reports from India. Gradually Douglas allowed himself to read whatever articles caught his interest, although he didn't feel up to reading about how ineffectively the government was continuing to function. There was a mysterious story in one of the newspapers from a town in Buckinghamshire about a field full of dead crows. The local gamekeeper, it was reported, said they'd had an unusually foggy winter's night. When the fog cleared around dawn and the gamekeeper went outside, a nearby field was strewn with an entire murder (ironically) of crows, lying lifeless upon the ground. The locals believed they'd died of disease. The crows at Darkwater Farm were certainly fighting fit; the farmer waged a constant war with them. Maybe he and George could build him an automaton scarecrow.

There came a distant banging of doors.

'Ah, here she comes,' said Douglas.

Molly stormed into the room, sat down beside Douglas, and attacked her ham and poached eggs with vehemence. She'd gone to the kitchen garden to pick vegetables early that morning, and was still in her gardening clothes. An opened letter was sticking out of her dress pocket, and Douglas could distinguish '*wood*' in the crumpled signature. That explained her tempestuous mood.

'How are you getting along with the landscape gardener?' Douglas asked after watching her for several moments.

'He's the most arrogant fool I've ever met,' she declared with her mouth half-full, while violently slicing a piece of ham. 'He is adamant about having an Italianate summer house. I have repeatedly said that I don't want one, but he still insists. I told him I won't have any of that ornate rubbish in my garden.'

George, having finished, leant back and slid his hands into his dressing gown pockets. 'Well, if you truly dislike him such a great deal, we will dismiss him.'

'No,' she said, a little too quickly. She fumbled with the napkin in her hands. 'I mean, I'll see how it goes a little longer. I might be able to convince him why my way of thinking is the correct one. I'm done.' She threw down her napkin and flitted out of the room just as quickly as she had entered it.

George frowned. 'I don't understand. Why does she ask us to keep Mr Greenwood on if she finds him so disagreeable?'

Douglas laughed. 'You really know nothing of the human heart, do you, George? She is a girl of seventeen, after all.'

'I hate it when you speak in riddles.'

'I think it's best if you learn to decipher this sort of behaviour for yourself,' Douglas smiled as he resumed reading the newspaper. His smile quickly vanished.

'What is it?'

'News from India.'

'Any mention of the android?'

'No. But there was a massacre of British civilians by the mutineers at a place called Cawnpore about a month ago. Their bodies were found down a well. God, to do something so barbaric to women and children…' Douglas shook his head in disbelief.

George looked into his teacup. 'There will be retribution. Revenge killings.' He said this as a matter of fact, with no indication as to whether he condoned or condemned this course of action, although Douglas believed he wasn't callous enough to approve of such slaughter.

'Hm. And the android shall probably be called upon to be the executioner.'

'There's nothing we can do about that.'

Douglas put the paper aside. He deliberated over whether to ask George the question that had been on his mind for some time.

'Say whatever it is you want to say.' George was looking squarely at him. 'You have that look on your face that you get when you're unsure whether to proceed with something or not. And you've been fidgeting with that teaspoon in your hand for the last two minutes.'

Douglas immediately dropped the spoon he was holding, and it clattered on the table. His brother's eyes had regained their usual power and they pierced straight through him.

'How long were you taking opium for? I know it was more than once.'

'Three weeks. It was only a few drops at a time.'

'Did you…did you steal Martha's drops?'

'Not intentionally. I found the bottle on the mantle in the drawing room. She must have left it there. I didn't know who it belonged to at the time, and I could not resist taking a couple of drops to see what effect they would produce. I knew the bottle probably belonged to one of the servants, and I left it there for them to find.'

'Was that how it started?'

'Yes. But I never used the housemaid's drops again. I had enough self-command to not keep the bottle, and purchased another from the apothecary. Has that information lowered your opinion of me even more?'

'No, I expected as much. I don't think that badly of you, you know. If I did, why would I want to help you defeat this addiction?'

For a brief moment, a flicker of emotion passed over George's face. Could it have been guilt? Whatever it was didn't last, as his face soon hardened again. 'I don't expect you to handle the commissions on your own for much longer. I've had quite enough of this inertia.' He left the dining room and went upstairs.

Later that day, Douglas saw him sitting at the desk in his study, fully dressed but still looking as tired as he had that morning. He had a ledger open in front of him and a glass of Molly's medicine beside it. (The medicine was so far proving to be as effective for George as it had been for Mr Neville.) George was shakily scratching away with his pen, fighting off sleep by the look of it. Douglas left him to it. It would be a relief not to be solely responsible for the business any longer. Not just because of the pressure this entailed, but because he'd felt George's absence more than he'd anticipated. He'd had no one to consult when he was unsure about something, no one to provide the missing clue when he was faced with a problem, and no one to rein him in when he was taken with a sudden idea. Even the peace and lack of arguments hadn't compensated for his absence.

Douglas finally allowed himself some time to work on the auto-carriage. The paint had been scratched and a front light smashed during that night he'd retrieved George. He had a sudden fancy to paint a white stripe along either side of the auto-carriage's red body, and it actually looked very stylish once he'd done it. Nodding with satisfaction, he closed the stable doors and returned to the Hall. He found Molly curled on a sofa in the oak parlour reading one of her textbooks. Douglas wanted to ask Molly about the state of affairs between her and Mr Greenwood – or Mr Arthur, as she now called him – but had no idea how to approach the subject. Then again, he was unsure he wanted to be privy to his sister's private business, and he had faith in Molly's judgement.

'Why don't you read in your own room?'

'Too warm.' She underlined something with a pencil and turned the page.

Douglas sat in an armchair adjacent to her. 'George seems better.'

'I wouldn't let my guard down just yet, although he seems to be cooperating.'

'What exactly is in that medicine you've been giving him?'

Molly lowered her book and leant her head close to his. A smile played at the corners of her lips. 'Nothing.'

'What?'

'Nothing except fermented ginger root, lemon grass and juniper, with a little sugar.'

'So there's no magic ingredient? Just ordinary plants?'

'Yes, but as long as George doesn't know that, it should hopefully continue to work. He doesn't seem to suspect anything at the moment.' She returned to her book.

Douglas stared at his sister for a moment, then laughed. 'You've managed to do the impossible, Mol. You've outwitted our older brother.'

'Don't underestimate me,' she winked.

Chapter Fourteen

Several days after the column's triumphant return, an envoy from Delhi arrived at the camp to offer terms and was sent back with an absolute refusal. What nerve those rebels had! But it was a sign of their desperation. General Nicholson's recent victory had evidently shaken the rebels' nerves and they were no longer confident that they could maintain their hold on the city. The siege-train had arrived a week or so after the column's return, delivering howitzers, heavy mortars, and much-needed ammunition. Copperton was one of those who went to greet the train in the early hours of the morning. He wondered how the train was to reach the camp when there were no railway tracks, but the 'train' was in fact an eight-mile-long procession of elephants and horses ridden by soldiers. Two elephants pulled each of the guns, and the ammunition was wheeled along in bullock carts. On the same day, the cloudless sky became overshadowed by black cloud, promising a storm, although little rain fell. The cool air brought the soldiers some relief from the heat, although one or two superstitious men muttered something about the thundercloud being a bad omen. Copperton failed to see how.

There was a palpable tension in the air at camp, as everyone anticipated General Wilson's announcement that the Delhi Field Force would launch a siege on the city. But no such declaration came. All the while, the number of sick men rose as cholera continued its invasion of the camp. Copperton caught glimpses of those afflicted by the disease when he took supplies to the camp hospitals and glanced at one of the cholera wards, seeing the wasted limbs and sunken faces, the blue-tinged skin. The Field Force's chaplain looked very uncomfortable as he read to the retching, groaning patients from his Bible. Copperton imagined death on the battlefield was more merciful and dignified than this lingering death – for many of those admitted to the hospital tent with the disease wouldn't leave alive.

Morale was waning. The bands thumped on with their cheerful tunes in the evenings, and some officers and men played various sports, although many did not have the heart for such frolics with so many of their friends in hospital. (Petey tried to encourage others from his regiment to join in, with some success. Nothing dimmed his high spirits.) Reinforcements had arrived from Meerut, but the Field Force could expect no more than that now. All was quiet at camp, with only the sporadic firing from the rebels to keep the men on their guard.

Despite professing his faith in the intentions of an officer, Copperton could not entirely take his eye off General Quincy. He began to notice how tense the man always seemed. His nervousness only seemed to increase. Petey had General Quincy's aide-de-camp continue to act as their informant, despite Copperton assuring him that it wasn't necessary.

'He doesn't think much of Quincy, and seems happy to do what I ask of him, in return for beer or cigarettes. Where's the harm in it?' Petey replied.

After several days, this watch had produced little result. Since there was little action, Copperton allowed himself to regularly wind down every other day, in order to save steam and oil, and reduce any unnecessary wear on his parts. If there was to be a siege, he would need to be in his prime. He resided in Petey's tent when he did this, entrusting his friend to wind him again at the start of the next day, which he did without fail for three successive mornings. Then, the day after the siege-train arrived, Copperton awoke to the faint buzzing of his dial and the gurgle of his boiler as usual...but found himself in the open night air. His wrists and ankles were bound with rope, his hands pinned behind his back. His sword was missing from its scabbard. Was Petey playing an elaborate joke on him?

'I'm surprised I was able to capture you so easily, given that you are worth a dozen human soldiers, or so they say.' A British infantryman with a dark, whiskery beard was watching him from a couple of yards away. He appeared to be a private in the Bengal Fusiliers, like Petey. The rifle in his hands was pointed at Copperton. Copperton's sword was thrust through the man's belt.

'I don't claim to be worth a dozen men.' Copperton thought that he must be to the rear of the camp, since he could see the Najafgarh canal directly behind the infantryman, and the bazaar a little further away. 'What is the meaning of this, sir?'

'Do you really have to follow any order given to you?' the infantryman asked, ignoring Copperton's question. He cocked his rifle meaningfully. 'Answer.'

'Only by an officer.'

'So I couldn't order you to run your sword through your own head?'

'No.'

'Pity. It would have been entertaining to watch.' He inched closer to his captive. 'I don't suppose you'd tell me your weaknesses? You must have some.'

'There are two places you could shoot me that would cause minor damage, but I fail to see why you wish to know that.' Copperton chose his words carefully. He had learnt to craft his speech from observing Petey. He'd even seen him trick a man into giving him his last bottle of beer.

'Because I intend to destroy you, you abomination,' the man sneered.

Copperton attempted to assess the man's emotional state. The rifle was trembling in his hands and he had a look that reminded Copperton of a wild animal. Copperton caught a glimpse of a tattoo on the man's wrist: an inverted triangle inside a circle with a cross struck through it.

'I am not the enemy,' said Copperton. Each length of rope binding his limbs was tied tightly. He moved his hands to create some slack on the rope, but when the rope caught against one of the bolts on his torso casing, he had a better idea. He rubbed the rope against the metal bolt with quick yet subtle movements.

'You *are* the enemy. You pose a greater threat than the Pandies. I know all about your makers and what they do. I intend to stop them.'

'How so?' Copperton tried to keep the man talking so that he did not notice what he was doing. The rope must nearly be about to break.

'I will make it look as if you tried to attack me but that I was able to bring you down in the process. First I will shoot you, and then I will shoot myself in the ankle.'

'I would advise you to reconsider, sir.' The rope fell from his wrists, but he kept his hands behind his back. 'If only for the simple reason that you cannot inflict such damage upon me.'

'I'm willing to try. If bullets won't work, I'm sure this sword of yours will.'

'Copperton!' another man's voice cried, a voice he knew well. Petey was strolling towards them, with his hands thrust deep in his trouser pockets. He was without a coat, and his sweat-stained grey shirt was half untucked. He removed a clay pipe from between his teeth. Evidently he'd run out of cigarettes, but he wasn't too particular about what form his tobacco came in. 'What on earth are you doing, man?' he coolly asked Copperton's captor.

'What needs to be done! This abomination must be annihilated.'

'That's a bit harsh,' said Petey, not appearing to grasp the severity of the situation.

'And you're a fool as well, Peterson, for treating it like it's a soldier. How do you know it won't turn on you and kill you?'

Petey sucked on his pipe. 'Copperton here has had plenty of opportunities to kill me.'

'Maybe it's biding its time.' He raised the rifle, which had been gradually lowering as he'd been speaking, and aimed his eyes at Copperton. 'Maybe it's planning on killing every one of us in our sleep. How do we know that it will obey its orders?'

'How do the generals know that any of us will obey our orders?'

'Because we have a sense of God-given duty, as soldiers of the world's mightiest empire and as Christians! Even the sepoys who are still loyal to us can be made obedient by the offer of regular wages. This thing has no such motive. We can't know what its intentions are.'

Copperton leant his head towards the man, having to stretch his neck out two inches. 'My intention at the present moment is to prevent you causing harm to anyone by your foolishness.' His arm shot out to grab his sword, which he used to cut the rope binding his feet. 'You might as well lower your gun. Bullets cannot penetrate me, so it does you no favours.' As long as he didn't manage to shoot him right in the eyes; those were his two weak spots.

'I shall not listen to you.' The rifle was shaking wildly in the man's hand. Sweat dripped from his brow. 'My brothers and I in the Sons of Adam League will destroy you and all of your kind. You're an abomination, you're an insult to God, you're—'

'Private Evans!' bellowed a voice from nearby. Colonel Kirk rode towards them. There was a look of fury on his face. 'What in God's name are you doing?'

Private Evans lowered the rifle. 'Nothing, sir.'

'Nothing? It looked as if you were trying to shoot the automaton.'

'I was only fooling around, sir. Peterson will tell you.'

'He was certainly acting like a fool, sir,' said Petey.

'And he made *me* look a fool charging around in search of the mechanical soldier after you reported it missing, Private Peterson. Go and make yourself useful, Evans, and report for picket duty, or I'll have you flogged.'

'Yes, sir.'

As Private Evans passed Copperton, he hissed, 'Mark my words – I will destroy you.'

Copperton watched him walk away until he was out of sight, disappearing amongst the rows of tents.

'Thank you, sir. But why did you defend me?' he asked Colonel Kirk.

'Because I saw how you saved countless soldiers from the Pandies at Najafgarh. I cannot dispute your skill on the battlefield, and you've carried out every task I've given you well. You might be an asset to us after all. God knows we can use whatever help we can get if we do attempt to retake the city.' He shook his head and then galloped off.

'Do you know what Evans meant by the Sons of Adam League, or whatever it was called, Cop?' Petey asked once the colonel was gone.

'I know what he was referring to. My masters warned me about his brethren. They're an organisation dedicated to the annihilation of my kind. They see us as a threat to humanity's way of life, saying we'll take away people's jobs. They also consider us a blasphemy against God, since we are said to be an improvement on the design He laid down for mankind.'

'Well, if they're all like Evans then I don't think you have anything to worry about.' Petey flashed him a reassuring smile. 'Although what he lacks in brains he compensates for in raw energy and drive.'

'I'll wager he was the one I heard lurking outside your tent that night. Why did you not tell Colonel Kirk that Evans intended to destroy me, Petey? He should have been disciplined accordingly.'

Petey shrugged. 'He wasn't worth it. And I have something important to say to you. That's why I wasn't there to wake you in the first place. I was detained.'

'What is it that detained you?'

'News from Harford.' Petey sounded serious. Copperton knew this must be of vital importance. 'He saw a man, an Indian, bring Quincy a message yesterday. When Quincy read it, he looked very pleased and said "Finally". He's been a changed man since then – or rather, much like he was before, Harford says. Not nervous or irritable at all.'

'So the message would provide a clue to the source of his anxiety.'

'Exactly.' Petey grinned like a jackal who was in sight of a limping sheep.

'You aren't suggesting that we…'

'Of course.'

'We cannot ask his aide to look at the message.'

'I wasn't suggesting that. I was suggesting we read it ourselves.'

'That is an outrageous suggestion! I won't hear of it!'

'But it would banish your suspicions once and for all, Cop.'

'I have no suspicions.'

'Good one. But if he is innocent, this will confirm it.'

Copperton couldn't deny that there was some sense in that. 'What if we get caught?'

'You told me you plucked a medal from Brash Brass's tunic right under his nose. Surely you can sneak into a tent undetected?'

'Well, no doubt I could, but even so—'

'We can ask Powell and Singh to see what they think. We'll put it to a vote – how about that?'

'Very well. But I shall only agree to the vote as I don't think they will approve such a thing as this.'

The others voted in favour of the plan, giving Petey a three to one majority. The vote was held on the edge of the Ridge, after Powell and Singh returned from picket duty.

'Now all we need is an opportunity,' said Singh, sitting cross-legged on the ground.

'I have asked our informant to tell us when one might be at hand,' replied Petey.

'Very well. Jatin and I must rejoin our regiment before anyone notices our absence. It might be better if the four of us avoid being seen together, in case we attract attention. I have already seen a few suspicious glances directed our way,' added Powell solemnly as he and Singh rose to take their leave.

Petey and Copperton made their way back to their tent without speaking. Petey whistled a tune that Copperton did not know. It wasn't until they were inside the tent that Petey broke his silence.

'I knew they would agree to the plan,' he grinned as he collapsed on his charpoy.

'I admit defeat,' replied Copperton, taking his sword out to polish. 'I've been meaning to ask you, Petey, what did Private Evans and Colonel Kirk mean by "Pandies"?'

'It's another name for the mutineers, after Mangal Pandey, a private of the 34th Native Infantry who shot and wounded two British officers, or something like that. He inspired other native regiments to rebel and kill their officers. This was months ago now.'

'What happened to this Mangal Pandey?'

'Tried and executed.' Petey was whittling something, or at least he was to begin with, for the scraping ceased after a while. Perhaps the heat was making it difficult for him to focus. Copperton consulted his internal thermometer, which informed him that it was thirty-five degrees inside the tent. Or perhaps it was not the heat that was affecting Petey after all. Every now and again in the past, Copperton had witnessed Petey take something from his trouser pocket and stare at it. It appeared he was doing so on this occasion, when he thought Copperton was too occupied to notice. Since Copperton was sitting directly behind Petey, he magnified his vision to see what it was. A locket brooch, with its lid open. Set inside it was a picture of a fair-haired young woman.

'Who is she?' Copperton asked as he retracted his vision.

131

Petey sharply turned his head, but didn't look cross. 'Spying on me, Cop?'

'My curiosity got the better of me.' Copperton sat beside Petey, who placed the brooch in his palm.

'Sally. My fiancée. She's the real reason I came here. I wanted a quick way to earn enough money to allow us to marry. The friend I mentioned – the one who died – was her brother.'

'I see.' Copperton handed the brooch back to its owner and Petey tucked it into his pocket.

'The lock of her hair inside it fell out when the fastener broke, but I still have the photograph, at least. She's even prettier in the flesh.' He smiled, but not his usual smile that could charm a laugh or a pint of beer from the most weary, hot-tempered man in the camp, the smile that was rumoured by some of the infantrymen to be capable of melting women's hearts. This smile was gentle, something private. However, it was quickly broken by a chuckle. 'But she's as sharp as a whip. Always ready with a quip if someone says something to displease her, but she's willing to be nice to anyone. She'd have all the boys here under her thumb. The lads at her father's inn fall over themselves to please her, but she never does more than joke with 'em. Sal only has eyes for me, although she never lets me get away with anything. When she gave me this, she said, quite sarcastically, "So you don't forget what I look like and take a beautiful Indian mistress."'

It seemed to Copperton that it was a relief to Petey to speak of his Sally. The men in camp thought him an easy-going chap who loved nothing more than a joke and a laugh, and who had no thoughts of settling with a wife. That was his defence. That was how Petey sauntered his way so effortlessly through life. Copperton understood that his friend was letting him see through the chink in his armour.

'You sound very fond of her.'

'I'd die for her. The way things are going, that might very well happen.'

'Have faith, Petey. The generals will soon form a plan to retake the city, and once your initial seven years of service are over, you can return to England to marry her.'

'If only it were that simple. It'll be six years before I'm allowed to marry – with written sanction from my commanding officer – and then it's back to

132

the barracks for me. Sal is tough enough to survive out here. She could be like a *cantinière* for the troops, selling them food and liquor, but I wouldn't want her living in the barracks, especially not in a place so hot and disease-ridden. It won't be much of a marriage, but she says she doesn't mind being a soldier's wife. A soldier can only retire after completing twenty-one years of service, assuming I survive the siege. Besides, I'm more concerned that it'll be cholera that gets me, not a rebel's bullet. I'm going outside for a while. Some of the lads in my platoon are having a cricket match. Don't let yourself wind down, in case any more madmen try to take you.'

'They shan't. Petey?'

'Yes?' He paused with the tent half-open.

'Do you truly consider me to be your friend? Be honest if I am a mere amusement to you. I have no feelings to be hurt – not in the same way as you do.'

Petey smiled. 'I confess at first I was merely curious about you. In truth I'm still not sure what to make of you, but now I do consider you my friend. I'm trusting you to look out for me if we do try to take Delhi, or my Sal certainly shan't be Mrs Peterson.'

'On my honour, I promise to defend you.' Copperton placed his gloved hand on his chest and bowed.

'I shall hold you to that,' said Petey as he left the tent.

Chapter Fifteen

The following day, after George returned to work, Molly and Mr Arthur spent the afternoon in the woodland. They'd debated the subject of the greenhouses for most of that time. Mr Arthur insisted that the only suitable place was the flat field near the woodland, and that meant a number of trees would have to be cut down, as they blocked the sunlight. Molly wouldn't hear of it, and insisted that the greenhouses could be accommodated near the lakeside.

'It will spoil the view, and the land isn't suitable. It's uneven and like a bog after the rain,' insisted Mr Arthur.

'What was the point of curing all the trees if we're just going to chop them down?'

'It was necessary to completely eradicate the infection first.'

'How much land do you propose we clear?'

'Half an acre.'

'*Half* an acre? I won't have it.'

'Then you won't have your greenhouses either.'

In the end they reached a compromise: they would cut down half the proposed number of trees on the border between the lake and woodland, most of which had been badly damaged in the recent storm. On his next visit the following week, Mr Arthur brought his labourers to do the cutting, and

Molly also recruited the farmer's son to help. That didn't mean Mr Arthur was expected to merely watch everything from afar. Molly had him assisting her in chopping up the trees once they'd been cut down. The sacrificed trees could be used as timber and firewood for the poorer townsfolk, so at least it wasn't a waste. Even so, there was a glint in Molly's eyes as she swung her axe, aiming her gaze at Mr Arthur while she did so. That put him on his guard. She was probably envisioning that she was chopping off his head. So she was still cross with him for delaying his return by several days. His father had demanded that he return home to advise him on some trifling matter. Mr Greenwood had vigorously questioned his son about the commission he had so proudly boasted of in his last few letters. He wanted to know about the Abernathys' wealth and connections. He'd also enquired if Miss Abernathy had a fortune. His son replied that he should imagine so, but he had no idea how substantial it was, and that it was no business of his. (He'd accidentally referred to her as 'Miss Molly' in front of his father once or twice, something that didn't escape the old man's notice.)

'I hope that your brother is improving, Miss Molly,' remarked Mr Arthur as he heaved a heavy branch into the cart.

'Yes, he is doing much better, thank you,' she replied as she split a trunk in two with some difficulty. Molly hadn't told him the nature of George's ailment. That was none of his business. When she'd met Mr Arthur on the day that George began to improve, she had been in a terrible temper. He hadn't deserved that, so she was more mellow now and willing to humour him. She'd even let him have his own way by allowing him to build on the meadow – or rather, in it. Mr Arthur had shown her his design for a 'meadow hideaway' on his previous visit. He'd painted a large watercolour of his vision. The structure was cut directly into the slope at the back of the meadow. Its face was made of wood and had only a single window. Tall grasses and flowers half-concealed it.

'I considered what you said about giving me a challenge and that you don't want anything ornate. That gave me the idea of working around the landscape, making it appear as untampered with as possible,' he explained.

'Well, it's certainly original, I can't deny that. I like it much better than your previous ideas.'

Another sketch showed the hideaway's interior. Mr Arthur indicated certain features of interest with his finger. 'It will be stone walls on the inside. Quite a snug little place, like an old cottage almost. A good place to observe the cows grazing. Moss should grow over time and hide its face, making it more inconspicuous. You could even stick the chimney inside a tree trunk.'

Having inspected the design thoroughly, Molly nodded approvingly. 'Very well then.'

Molly and Mr Arthur chatted amicably from time to time as they cut up the trees and tossed them into the cart. Both were covered in sap and dirt but Molly wasn't the least bit embarrassed. Their conversation eventually subsided as they grew tired and were eager to finish their work. Each fallen tree left them more exposed to the hard blue sky and glaring sun. Every so often there would be a loud crack, and they'd pause to watch as another tree thundered to the ground in a burst of leaves, accompanied by the workmen's triumphant shouts. Molly occasionally stole a glimpse of Mr Arthur to make sure he was still working. He wore fawn trousers and a white shirt with the sleeves rolled up. The back of his shirt was grey with sweat. Under the radiant sun his hair lightened from barley to golden hay, although it looked feather-soft, and at that moment was rather tousled. He might have been mistaken for a labourer rather than a landscape gardener. To his credit, he hadn't complained once. Molly was quite aware that he was also occasionally glancing at her.

When Mr Arthur next looked up to ask if his client approved of his efforts, she was scaling a nearby apple tree.

'What are you doing, Miss Molly?' he shouted.

'Procuring refreshment. I can see the labourers have paused to have their bread and cheese, so we can do likewise.' She plucked a green apple off the tree and tossed it down to him. He just managed to catch it. It tasted tart but sweet when he bit into it, the juice relieving his parched mouth. Molly ate hers from her perch on the branch, tossing the core to the ground afterwards and narrowly missing Mr Arthur's head. A noise suddenly caught her attention, now that the sound of crunching apple no longer filled her ears, and she climbed a branch higher. 'There's a sparrow's nest up here! Three chicks!' she called down. 'Come and take a look.'

Mr Arthur suddenly looked nervous. 'I confess I'm not terribly good with heights.'

'You're not?'

'Not everyone is as adventurous as you, Miss Molly.'

'Does it frighten you?'

'It certainly unnerves me. In fact, I was surprised I managed to get over the kitchen garden wall that day I first arrived here.'

Molly drummed her fingers on the tree trunk, then hastily climbed back down. She saw how anxious he was at the speed and ease with which she moved. He was probably prepared to leap in to catch her at any moment. But she was no damsel.

'Is it the thought of falling that unnerves you?' she asked, landing lightly on the ground.

'That is part of it. But even if I don't look down, I still feel light-headed. It's rather unpleasant. I've been like it since I was a boy.'

'Hm.' She ran her finger along the jagged end of her thumbnail. 'Well, I suppose we'll have to see about that.'

'Everyone is afraid of something,' he smiled.

'You don't have to justify yourself to me, Mr Arthur.'

'I'm not. I'm explaining why I'm not ashamed of it. I'm sure even you are frightened by some things.'

'Not much.' The sight of George when Douglas brought him home on that stormy night had frightened her out of her wits, although she'd had to force herself to remain calm in order to do what was needed of her.

After a brief luncheon, they resumed their work. The clocktower's bell rang twice in the distance as Molly's axe bit the thick branch of a fallen tree. She allowed herself to lapse into thought. She wondered about her brothers' mechanical soldier in India. There had been no mention of it in any of the newspaper reports that trickled from northern India. She wished her brothers hadn't had to be involved, even indirectly, in this horrible, bloody mutiny. (Then again, maybe every English person was implicated somehow. Their tea had to come from somewhere.) At least George and Douglas had learnt to take her into their confidence, after they had concealed George's wager with Lord Leyton until the night before the earl arrived to inspect Maestro. They'd told her about their interview with General Brassington as soon as she returned from the Royal Botanic Gardens that same day.

Molly heard something thump to the ground behind her. It was loud enough to make her look up. Mr Arthur clutched his wrist and sucked air through his teeth. His axe was lying on the ground.

'What did you do?' she asked.

'I caught myself on the sharp edge. It is only a scratch.'

'Let me see, Mr Arthur.'

He seemed about to comply, then retracted his arm.

'Stop trying to be brave and let me see.'

After hesitating several moments, he offered her his hand. The palm of his other hand was smeared with blood from where it had been pressed over the wound. There was a deep cut on the outside of his thumb on his injured hand, but nothing too severe.

'Keep hold of it a moment,' she ordered, retrieving her water bottle. Molly rinsed the wound with water, the red line welling with blood again almost instantly. She snapped the stem of a golden yellow flower growing at the base of a tree and took Mr Arthur's hand. 'This will sting but it'll help it heal.'

He winced as she squeezed a yellow substance from the flower's head over the cut. She then dripped the white sap leaking from the end of the stem over the wound, and a waxy, white seal formed as the sap set. 'You shouldn't need a bandage, but just be careful and try not to move that hand too much.' Her gaze fell on her white hand cupping his browner one. Both their hands were sticky with tree sap.

Mr Arthur was examining her work and stroked the side of his thumb. 'You seem to have a remedy for everything, Miss Molly.'

'Only some things. I used the honey flower's nectar and sap when I cut myself while dissecting a specimen yesterday. See?' She held up her other hand for him to see the scabbed line on the back.

'What did you call it?'

'A honey flower. One of my own creations.' She glanced at the cluster of golden flowers on the woodland floor. 'I identified the substance in honey that helps wounds heal, and transplanted it into the flowers. The nectar cleans the wound, and the sap acts as a bandage. It'll dry and fall away in a few hours.'

'Your knowledge of healing is certainly impressive.'

'I learnt a good deal about healing from an Irish gypsy woman when I was young, but I've built on her teachings over time.'

Poor Mrs Dempsey. Molly hoped her sons in America had really sent for her, although she suspected that was a lie told to her by Mrs Dempsey's neighbours to spare Molly the truth that her mentor had died – probably from a sudden illness. It was around the time of that terrible cholera outbreak.

'A gypsy woman?' said Mr Arthur. 'How extraordinary. I dare say you'd make a good nurse.'

Molly sighed to herself. She'd had her fill of nursing after caring for her consumptive mother during her last days. But Molly had had the patience of a saint throughout that week when George was in the fever's grip. Once he was starting to recover, she'd dared to read while she sat at his bedside. She'd become frustrated at not being able to comprehend something in the textbook and she must have been grumbling loudly, because George asked her what was the matter. He told her to show him the book and he explained it to her as clear as day. It was an unusual little moment between the two of them.

'I wouldn't have the patience,' she replied to Mr Arthur.

'Hm, maybe there is some truth to that.' He smiled playfully. 'If you'll forgive me for saying so.'

'You forget yourself, Mr Arthur.' Molly released his hand. 'You can load the rest of the branches into the cart one-handed, can't you?'

'I can.'

'Get back to work then.' She failed to suppress her smile as she gave this order. The heat must have been making her head giddy, as she struggled to maintain a sober enough demeanour to check him for his cheek. Nevertheless, he meekly did as she commanded and started hauling branches into the cart.

Chapter Sixteen

A Council of War was to be held to decide whether to launch an assault on Delhi or not. It was a prime opportunity for Copperton and his comrades, since General Quincy, like every other general, was required to attend, and the four of them meant to make the most of it. Copperton told Powell and Singh to watch the north and west sides of General Quincy's tent while he and Petey watched from the east side, to make it look less obvious what they were doing, and also so that the other three could keep watch from all sides while Copperton undertook his mission.

'It seems wrong to spy on an officer,' remarked Copperton, not taking his eyes off General Quincy's tent.

'But we have good reason to,' Petey pointed out. He pushed up his forage cap and patted the havelock to make sure it covered his neck.

'I suppose.' Copperton magnified his vision to see how the other two were faring. Powell was smoking and looking bored. Singh had his little book open and was writing away. He never scribbled furiously in an attack of genius when he wrote his poetry, but leisurely let the words flow from the pencil. Copperton had sometimes watched as the elegant, curling characters graced the pages (which reminded him somewhat of musical notation). He hadn't a hope of comprehending them, even after Singh had tried to teach him to read Nasta'liq script.

'This makes no sense to me, Singh. Why do you not write in English now you know how? I see you make your linguistic notes in English,' Copperton had remarked one night.

Without stopping writing, Singh had humbly replied, 'Your English letters are too hard and stern. They are for writing lists and telegraph messages, not for verse. Only Urdu is a worthy vessel to contain the poet's words. It does not work otherwise.'

'Surely you are able to translate your verses into English?'

'Not fully. You misunderstand, Copperton. A translation is imperfect – something is always wanting. Something is lost.'

'I confess you have quite lost *me*, Singh.'

'Your English is not the most beautifulest language.'

'You mean the most *beautiful* language,' corrected Copperton. 'And it is the language of the greatest and most advanced nation in the world. Surely that supports its merit?'

Singh only shook his head as his pencil softly scratched away.

Copperton marched to and fro before sitting on the ground beside Singh, who was leaning against the mud wall of the sepoy's lines.

'Something has been puzzling me. Why do you remain loyal to the Company? You have as much cause to rise against them as any of the mutineers, if not more, since the Company took your family's land when they annexed Oudh. Surely it is not because of kinship with your brother soldiers that you remain with us? So many sepoys elsewhere have risen against their officers. Even some sepoys in the Field Force were suspected of harbouring mutinous intent and sent away.'

Singh put away his book and sighed. 'Kinship is part of it, and I need the money now my family have lost their land. I feel more loyalty to the British than the *Purbais* – the "outsiders from the East",' he explained, noting Copperton didn't recognise the term. 'They cheated us for their own selfish reasons. It was because of them that the Sikhs were defeated and the Punjab lost to the British in the last Sikh war. I was only nine when it happened, but I remember it clearly. When my family heard that the Punjab had fallen, I'd never seen my father so bitter and angry – it frightened me. And now the *Purbais* have started this ill-fated revolt. I do not think the Company are good to us, make no mistakes. I have thought once or twice that it would be good to overthrow them. But what then? We cannot go back to the old ways. The king is like his kingdom – in his winter. When he dies, it will all wither. And sooner or later, more ships from England will arrive and they will crush the mutiny. And…I do not agree that the Christians deserve to die. Both the English and the people of this land will have to answer for what they have done when they depart this world.'

'I see,' said Copperton, although he felt like he was seeing through fog. 'You and your family are Sikhs, I presume?' Copperton had assumed Singh was a Sikh – there were many in the column, along with Gurkhas and Punjabi Muslims.

'My father is, but my mother's relations are Rajputs. She converted when she married my father. When I was young, my mother said to me that there are many paths to God.'

'And what path do you take?'

Singh smiled. 'I am undecided.'

Copperton's head was in a whirl. He could practically hear his gears jarring or rotating at full pelt. This was too puzzling for him. Religion was a human affair and something too complex for his understanding; he simply knew to obey the British officers. But his greater concern was whether Singh was in earnest. Was he secretly plotting with the mutineers and trying to blind Copperton with his poetic words? If he, or any of the sepoys at camp, showed the slightest sign of disloyalty, he'd sworn he would immediately inform Colonel Kirk. Since that night, however, Copperton had only found reasons to trust Singh, who showed himself to be an intelligent and observant young man. There was no savagery in him; he'd even been giving Copperton Hindi lessons. (Singh had explained during their first lesson how Hindustani was 'bazaar talk', while Urdu was a more formal manner of speech. He had been in rhapsodies about whether a certain word was borrowed from Persian or Sanskrit, showing Copperton the lists he'd made in his *kitab*, and then apologised for deviating from their lesson.)

Copperton turned his magnified gaze from Singh and Powell to look around. Their watch had been a long one; nothing much had happened all morning. If they remained in their current position much longer, some of the other soldiers would certainly begin to notice that they were up to something. A black dog that Copperton had sometimes seen wandering around the camp became curious about them. It kept pawing and gnawing at Copperton's legs (at one point it cocked its leg against Copperton's and left a small puddle). He patted the animal on the head and followed Petey's instructions to make it submissive, petting it as gently as he could. He was acutely aware that he could easily crush its bones if he applied too much pressure. The dog's loyalty was soon gained, however, and it remained at Copperton's feet, panting heavily. He feared that it would bark or try to follow him into General Quincy's tent. Petey was kneeling down, scratching the dog's side, when their target suddenly exited his tent and shouted to his servant. After a short exchange between them, General Quincy marched off in the direction of General Wilson's tent.

'Here's your chance, Copperton,' said Petey, the dog quite contentedly sprawled on the ground beside him. The android nodded and flitted across to the tent, slipping inside undetected. It was undoubtedly nicer than a regular soldier's tent. There was a hook for hats and garments along one wall, and even a framed picture. The only furniture was a charpoy, a writing desk and a large trunk – the charpoy precariously balancing on the other two items. The general's possessions were scattered about: a couple of books, a bottle swathed in cloth, a handsome rosewood dressing case, a pair of discarded walking shoes and stockings. There was a sponge bag, hairbrush and dress comb on the messy bed. Several flies drifted through the air, buzzing drowsily. Copperton swatted them when they landed on him. There was a half-finished letter on the writing desk that was addressed to 'Eleanor', who was apparently General Quincy's fiancée, judging by the letter's contents. That was of no value. But the note beside it was of far greater interest. It was slightly crumpled, and written in a hasty scrawl that was markedly different from General Quincy's neat hand. The note appeared to be written in a cipher.

PDA KPDAN KBBEYANO OQOLAYP JKPDEJC WJZ WJ WOOWQHP KJ ZAHDE OAAIO EIIEJAJP. PDA PEIA PK OPNEGA SEHH OKKJ XA WP DWJZ. PDA SAWLKJ EO NAWZU PK XA LQP EJPK WYPEKJ. E ODWHH EJBKNI UKQ KB PDA YDKOAJ OEPA WO OKKJ WO LKOOEXHA.

Copperton scanned his eyes over the text multiple times until he was sure he'd memorised every letter. There was nothing on the note to indicate who had sent it. He searched the rest of the tent, even rummaging through the already disordered bedsheets, but found nothing else of any relevance – not that he expected to. There was a moment of excitement when Copperton found a crumpled piece of paper inside a pair of trousers, but it turned out to be a note stating that General Quincy owed another officer five pounds after losing to him at cards.

With his mission complete, Copperton was about to make his exit when he spied something on the ground, half-trapped under the tent's canvas. He extended his arm to retrieve it, and saw it was an ivory figurine of a sowar mounted on a horse, with his curved sword in his right hand and the horse's reins in his left. He wore a round hat and kurta, with shoes that curled inwardly at the toes. A circular shield hung on a strap from his right shoulder. The intricate detail and smooth finish on both horse and rider were remarkable. The figurine must only have been about two inches tall, and was fixed to a black base. Without really thinking why, Copperton pocketed the little ivory sowar. He slipped out of the tent and walked on. His fellow conspirators dispersed, as they had agreed beforehand.

Copperton made his way back to Petey's tent, knowing his friend would be elsewhere. He copied out the message on a scrap of paper. He'd read that Julius Caesar encrypted military messages by substituting each letter of the alphabet with the letter three positions further along, and suspected that this cipher worked in a similar way. Without knowing the number of positions the alphabet had been displaced by in the note, however, some ingenuity was required to decipher its contents. Copperton began by looking for the frequently repeated letters that also appeared in two-letter words, which suggested that they were vowels. Once he was confident which vowel matched which letter, he looked for other repeated sequences to uncover letters such as 't' and 'h' in 'the'. From there, it was a matter of inserting the already deciphered letters into the remaining words and deducing what the other letters were likely to be. He was confident that he'd correctly deciphered the entire message, which ran as follows:

The other officers suspect nothing and an assault on Delhi seems imminent. The time to strike will soon be at hand. The weapon is ready to be put into action. I shall inform you of the chosen site as soon as possible.

What weapon? No one had spoken of a weapon, other than the heavy guns that the Delhi Field Force had captured. Copperton doubted that was what the message referred to. This shed no light on General Quincy's strange behaviour; if anything, it only deepened the mystery surrounding the man's actions. But this message suggested that there was a traitor amongst the Field Force. Whether Quincy was the traitor, a go-between for the true perpetrator and the rebels, or a loyal officer trying to apprehend the writer of the note was yet to be seen. Deep down, however, Copperton couldn't believe it was the last option. He hid the message under his glove. He would have destroyed it, but he wished to consult his friends about the message, since he was curious to see what they'd make of it.

The four of them did not reconvene until that night. The Council of War had decided on a course of action: an assault on Delhi was to be launched on the fourteenth of September, in seven days' time. Work to construct batteries near the city walls began at once, in accordance with the engineers' plan of assault. The plan was to eliminate the bastions along the stone walls that enclosed the city, and to make breaches in the walls for the assaulting columns to enter the city through once the attack commenced. Practically every available man was helping to construct the battery wall from earth and gabions, shovelling soil or filling sandbags in order to entrench the heavy guns. The enemy unrelentingly fired on them with shot and shell all night as the work was carried out. Copperton proved his usefulness by helping to speed up the wall's construction and by aiding the covering party.

The four friends had different duties, but congregated shortly before sunrise in the almost-completed battery, 700 yards from the Mori Bastion. Before them was Ludlow Castle, a splendid white fortress that had once served as the Resident's house, and which had been neglected by the rebels. Powell and Singh were plastered in dirt. Petey, who had been in the covering party providing protection for the workers (or exchanging dirty jokes with them), was comparatively clean. They distanced themselves from the other men, who were far too occupied positioning the siege guns to notice them

(Copperton was able to lift the twenty-four-pounders single-handedly). In that single night, a wall had been formed from earth, stone and sandbags that was thick enough to protect the guns from enemy fire. The guns' barrels rested just above the top of the wall. Petey pretended to rebuke Powell and Singh for their slowness as someone threatened to approach. Copperton extended his neck several inches to gauge how many rebels, who were armed with muskets, were around. The enemy were primarily positioned in the Mori Bastion and Kashmir Bastion above. Their guns had fallen quiet. Most likely this was only another brief reprieve, and they would resume firing before long.

Copperton's head settled in its proper place on his shoulders.

'It's still strange to see you do that,' said Petey, remembering to add, 'Work faster or we won't have this finished by sunrise!' with convincing ferocity.

'What did you see in General Quincy's tent, Copperton?' asked Singh eagerly.

'A note.' He showed them the scrap of paper. His decryption was written beneath the original message. Powell deemed Copperton's decryption to be correct, since he was familiar with Caesar's method of coding messages.

'Are you sure he wasn't referring to you, Cop?' said Petey. 'You are meant to be a secret weapon.'

'Hardly a secret now, is he?' Powell handed Copperton the note. 'Half the army has caught sight of him.'

'I am sure this has nothing to do with me,' said Copperton. 'It appears General Brassington wasn't the only one who sought to use the mutiny as a test.'

'Do you think General Quincy is a traitor?' asked Singh.

'There's no way of knowing that for certain with the limited information we have gleaned,' replied Copperton.

'Should you not tell Colonel Kirk, Copperton?'

'Best not, Jat,' said Powell. 'If there is a conspiracy, who knows how deep it goes? There's no telling who sent Quincy that message, for one thing. We can trust no one outside of the four of us.'

'So what do we do?'

'Copperton?' Petey demanded. Copperton had been staring into the distance, but turned his head on hearing his name. 'Penny for your thoughts?'

'I was thinking that perhaps there might be someone we can trust, who can try to find information on General Quincy.'

'And who might that be?'

'My makers.'

'And how do we reach them, exactly?' asked Powell. 'By the time word would reach them, possibly two or three months from now, Quincy will have used this weapon.'

'There are far faster means than a letter.' Copperton pressed down on the panel in the middle of his chest, which opened like a cupboard door. He plucked something from his chest, seeing the slightly disturbed faces of the three men. He supposed it was as if any of them were to rip out one of their organs.

'Fear not, this is not part of me, it was simply stored in there,' Copperton assured them as he closed his chest panel. He set the wooden box, which was slightly larger and thicker than a tobacco tin, on the battery wall. There were two gold dials on one of its sides and a number of brass buttons on the topmost side. Three small brass trumpets popped out of the top when Copperton pressed one of the gleaming brass buttons, along with a tall antenna. The middle trumpet in the crest was the largest, this being the speaking trumpet. Copperton turned a dial and the device started to make a peculiar, fuzzy noise.

'Is that a wireless telegraph?' asked Petey excitedly.

'That's precisely what it is.'

'Incredible!'

'But it is rather precarious. My masters entrusted it to me should an emergency arise. I never seriously thought that I would need to make use of it.'

'Well, they obviously had incredible foresight.'

'I'll need to tune it, though, if we are to reach them. The transmitter is kept on at all times back in England, just in case. There's another receiver in the airship, which could cause interference should it be in use.'

'Airship?'

'Now is not the time to explain, Petey. Wait, I think I have tuned it,' declared Copperton as the device's fuzzy crackling diminished. He shouted into the speaking trumpet. 'Hello! Can anyone hear me?'

Chapter Seventeen

The three of them were dining together that night – an infrequent occurrence, since they each tended to be busy with different things. Yet Molly thought her brothers had tried to be as far away from each other as physically possible by sitting at opposite ends of the long dining table. (She suspected they'd had another argument about something.) Molly was sitting on Douglas's right.

'Are you and Mr Arthur making progress with the garden?' Douglas asked her.

'Some,' she shrugged, toying with the cabbage on the end of her fork. 'Although he didn't arrive today as his father requested his presence at home. Again.'

'Oh well, that can't be helped, I suppose. As long as he isn't proving unreliable.'

'This project is too important to his reputation to be taken lightly.'

There was a lull in the conversation. This wasn't right; this felt too normal.

'So what have the two of you been doing all day, since your current project for the soap manufacturer is on hold?' she asked.

Douglas's face brightened. 'I made this.' He placed something on the table that looked like a leather gauntlet lined with metal. Holes had been cut out for the various controls on the back of the hand.

'Why?' Molly asked, letting her cutlery rest on her plate. How long had he been waiting to unveil this?

'Just watch.' He slid his hand into the gauntlet and wriggled his fingers. It seemed to shrink around the outline of his hand so that it fitted him perfectly. 'It's powered by electromagnetism.'

'I still don't understand...' Molly stopped speaking as her knife and fork began to tremble, then every item of cutlery on the table levitated into the air. Douglas held his palm upwards and flexed his fingers, looking very much like a sorcerer.

'You can use it to pull objects towards you or to suspend them in mid-air,' he explained.

'Makes clearing the table easier.' Molly watched the knives and forks hovering above her head.

'But not useful if you're still in the middle of dinner,' observed George.

Douglas attempted to lower the cutlery, but instead every item stuck to the gauntlet. 'Oh, for God's sake.' He disconnected the gauntlet's battery and the knives, forks and spoons clattered on the table.

Molly sorted through the silverware and passed a set down to George. 'Good thing you didn't attempt this demonstration when we had guests for dinner,' she said. 'It looks like your gauntlet might need refining.'

'But I spent all afternoon working on this and I wanted to show it to you.'

'Then you wasted an afternoon,' remarked George as he resumed dinner.

'Well, I had nothing else to do, and I've had this idea for a while now. It might prove useful in some way, like finding lost screws or helping in the construction of heavy machinery. You can also reverse the polarisation to repel objects instead.'

Molly gripped every knife and fork around her.

'See this?' Douglas held up a pea-sized black metal ball. 'You put it in this slot here.' He slotted it into the back of the gauntlet. 'Now watch.'

He aimed his index finger in George's direction and made a quick movement with his hand. The next second, a glass of water on George's left smashed.

'Are you quite done destroying the tableware?' Molly demanded. 'Or were you trying to kill your brother?'

'If I was trying to shoot him, I wouldn't have missed,' Douglas winked.

Molly shook her head and continued eating. 'You're mad.'

Douglas only laughed to himself.

'Can you hear that?' said George abruptly. His brother and sister strained to listen, detecting a faint, intermittent buzzing.

'Is that the wireless transmitter?' Douglas asked.

'I believe so.'

Douglas was instantly on his feet, and bolted out of the room. The transmitter was on the mantel in the oak parlour – flanked on either side by an ornamental vase containing lead plates submerged in sulfuric acid (these makeshift batteries were connected to the transmitter by discrete metal wires). The bulb that looked like a nose on the transmitter's walnut face was pulsing in time with each buzz. George and Molly followed their brother into the parlour moments later.

'It must be from the soldier!' Douglas pressed the button to receive the transmission. The device made a warbling noise and a voice crackled through it.

'Hello! Can anyone hear me?' called a familiar, brassy voice. 'Hello?'

'Soldier! We hear you. Can you hear us?'

'Master Douglas!' the soldier's voice crackled.

Someone in the background exclaimed, 'Good God! It works!'

'I trust you are all well back home?' said the soldier.

'Indeed we are. It is good to hear from you, although it sounds as if you're not alone?'

'There are three listeners here with me – my fellow soldiers, who can be trusted absolutely. I must speak quickly – we could be discovered at any moment. We have reason to believe that one of the officers here may be a traitor. There is evidence that he has created a weapon without sanction from the rest of the army.'

'What sort of weapon?'

'We're unsure, although I once saw him surrounded by a wall of mist, away from the battlefield, with several unconscious men at his feet. We need you to find out the officer's history and try to uncover what he intends to do, if what information we have on him so far is accurate.'

'What is the man's name?'

'Major-General Quincy.'

'Copperton! Watch out!' Douglas heard someone shout, accompanied by the sound of gunfire.

'His name is Quincy! Report back to us when you can—'

The line went dead. Only the transmitter's usual scratchy hum sounded.

'Soldier!'

Douglas received no answer.

'What happened?' George asked.

'We lost them. It sounds as if they were under attack.'

'The receiver might have been hit.'

Douglas fiddled with the controls, but to no avail. 'Let's just pray that they survive that attack.'

George leant over him and switched the transmitter off. 'Don't dwell on that possibility. We've been given a task that we must complete as quickly as possible, and hope they respond to us once we have something to report.'

'Hardly an easy task, is it? Where do we even start looking for information on this Major-General Quincy?'

'Quincy...' Molly's brow crinkled. 'That sounds familiar. Oh! I know!'

She shot out of the room, passed a startled Martha in the hall, and ran upstairs. Martha had almost finished clearing the dining table by the time Molly returned to the parlour, brandishing a book.

'Dr Quincy is the author of one of the books it was recommended that I read before starting my studies.' She placed the book on the table for her brothers to examine. 'He's been a lecturer at several universities, but apparently he is not currently teaching, after an experiment of his went wrong and caused an explosion. His research is about improving crop yields. Do you think he and this officer could be related?'

'More likely than if the officer was a Smith or Brown,' remarked George as he briefly studied the volume. 'And this man's work suggests that there could be a promising link between them.'

'So what do we do?' asked Douglas.

'Find a way to secure an interview with this Dr Quincy,' his brother answered.

'You could ask to meet under the pretence of a business venture?' suggested Molly.

'We'd have to know precisely what.'

'Or perhaps we could simply claim to be interested in his research,' Douglas suggested.

'I'd need to tell you what to say,' said Molly. 'You'll risk exposing your ignorance.'

'I'm sure you could let us borrow your textbooks.'

'It'll take more than a few textbooks to convince him. I'll have to play teacher.'

'Maybe it'll be preparation for the future, should you become an academic one day,' teased Douglas.

'Don't be stupid. The university have already made it clear that I won't be eligible to graduate like a real student. I'm exempt from taking Moderations, which means I can't take all of the required examinations for a degree.'

'A convenient excuse,' muttered George.

'Don't you go offering them even more money,' she warned.

'Fear not. You've made your feelings about that perfectly clear.'

'Not that I feel capable of learning Thucydides or Herodotus by heart. I can't imagine anything more tedious.'

'I'll write to Dr Quincy saying we'll be in London on business next week and wish to call on him. You had better prepare your first chemistry lesson for us, then, Dr Abernathy.' Douglas smiled at her.

Molly put her hands on her hips as she looked at him. 'Only if you promise not to call me that again.'

To their surprise, Dr Quincy more than readily invited them to dine with him at his residence in London that Wednesday. It was only as Douglas put down Dr Quincy's letter that he became apprehensive about the plan. There would be drink at the dinner, unless the man was teetotal. It would be too great a temptation for George. Douglas was still surprised that George was cooperating with their efforts to keep him sober. When he'd asked him why, knowing how stubborn his brother was when he didn't wish to do something, George replied, 'I don't want to remain dependent on the spirits. I know I can do without them.' What George omitted to mention was that, as well as wanting to show self-command, he didn't want to cause his brother or sister any more concern. He'd seen now that they couldn't ignore his habits and trust him to himself. This strengthened his resolve to learn to calm his mind when he was without work or faced with a problem he struggled to solve. If only he still didn't desire spirits – that was the obstacle to overcome. He might not want the alcohol any longer, but his body still did. It had grown too accustomed to it. Before they'd even left Soho, George had reached a stage where, even if he wasn't particularly overwhelmed by his thoughts, he still felt the need to drink. He had started to lose control, and he vowed never to let this happen again. Fortunately, Molly's tonic helped curb the yearning whenever it started to gnaw at him.

Douglas's hopes of dissuading him from attending the dinner, however, were swiftly dashed.

'The man could potentially be dangerous. It will be better if there's two of us,' George argued.

'Not if you lose control of yourself.'

George gave him a glacial stare. 'Do you think I'd consider this plan if I thought there was a chance of that happening?'

Douglas sighed and gave in. Evidently his older brother still felt he had to watch out for him – either that or George thought he couldn't be trusted to carry out the plan alone.

As they soon discovered, however, Dr Quincy was far from dangerous – on the surface, at least. He was a short, stout man with downy fair hair. He seemed to have never fully grown into his face, having small features and spectacles that were too large for him. He had his back to them as the butler led them into a well-furnished drawing room, but quickly spun around and gave them a lavish smile. They'd been unsure whether they would be part of a larger party or not, but it appeared it was to be just them. Waddling across the room, their host shook each brother enthusiastically by the hand.

'Good evening, gentlemen. It is an honour to meet you both. I had hoped there would be a couple of friends joining us, but they had a last-minute change of plans, it seems. No matter – I'm sure that we shall do just as well with three people. I have a great deal to ask you,' he said sanguinely. 'Dinner should be ready shortly. Might I offer you a glass of something?'

George asked for Madeira. Douglas had to fight to conceal his disbelief. What in God's name was he doing? He was supposed to have declined and explained that he didn't drink spirits.

'So, I have heard much about that automaton composer of yours, The Mechanical Maestro. I tried to see it on stage but tickets sold out almost instantly!' said Dr Quincy once the three of them were seated.

'I am sorry to hear that, Dr Quincy,' Douglas replied. He glanced at George and saw that the glass in his hand was still full. 'Perhaps there might be an opportunity to see him in the future when he has returned from his travels abroad.'

'Do you have any new projects currently in progress?'

'Yes, we have quite an interesting commission from a man who owns a soap-making company. He's recently invented a new form of shampoo that he claims not only washes and strengthens hair but prevents loss of colour and hair, and damage from heat. He wanted us to create a device that can wash, cut, dry and style hair, to help promote his new product.'

They had tested the device on poor Martha after part of her hair caught fire during a kitchen accident. She had seemed rather apprehensive when she saw the chair brandishing several arms, one wielding a pair of scissors. But by the time her hair was under the metal hood, she was contentedly reading a magazine. Only, when the hood was lifted, they saw that her hair was pink. They thought the fault was with the man's product rather than with their machine. Now the poor girl wore her bonnet indoors instead of her cap, although her hair was still visible from the front. The new kitchen maid had been repeatedly rebuked for laughing at her. Molly was trying to find a way to return Martha's hair to its original colour, and had berated her brothers for not questioning what was in the shampoo in the first place.

'How interesting! I should like to see this hairdressing machine when it is finished.' Dr Quincy smiled broadly.

'It may be some time yet before it is completed.' When Douglas next looked across at George, the liquid in his glass had gone down a fraction.

Douglas cleared his throat. 'So, Dr Quincy, I understand that you are particularly interested in using nitrogen to increase crop yields?'

'Yes, that was the former focus of my research. But I have since devoted my attention to other projects, most notably the development of an alternative anaesthetic to chloroform during surgery, one that only numbs the part of the body to be operated on rather than leaving the patient completely numb. It is less dangerous for the patient that way, you see. I confess I have discontinued my research on the subject for the present, but I remain hopeful.'

'I hope you won't think me intrusive if I ask why you discontinued that line of work?'

There was a slight tremor in the man's face. The jolly smile contracted slightly and the eyebrows pinched. His countenance smoothed out in seconds, though.

'Not at all. It was merely that I was struggling to make much progress in that quarter. The substance I created was far too strong. The university was not willing to fund me for much longer without a result. I assure you that I do see some projects through to completion. For example, I have created a number of highly effective methods for killing pests. If only I was as good at preserving life as exterminating it.' Even his laugh was like a duck's quack. 'Then again, I suppose it ensures that nothing will eat farmers' crops and that food does eventually reach the table.' Again came the duck laugh.

Each time Douglas darted a look at his brother, the volume of liquid in the glass had decreased. After the sixth time, however, he caught George pouring some of the liquid into the pot of the fern on the table behind him. He'd chosen his seat carefully. Dr Quincy continued to digress on the subject of his current research until the butler announced dinner. The butler brought a bottle of wine to accompany the meal. George and Douglas devised a system, via a lot of subtle gesturing, whereby Douglas would occasionally hold his partially empty glass out to George, who'd then tip some liquid from his own glass into it. Their host was too preoccupied in his own ramblings to notice. This meant that Douglas was drinking slightly more than he knew he ought to be, but not enough to put him out of his senses. He'd feel it in the morning. Their host found it incredible to believe that neither of his guests had received any kind of formal education. (Apart from a single week at a grammar school run by an authoritarian, sadistic vicar, Mr Meddlings, who was very able with his cane. George and Douglas were expelled following an incident where a gargoyle miraculously sprang to life during Sunday prayers and terrorised both teacher and pupils. It had been in retaliation to Mr Meddlings' constant cruelty, and his insistence that the two boys attend useless Greek and Latin lessons when they wanted to work on their own project: a bird remotely controlled by electromagnetic waves.)

Dr Quincy pushed his glasses up his snub nose. 'Truth be told, I am glad to not have to teach for the present moment. Were the students to show any enthusiasm for chemistry, I might have a greater passion for teaching, but one is lucky if there are one or two dedicated scholars in an entire class.'

'Our sister is to attend Oxford shortly to study natural sciences,' remarked Douglas.

Dr Quincy looked at him quizzically. 'Your *sister*?'

'Yes. She is exceptionally bright and so they admitted her.'

Dr Quincy was evidently at a loss to know what to make of this.

'She has an interest in growing flowers and vegetables, and has read your writings on the subject with great interest,' Douglas added.

Dr Quincy brightened on hearing his work praised. Would he take the bait and return to the topic of his abandoned research? It appeared not.

'I am most flattered. My own younger sister is terribly fond of music. She has poor nerves, and playing helps to keep her calm. I can never get her away from the pianoforte. She is engaged to our cousin who is a general in the British Army. He's caught up in that dreadful mutiny business over in India, where your new weapon will no doubt be of great assistance. The last time my cousin was here, my sister played for us. I had never heard her play so well before, and she sang so beautifully. The effect of being in love, no doubt. My cousin had a friend with him who is also an officer. I've forgotten his name now. I dare say he was in danger of falling in love with her himself, so struck was he by her playing and her voice. They even sang a duet together.' He laughed nervously, but his affection for his sister shone through in his tone of voice. While this had not been the desired response, it had yielded some interesting information nonetheless. How the hell did Dr Quincy know about the soldier? Surely George had misheard him. He looked at Douglas, whose lack of surprise showed he'd not grasped the significance of what their host had just said. It was hard to conceal his disbelief at his brother's obliviousness and resist the urge to kick him in the shin. They needed to draw their host into revealing the extent of his knowledge. Dr Quincy was quick to begin a fresh turn in the conversation, however, and was soon lost in a narrative from his days as a student. Perhaps George had imagined his remark about the soldier after all.

George sensed an appropriate time to make his move. 'Excuse me,

Dr Quincy, but I appear to have left my pocketbook in the drawing room. Might I please retrieve it?'

'Oh, of course, Mr Abernathy. I trust you remember the way? I could send my butler to search for it?'

'That won't be necessary. I can remember the way.'

Dr Quincy was quick to recover the previous thread of conversation, and was fully engrossed in a fresh narrative as George left the room. Making sure that no servants were around, he made his way straight past the drawing room and ascended the stairs. They'd decided that Douglas would be the one who'd keep Dr Quincy entertained and George would be the one to examine his study. They had identified the study window on their descent in the airship earlier. He picked the door's lock with the file he kept in his coat pocket. The study smelt of coffee and undisturbed dust. Bookshelves lined the walls and a large, mahogany desk occupied most of the room. A sun-faded Persian rug was spread over the floor. Everything except the desk's surface was coated in a thin film of dust; clearly Dr Quincy had forbidden his maid to enter his study, as was the case at Ravenfeld Hall. George stepped cautiously, reminded of when he had entered his sister's old room in search of Professor Penrose's letter. He even ran his eye along the bookshelves, but none of the volumes had been disturbed for a long time. He carefully sifted through the jumble of papers on the desk, and made sure to replace everything as it was. The papers were mostly correspondences from universities and fellow academics. As George replaced the uppermost leaf, his eye landed on the desk drawers, which proved to be locked. The file made short work of the locks. In the top drawer there was the draft of what looked to be Dr Quincy's latest paper – nothing relevant, from what George could tell. In the drawer below there was a letter.

Sir,

Further to my previous letter, I request that you recreate the anaesthetic mixture in its entirety. Ten gallons is the desired quantity. Have it ready for the 29th and deliver it directly to Brigadier-General Fowler's residence at 39 Pall Mall. Your part in the business shall then be complete. I remind you that, should you fail to comply or tell anyone about this matter, then the union between Miss Quincy and myself shall not take place. Destroy this letter once you have read it.

Major-General Horatio Quincy

George searched for any other letters from General Quincy, but found none. Perhaps his cousin had been ordered to destroy any previous correspondence. The letter was dated October of the previous year. More than enough time had passed in which to dispose of it. If Dr Quincy hoped it could one day serve as evidence of blackmail in court, he would have to ensure a strong case was built around it. Replacing everything as he had found it, and making sure to lock both the desk drawers and study door, George made his way back downstairs. He took his pocketbook from his coat pocket and displayed it to his host as he entered the dining room. He had only been gone twelve minutes.

'Ah! I am glad that you recovered your pocketbook, Mr Abernathy. Your brother has just been telling me about your so-called airship. I assume that's how you travelled here this evening?'

'Yes, that is correct.' George resumed his seat and decided it was time to take a more dominant role in the conversation. While he was talking they did not have to continue their routine with the glasses – a fleeting glance at Douglas had shown that it'd gone on for too long. George even dared to actually sip the Madeira in his glass towards the meal's conclusion. This was partially a test of will, and he was surprised that he received it with indifference – even revulsion – but knew that several more sips would see the return of those familiar sensations, and he would not be able to prevent himself then. He was relieved when the evening drew to a close.

As they rose, Douglas held the airship keys out to him. 'You're driving home.'

George took them wordlessly.

'Well, gentlemen, I must thank you for a most pleasant evening. I should be happy to receive you again whenever you are next in London,' their host smiled.

As they were shown out, George paused in the doorway. 'The man who accompanied your cousin on his last visit – his name wasn't Fowler by any chance, was it?'

Dr Quincy's eyebrows raised. 'Why, yes. I believe the officer's name was Fowler. Why do you ask?'

'The man is an acquaintance of mine, and I have heard him speak of a Major-General Quincy. I only made the connection this minute and simply wondered if it was indeed him.' George's usual indifferent manner added weight to the lie.

'Oh, quite the coincidence!' Even George could tell that the man's enthusiasm was forced. As they walked past him on their way out, he perceived the chemist's hand was trembling. Those two officers had him truly frightened.

The following afternoon, George found his brother at the dining table nursing a throbbing head over a cup of strong coffee.

'Here's a change. You completely sober and me having to suffer,' said Douglas.

'It will soon pass.' George sat down opposite him.

Douglas's head slumped forward onto the table. 'Why did you accept a drink when Dr Quincy offered?' He spoke in a muffled moan.

'I reasoned to refuse would appear impolite, especially after he had suffered the disappointment of two guests failing to attend. It could have made it harder to get him to talk.'

Douglas lifted his head sharply. 'Oh, so now you show an understanding of social etiquette? More likely you wanted to test yourself.' Just for a second, he thought George was smirking at him. George was dressed as if he'd just come back from a meeting. (He still wore the same black frock coat with white piping to meetings that he'd worn to Lord Leyton's ball. Douglas wondered if he was fond of it or if he simply wanted to avoid paying a tailor to make him another coat.) The smell of coffee and tobacco clung to him. Douglas tried to recall if they'd had any appointments that morning, but it caused his head to hurt too much.

George was studying him intensely. 'If you are feeling that ill, you could try one of Molly's remedies? I can testify to their effectiveness—'

'No. I'll be fine. Anyway, we learnt what we needed to from Dr Quincy.'

George had told him what he'd found in Dr Quincy's study on the way home. He was surprised that Douglas remembered it.

'So his cousin was blackmailing him to recreate the formula for the anaesthetic he's been working on, or he wouldn't wed his sister. Dr Quincy couldn't afford to refuse as it would destroy her future security.'

George began pouring himself coffee (his coffee consumption had increased slightly since he'd stopped drinking spirits, but it was the one vice he was allowed). 'Do you recall General Brassington saying that only two other generals knew about the automaton soldier?'

'I think so.'

'What are the chances that they are General Quincy and General Fowler? Dr Quincy knew we had built something for the army, for one thing. It's likely one of the men mentioned Brassington's idea to him in passing without giving away too much detail.'

'Oh God! How did I not pick up on that? That was no insignificant remark, considering that the soldier is supposed to be a secret.'

'Most likely you were too busy watching my movements – I didn't mention it on the journey home as I deemed you too intoxicated to accurately recall what you'd heard Dr Quincy say. Then again, now that the android is in India, news of its existence will find its way back to England somehow. Letters to relations back home and so forth. I'm surprised that it hasn't been detected by the papers yet.'

'Yes, I'm not sure how General Brassington thought he was going to conceal him for that long.'

Their soldier hadn't appeared in any of the publications they'd read. The benevolent British public were too busy baying for Indian blood; or at least, that was the impression Douglas received from the newspapers and snippets of conversation overheard during business trips to London.

'I investigated Brigadier-General Fowler's background. His family owns an estate in Buckinghamshire. They made their fortune trading with Africa and India, but Fowler has recently invested in several ventures, none of which have proven terribly successful, including an engineering works,' George continued.

'Ideal if you want to build something covertly. What are the chances that there are any plans or notes relating to this weapon somewhere on the estate?'

'Very slight. I doubt the man would be that foolish. It might be worth visiting the estate nevertheless. Do you recalling showing me a newspaper story about a field full of dead crows?'

'Vaguely. It must have been weeks ago.'

'The story was reported from Spurwick, the same town where the Fowlers' estate is.'

'That's an intriguing coincidence. How did you find all this out about Fowler so quickly?'

'I deduced that Fowler's residence on Pall Mall was a residential club for army officers, since most of the buildings on that street are clubhouses. I copied General Brassington's hand from a letter he sent to us during the android's construction to forge a letter of recommendation. It was sufficient for me to be admitted when I arrived at the club this morning.'

'Do you mean to say you flew Spuggy back to London after we'd only been there not twelve hours since?'

'Yes. The journey is only a couple of hours long. Not to mention it was preferable to wasting time and money trying to find a hotel in London at such a late hour last night. I also needed General Brassington's letter to copy from.'

'True, but you know the engines could have run dry mid-flight? I've been meaning to replenish their fuel supply.'

'There was sufficient fuel for the journey – I was certain of it. As I was saying, some of the club members knew Fowler, and it didn't take much time to gather sufficient information about him before anyone grew too suspicious of who I was.'

'With your memory and powers of perception, you'd be the finest criminal in England if you chose to be,' Douglas smiled. 'But you know there will be a great deal of confusion when General Brassington learns about that letter.'

'I'll address that later. We'll leave for the train station tomorrow morning. We should reach Spurwick by late afternoon.'

Douglas took a swallow of coffee. 'There might not be much to discover, considering how long ago that incident with the crows was.' Neither did the idea of a long train journey sound appealing to him at that moment.

'I'm aware, but is it not logical to rule out every possibility?'

'I suppose so… Fine.' Douglas gave him another tired smile. 'As long as we can leave after breakfast. Molly should be fine on her own for one night.

She'll have the servants for company.'

'I shall see to the necessary travel arrangements. All you're required to do is pack your things before we depart.' George considered his brother's slouched position. 'Go and lie down, or I'll repay you for your treatment of me when I was incapacitated by that fever.'

Chapter Eighteen

When Mr Arthur visited the following day, an impatient Molly whisked him into the woodland to inspect the half-finished greenhouses before he could even say 'good morning'. The weather was far milder now it was early September, but everything would be in bloom for several weeks yet. The flowers carpeting parts of the woodland floor consisted of native species and Molly's creations, both thriving and without one usurping the other. Different scents mingled in the air: delicate, sweet, musky, creamy, acidic. Surprisingly, they all mixed well together. The bees flitting between the flowers weren't fussy anyway. The greenhouses' timber and cast-iron frames had been completed; now they were waiting for the glass to arrive. Mr Arthur had neglected to make the necessary arrangements for this, and was promptly scolded by his client.

'And I still don't understand why you insisted on such elaborate pieces of metalwork.' Molly pointed at the iron spandrel brackets far above her head. Inside the iron curls were flowers and gears. 'What use is that?'

'There's no reason why a thing can't be useful *and* aesthetically pleasing. Besides, I added plenty of practical features to the greenhouses – like ventilation and the tank that catches rainwater to feed the boiler,' said Mr Arthur.

'That was my idea.'

'And I was the one who gave a thought to underfloor heating in the first place. I do have some good ideas, Miss Molly.' He followed her as she wove in and out of the empty frames. There were six greenhouses in total.

'True, but the rest of your ideas are sheer nonsense.'

'I'll accept having some of my ideas deemed to be good. That is practically a compliment, coming from you.' He smiled as he readjusted his hat.

She preferred how he was that day they were chopping up trees together, without his usual suave, cocksure manner, which suited him as well as that stupid olive hat did. 'Well, you still cling to your formal training,' she said.

'That's not true. I have begun to see things rather differently now.'

Molly spun around to face him and rested one hand against a greenhouse's frame. 'In what way?'

'Well, I always viewed a garden as I would a painting.' He formed a frame with his fingers and, from his view of the lake, made a picturesque little scene inside them. 'The two are both compositions – you must think about line, space and colour. Actually, in that regard I broke away from my contemporaries, who are all for marble and greenery. Other designers cram as many foreign specimens into a garden as they can manage, with no regard to the overall picture. Each group in turn moulded me to their way of doing things when I was at Edinburgh. But you've made me consider how to work with what is already there and to be more sympathetic to the plant life.'

Molly's anger abated surprisingly quickly as she listened to this speech. 'You don't have to flatter my vanity,' she said, leaning her back against the frame and gazing at the lake. Diamonds danced on the water.

'I'm not. I mean what I say.'

Molly smiled softly. 'I like how passionate you get when you're caught up in something, as you were just now. Your eyes brighten, and you talk a lot faster.'

'Do I?'

'Indeed.'

'Like how you pick at your nails when something bothers you?'

Her smile faltered, and her cheeks tinged pink ever so slightly. 'And what else have you noticed about me?'

'Nothing that comes to mind immediately. I simply couldn't help noticing that one particular habit of yours, that's all.' He shrank with embarrassment, fearing he'd said something thoughtless.

He might act like a confident businessman, but it's a façade. Sometimes he has absolutely no tact about him, thought Molly.

They left the greenhouses and wandered along the lake's edge, walking alongside one another. Little did Mr Arthur know that Molly was deliberately leading him back towards the woodland.

'When are you going to let me do something more substantial than designing greenhouses and such?' Mr Arthur asked this question coolly enough, but Molly sensed his impatience seething beneath.

'Am I not giving you free rein over the orchard's design?'

'Well, yes. I suppose there's that.'

'Don't complain then. If you make a decent job of the orchard, then I might give you something more substantial to do.'

'You *might* give me something? That's an empty promise.'

'So is "Oh, the greenhouses might be completed by the end of August".'

'I didn't commit myself wholly because I was unsure.'

'Precisely – an empty promise. Are we not over a week into September?'

'You are incredibly difficult to please, Miss Molly.'

'And you are incredibly difficult to pin in one place, Mr Arthur.'

They walked in silence for a few seconds, but neither could act cross for long, and they both burst out laughing like children. Molly wondered if he secretly enjoyed teasing her. She rather liked the playful tit for tat they sometimes had. But when she was truly angry with him, she let him know. They'd entered the woodland and meandered their way through the trees, often straying from the paths. Most of the birds didn't pay them any mind, although some flew away as they approached. Molly wondered why the Hall was named 'Ravenfeld' when she had never seen any ravens. There were plenty of rooks and crows strutting across the meadow, cawing at passers-by in defiance. Perhaps the Hall's original occupants had mistaken them for ravens.

Molly stopped before the apple tree she'd climbed that day the trees had been cut down. A number of green apples were half-rotten on the ground but there were still plenty on the boughs.

'I've thought of a method to help you overcome your fear of heights,' she said.

'How so?'

For answer, she held up a leather harness that had been concealed behind the tree trunk – or, at least, Mr Arthur thought that was what it was. It was attached to a length of steel rope, which stretched into the treetop.

'This will ensure that you won't fall. That rope is more than able to hold your weight. It supports my brother fine, and he's probably slightly heavier than you.'

Everything inside Arthur recoiled from the idea, yet he was hesitant to refuse her.

'At least try it on and see how it feels. You use this strap to tighten it, like a belt.'

He took the harness from her and slowly stepped into it, fumbling with the belt buckle. His hands were already shaking.

'You twist that to go up, that to go down. You can adjust the speed with this clasp here, which creates some resistance. If you don't want to be carried up or down, you can climb.'

She easily climbed the first four branches and waited for him. 'Just try going up to this height.'

Arthur swallowed. His heart was beating so hard that it was painful, and he was in a cold sweat.

'Look at me,' she said firmly. Those bright, emerald eyes easily captured his full attention. She had a look, a way, about her that was utterly compelling. But there was also a gentle warmth in her eyes when she was not angry with him. If her temper were sweeter and her character more docile, many gentlemen would find a charming little lover in her. But such girls did not suit all men. It would be a shame to see that fire in her extinguished. 'Just keep looking at me,' she said.

He drifted to the trunk and placed a hand on its bumpy surface. He began to climb shakily, and was certain that he'd lose his footing at any moment. His head spun.

'You'll only fall if you think you're going to fall.' Miss Molly said the words with such firmness that he couldn't help but believe her. His fear of looking like a fool in front of her was gradually surpassing that primitive, obscure fear of heights. When he was on the branch below her, she reached out her hand and helped to pull him up to where she was.

'Are you all right?' she asked.

'I suppose so.' His limbs were shaking.

Miss Molly had her hand on his shoulder. 'That wasn't bad at all,' she grinned. 'Ready to go higher?'

'Perhaps not now. This has been a significant enough step—'

Arthur felt himself being catapulted into the air, stopping just short of a branch above his head that the other end of the rope was wrapped around. Without meaning to, he looked down. He was suspended thirty feet above the ground. White-hot fear filled him and he gripped the rope for all he was worth. He was falling; even though he knew he hadn't physically moved, his mind told him that he was plummeting to the ground. His stomach fell away from him and he prayed over and over again that all of these feelings would just go away. *'Please stop, please stop'* pulsed through his head (and at the back of his mind a voice whispered, 'Don't let me faint in front of her').

'Arthur.'

He spun his head around to see Miss Molly sitting on the branch above him. For one awful second he thought she was about to unfasten the rope. 'If I hadn't done that, you'd never have gone higher. Here, I'll pull you up.'

'That was still a rotten trick,' he said crossly, slowly releasing one hand from the rope, which he was still desperately clinging to.

'You'll thank me eventually.' She beamed down at him. Strong sunlight slipped between the leaves behind her, like a halo around her wild mane of hair. What a peculiar girl she was. But she had given him the courage to face his fear. He was ashamed that she would be able to feel him trembling as she helped him onto the branch beside her. His ears rang and his head swam. She had her arm anchored around his elbow. When his heart was calmer, he dared to lift his eyes from his hands to her face.

'Look here.' She turned her head away from him towards the nest perched in a forked branch on her left. Inside it were three tufty little chicks, squeaking and crying out for food.

Molly smiled at them. 'When I saw them last, they looked as if they had only just hatched. Now they look like they'll be ready to fly soon.'

'They certainly do.' He leant closer for a better view, feeling strands of her hair tickling the side of his face. He warmed at being so close to her. It felt improper. *She* certainly didn't care for decorum a great deal. That said, there was no pretence about her. He admired that. Sometimes he forgot that Miss

Molly was mistress of Ravenfeld Hall. She was so unlike the refined young lady that he'd first imagined before he actually met her. 'Will the parents not return if they see us here? Or attack us?' he asked.

'They won't return for some time, but it might be better if we didn't linger too long.'

Arthur expected her to move immediately but she didn't stir, apparently too engrossed by the chicks. Her arm was still entwined around his. He'd (almost) forgotten to worry about losing his balance and had slackened his grip on the branch with his free hand. He'd stopped shaking, although his thudding heart refused to be at ease. He could only guess why.

'Are you pleased that you've made some progress towards conquering your fear?' she suddenly asked.

'It's not something you can ever really conquer, Miss Molly. That said, I never thought I'd be able to do this.'

'Well, that counts for something then. You should be proud of yourself, Mr Arthur. How do you wish to make your way back down?'

'Slowly.'

She grinned at him, her eyes flashing.

Arthur's hand instantly flew to the controls on the harness.

Molly held up her hands. 'I promise I won't do it again. We'll make our way down together.'

She kept her word, although she had to slow her pace for him.

Chapter Nineteen

The vicar of Spurwick went home to his wife on Friday evening and reported having met two young men in the road. From the way that they were dressed, he assumed they were farmworkers. One was a pleasant, red-haired young man while the other was rather surly-looking with raven-black hair. It was the red-haired brother – for he believed that they were brothers; they had a similar look about them, anyway – who addressed him. He enquired about the location of Spurwick Abbey, saying they had come to help with the harvest at the nearby farm. The clergyman directed them as best he could and the young man (did he say his name was William?) thanked him sincerely.

Meanwhile, the girl who worked in the kitchen at the local inn was boiling mutton and listening to a conversation between the landlord and his wife about their latest guests.

'There's two gentlemen. They say they're on their way to London on business,' said the landlord, his pipe clicking between his teeth.

From behind the bar, his wife squeakily wiped a glass with a grey rag. 'What sort of business?'

'Didn't say. Just…business.' He waved his arm emphatically, being unfamiliar with the world of industrialists and learned men.

'What was their name?'

'Denman. That's what the red-haired gentleman wrote in the book, anyway. You know what I think? I think they're police – detectives.'

'Heavens above! What would two detectives be doing here? The most trouble we've had round here is with those poachers who keep stealing the abbey's chickens.'

'But listen to this.' Her husband took his pipe from his mouth and aimed it at his wife. He loved to invent grand stories. 'I was talking to John earlier, and he'd seen them all about the town. Talking to people. Asking questions.'

'Questions about what?'

'About the town and the abbey.'

'That doesn't mean they're detectives.' She thumped a glass on the bar. 'Perhaps they're looking to buy land in the area.'

'I bet it's to do with all those dead crows last winter.'

'How on earth could it be? Why would the police be interested in that?'

'Well…it was strange, wasn't it?' Her husband's reasoning was starting to unravel. But the girl in the kitchen was thrilled by the idea that there were two detectives under their roof, for she'd taken a fancy to the tall man with auburn hair, and this revelation only fanned the flames of her girlish admiration.

None of them heard the thud from outside later that night as the two young men in question exited the inn by the means of a window. The moon lit their way as they crossed the open fields towards the abbey. Ankle-high stalks bristled around their feet. The harvest had been and gone already.

'I still feel guilty for writing an assumed name in the guestbook, although it is rather exciting,' said Douglas, swinging an unlit lantern in one hand.

'Hardly,' returned his brother as he twisted the two halves of his ebony cane together, which he'd concealed inside his coat until then. 'William is your other name, after all, so it's not entirely an assumed name. And you borrowed from my other name to make Denman.'

'It's still strange passing father's name as my own, though. At least Denman was less suspicious than using Dennington. Someone familiar with nobility might have made the connection and realised who we are.'

It was no surprise that their mother had bestowed both the name that every eldest son in her line was given *and* her maiden name on her firstborn. Perhaps it had been prophetic, ensuring that George became his uncle's heir. He certainly took after their mother's side of the family in terms of looks.

'I don't care for my other name,' said George brusquely.

'You know, it's a good thing that you didn't accept the dukedom after all, since, in accordance with our uncle's wishes, you would have had to change your surname to Dennington. Then you'd be George Dennington Dennington.'

'Lower your voice. Someone might hear us.' When George whipped his head around to snap at his brother, he could see something covering Douglas's right hand. George stopped in the middle of the field. 'Why did you bring that ridiculous toy with you?'

'I thought it might be useful if we find ourselves in a scrape.'

George sighed. 'As long as you only use it to fire projectiles and not to attract anything magnetic. Is that your only means of defence?'

'Yes.'

'You fool.'

'You have no right to criticise me for being unprepared for a fight. You brought a stick.'

George sharply caught Douglas under the chin with the cane's topper. The metal disc was ice-cold against Douglas's skin.

'You have no idea of half of what this cane can do, although I doubt I'll need to resort to any of the devices concealed inside it.' George walked on, his brother trailing after him.

Douglas stifled a yawn. After an early start, a long train journey and a good dinner of boiled mutton and potatoes, he would have happily been asleep on the hard bed the inn had provided him, instead of stalking through a field. But there was work to be done. The two of them had changed back into the farmworker disguises they'd worn to interview the gamekeeper and farmers, thinking they'd be less suspicious of two lowly farmworkers than of two frock-coated gentlemen. Molly had procured the clothes from the rag and bone man in Holtbury. It was strange seeing George in a rough brown coat and trousers, with a cloth cap and scarlet neckerchief. Douglas had only ever known his brother to wear black, grey, white, dark blue and, occasionally, dark red. Until the age of fourteen, he'd often had to make do with George's hand-me-downs. Then he'd experienced the triumph of growing taller than his older brother. ('And you haven't stopped gloating about it for nearly ten years,' George said whenever Douglas reminded him of the fact now.)

Ahead of them was the Fowlers' estate, sleeping in shadow. It might be called Spurwick Abbey, but if there ever was an abbey on the site, it must have been torn down centuries ago. A Palladian mansion squatted on the ground in its place. They'd seen it in the daylight; the ivory and grey façade, adorned with glistening marble columns and a portico, looked splendid in the sun. Two long wings stretched out on either side of the main building. Spurwick Abbey was a white dove compared to Ravenfeld Hall. The grounds were enclosed by a brick wall and tall gate at the front, with hedgerows and fences around the sides. But George and Douglas's objective was the field on the periphery of the grounds. It was barren, containing only black soil. Either it had been dug over after its crop was harvested or the soil was too poor to grow anything. A section of the fence had recently been repaired but not terribly well, and it collapsed at a single tap from George's cane.

They trod across the field. Douglas lit the lantern but it showed only uncombed soil. He kicked a stone with his shoe. 'Well, I'm not sure what you were hoping to find, but unless we can dig the entire field in a night, I doubt this trip will have been of much use. And the locals were able to tell us nothing.'

'We can still get a soil sample for Molly to analyse.'

'I suppose.' Douglas pulled a small glass jar out of his coat pocket. Kneeling down, he scooped some of the soil into the jar and twisted the lid over the top. Now the lantern was closer to the ground, he realised that what he had thought were sticks were actually small bones. Bird bones, most likely.

George had wandered to the centre of the field. Unsure what to do, Douglas fiddled about with his gauntlet, still smarting slightly from George's dismissal of his invention. He'd show him that it wasn't as unwieldy as he thought it was. Sliding the knob connected to the coil inside the gauntlet, he decreased the voltage until the electromagnetic field was weak enough not to send every magnetic object within a radius of several yards flying towards the gauntlet. He let his hand hover over the ground as he walked, wondering if he could find anything metal buried below the soil. This was more for his own amusement than anything else. He felt a tug on the gauntlet. Douglas glanced at a patch of soil behind him, then waved his hand over it. Something was pulling at the gauntlet – something buried from view.

'George! Come here!' Douglas called, regretting having done so instantly. His shouting could have alerted anyone who was nearby. However, none of the windows from the abbey lit suddenly.

George had been prowling along the edge of the field but looked up on hearing his brother's command. He made his way towards him, walking with quick, purposeful strides.

'I think I've found something,' Douglas informed him. 'Something metal.'

George's gaze travelled from Douglas to the patch of ground Douglas was pointing to. He'd dragged his finger through the soil to make a cross over the spot.

George knelt on the ground beside the cross. 'Turn that gauntlet of yours off.'

Douglas did as ordered, once again annoyed at George's refusal to acknowledge that he'd done something useful. George dug through the soil while Douglas held the lantern over him. A smooth piece of metal emerged from the earth. George brushed away more soil; the object that he lifted out of the ground was a broken glass canister, oblong in shape with a brass and iron frame.

'What is it? Some sort of lamp?' Douglas asked as George offered it to the lantern's light.

'No. If I were to guess, I'd say these are the remains of the weapon. This is the shell that contained the anaesthetic. Look here.' George rotated the canister to show him what was on one side: a golden pocket watch with the front of its case removed. It was attached to a long lever and a spring.

'A timer.'

'Precisely.'

'So it can be detonated remotely. Fowler must have clever engineers. This is quite a complicated mechanism. As soon as the watch struck three, the hour hand would come into contact with a hair trigger to release this long copper lever. The lever then releases the tightly wound spring with a nail attached to the end of it. The nail would shatter a hole in the glass to release the anaesthetic gas.' Douglas indicated the nail in question.

'The mechanism is simple, really. It appears they had good taste in timepieces.'

'What do you mean?'

For answer, George turned the canister until the back of the watch was visible through the glass, so his brother could see the maker's mark. The glass warped the initials slightly, but Douglas could discern them easily enough: *AB.s.* The watch had been made two years ago.

'One of ours?' Douglas blinked in surprise.

'One of mine, more specifically.'

'Do you know who bought this?'

'No. You were usually the one behind the shop counter, so the selling of the watches mostly fell to you.'

'Yes, because your manner of dealing with customers is very lacking. I still have to take charge at meetings with clients now, although maybe I won't as much in future after seeing the way you handled Dr Quincy during dinner. You're certain this watch wasn't a special commission?'

'I'm certain. It's rather simple and plain.'

'There could be a receipt or ticket for it in our old paperwork. I'm glad we decided to retain everything.'

'That might not tell us a great deal. It could have been purchased as a gift, after all. Nevertheless, we'll consult our paperwork when we return.'

Douglas was about to speak when a gunshot ripped through the night air. It sounded like it had been fired from a hunting rifle.

'I know you're there!' shouted the gruff old gamekeeper they'd interviewed earlier. 'Filthy poachers!'

'*Run.*'

The gunshot still reverberated in Douglas's ears, but he heard George's command clearly enough. The two of them sprinted across the field as fast as they could.

'Not bragging about your cane now, are you?' Douglas panted, with one hand clamped on his cloth cap.

'He's seen us. We can't face him head on.'

Another explosive pop filled the air. Douglas heard dogs barking.

The two of them ran in the direction of the hedgerows at the far side of the field, George leading. Gripping his cane's topper, he broke the cane apart. Douglas saw that the top half had transformed into a sword with a long, thin blade. George severed part of the hedgerow with two strikes, creating an exit. They'd cleared the field and the gamekeeper's line of fire. They reached the main road through a gate in the next field, and didn't stop running until they were certain that they weren't being followed by the dogs.

When Douglas regained his breath, the first thing he said was, 'How did you conceal a damn sword inside your cane? There's no way that blade could fit inside the top half.'

George showed him the steel blade. There were three seams across it. 'The blade retracts,' he explained, hardly sounding out of breath at all. He collapsed the sword with a swift movement of his wrist. Douglas watched each part of the blade slide seamlessly into the next from the tip downwards, until it had disappeared inside the ebony cane.

'We had better hurry back to the inn. I'll certainly sleep well after this.'

George put the cane together again. 'Don't forget we're departing first thing in the morning.'

'You needn't remind me. I suppose we can sleep on the train,' Douglas sighed as the two of them ambled down the road.

The next morning, the landlord was listening to a tale from one of the inn's regulars about the poachers' latest appearance, just as the two 'detectives' were leaving. When George and Douglas returned home that afternoon, they immediately rummaged through the battered trunk that contained paperwork from the old shop. Different kinds of documents were methodically bundled together with odd strips of plain cotton. Flicking back two years, they did find a ticket that matched the watch. It had been sold to a Mr Beechcroft for four guineas. This told them nothing important. The name was of no significance, as far as they knew. A military title, rather than a plain 'Mr', might have been promising. George, after deliberating at length, voiced a thought that refused to be silenced. He'd seen a similar watch before, although he had not paid much attention to it at the time, nor had he seen its hallmark. It had belonged to Professor Gottfried, the enigmatic chemistry professor who had been part of the plot to steal Maestro. The professor had not been seen or heard of since, although a curious report in a science journal claimed he hadn't left

Prussia since last winter. He'd told George that his watch had been a gift and that it had come from the brothers' clockmaker's shop. Douglas agreed that this was not a productive line of enquiry, especially if George couldn't be certain it was the same watch. More than likely, the fact that the watch used in the bomb was one of theirs was probably a coincidence. Any watch of high craftsmanship would have been sufficient for the purpose. What was important, however, was that they had an insight into how the device, and presumably the one General Quincy possessed, worked. And how it could be stopped.

'All you'd need to do would be to stop the hour hand making contact with the trigger,' said Douglas. The dissected remains of the bomb were on their workshop table. Each piece of clockwork had been removed and cleaned to dislodge any remaining soil.

'Straightforward enough,' remarked George from across the table. 'Assuming our soldier can reach the device before the timer activates the mechanism.'

There came a knock at the door. Molly entered without waiting to be asked inside. 'I've had a look at the soil sample. Thanks to my chemistry reading, identifying the chemicals within it was relatively easy – *your bird is on fire.*' She pointed at the metallic bird standing on a perch near the window. It was about three feet high, with red copper feathers and a gold beak. Red, phosphorous flames with a pinkish hue enveloped the bird. Seconds later, it disintegrated before their eyes into a heap of metal. Molly looked questioningly at her brothers. Neither seemed terribly concerned that one of their creations had just been reduced to a pile of clockwork and metal feathers as they calmly regarded the bird's remains.

'Just watch, Mol,' said Douglas.

The clockwork started to quiver. Gears rose into the air and fitted themselves together. The bird's feet reappeared, followed by its body and wings; everything down to the last scale-like feather fitted back into place. The clockwork inside it locked together. Its head reformed last, and the bird let out a squawk when it was whole again.

Molly walked around the table to get closer to the bird. She watched it open and close its jet eyes. Now she was close enough to see the tiny rubies that were studded on its feathers; the covering of feathers was thin enough for her to glimpse the clockwork beneath its frame when it ruffled them.

'How did you make it do that?' she asked.

'Very strong magnets and a lot of clever trickery.' Douglas winked. 'The phoenix was a request from a friend of Lord Leyton's. He saw the purple peacock we made for the earl's birthday ball and wanted something that could rival it.'

'Won't Lord Leyton be annoyed when he finds out about it?'

'There's every chance – in which case he'll ask us to make him something even more magnificent that'll eclipse the phoenix.'

'But I thought you weren't going to accept any more unchallenging commissions from the nobility for jewelled animals?'

'Regrettably, such commissions are still sometimes necessary,' said George, 'since it costs a considerable amount of money to run this house, including paying domestics' wages.' He shot a meaningful glance at his brother.

'Besides, this commission for the phoenix presented a bit of a challenge,' added Douglas.

Molly hovered her hand over the bird, and when neither of her brothers cautioned her not to touch it, she stroked its hot head.

'How did you produce those flames?'

'Lithium salts,' answered George. 'It's easy enough to do.'

'The phoenix is on a timer so that it'll combust every hour. In fact, the trigger that ignites the flammable liquid and releases the lithium salts inside the bird is similar to what was used in this device.' Douglas indicated the remains of the bomb. 'Anyway, you were saying what chemicals you'd identified in the soil sample, Mol?'

'Oh, yes. From my analysis of the sample, I'd say the thing that killed those crows was the anaesthetic that Dr Quincy was working on. Once the liquid inside the canister vaporises, inhaling only a small amount would prove fatal. If you were a soldier on a battlefield, you wouldn't stand much of a chance against it.' She shook her head sadly.

'Presumably the canister that is in India will be larger, or there will be several such devices. We know ten gallons of the mixture were requested and I estimate the canister we found held one gallon at most,' said George.

Molly shrugged. 'I'd say so.'

'Did you find out anything else?' Douglas asked.

'Not really – then again, chemistry isn't my speciality. I'll let you know if I discover anything useful.' Then she flashed George an impish smile. 'I've given the cook her instructions for tonight.'

'I don't expect you to go to any great trouble,' her eldest brother replied.

'I know – don't think I've ordered a banquet. I know you only eat out of necessity. You can moan as much as you like, but everything has already been settled.' She flew to the door and slipped out of the workshop before he had the chance to moan at her.

George ran a hand through his hair and sighed. 'We must inform the soldier of what we've discovered.'

'Well, I hope you have a means of contacting him,' said Douglas drily. 'Unless he reaches us first.'

George rose to his feet. 'There's nothing to be done other than keep the communication line open at all times. I'll make sure the transmitter downstairs is working. You can start revising the plans for Mr Richard Owen's order.'

'I hope Mr Owen appreciates that the plans for those megalosaurus and pterodactyl automata required a lot of research and some guesswork, since we're not palaeontologists. He might disagree with us on the look and movement of the creatures, but I'm sure we're right. I don't know what he's rushing us for – it'll probably be years before his new Museum of Natural History is even built.'

'Most likely. I'll join you shortly.'

'You know, you are allowed to have an evening to yourself on your birthday, especially after what we've been through these last couple of days.'

George frowned. 'You know I attach no importance to birthdays.'

'I'm aware. But Molly and I will uphold our usual tradition of giving you a day of peace and having whatever you like best for dinner.'

'Make sure that is all you do.'

'Well, we have more motivation to celebrate your birthday than usual, since you might not have seen your twenty-sixth year had I not rescued you that stormy night.'

'As grateful as I am to you, don't expect any exceptional treatment when it's your birthday in December,' said George dryly.

'I wouldn't dream of it,' his brother called after him as he walked out of the room.

Chapter Twenty

'Jt's the Pandies!' Petey cried as a storm of bullets and shells rained down from the Mori Bastion. They pounded into the battery but did not penetrate it.

'Copperton! Watch out!' exclaimed Singh as an enemy shell burst within several yards of them, sending soil and shrapnel in every direction. Smoke screened the enemy.

Copperton knew he had to hurry and conclude the transmission. 'His name is Quincy! Report back to us when you can—'

A bullet struck the wireless receiver and sent it tumbling off the wall.

'Damn!' Knowing there was nothing to be done about it for the present, Copperton turned his attention to the situation at hand. 'I'll see to them.'

Copperton launched himself over the battery wall and sprinted towards the bastion with his sword drawn. He danced nimbly between the bullets and shells streaming towards him. He was fairly confident that he could withstand such an intense bombardment from heavy guns, although now was not the time to test this idea. All he needed to do was draw the rebels' attention away from the battery until the guns could be made ready. But, to his great astonishment, the battery's guns thundered in a glorious chorus behind him. Copperton beheld pieces of the stone walls surrounding Delhi fall into the ditch below. At last! The enemy guns fell into a stunned silence, short-lived as it was. The guns from both sides seemed to join in a duet. Copperton was now within range of the ramparts on the walls and the advanced trenches, where he was greeted with musket fire. He took aim with his hand and shot at one of his attackers, who vanished behind the rampart before the bullet was even fired at him. The rest of the gunmen fled like startled deer.

'I thought as much. Cowards.' Copperton raced back to the battery, but was now caught between two opposing lines of fire. Fountains of earth shot up around him. He hurdled over the battery wall and landed on the ground with catlike dignity.

'That was a foolhardy thing to do, Copperton!' Powell shouted above the racket of the guns.

'Where did you get a gun from? I saw you fire a shot,' remarked Petey when there was a lull in the battery guns' firing.

'Observe.' Copperton made the shape of a pistol with his hand. He took aim at a fallen sandbag on the ground, and a bullet pierced a hole in it. Smoke curled from Copperton's index finger.

'Your hand *was* the gun?' Singh exclaimed.

'Correct.'

'So why have you been using actual guns all this time?' asked Petey.

'I was always being given them and ordered to use them, so I complied. I can only hold about six bullets at a time in my hand anyway. It gives me the advantage of surprise when a foe believes me to be unarmed.'

Petey chortled.

'Shame about your machine.' Powell knelt beside the receiver and picked it up. The trumpets were badly dented and there was a hole in one side of the casing where the bullet had struck it. Copperton could hear it rattling around inside the device. Miraculously, the antenna was intact. 'Even if your makers do respond, they have no way of reaching us.'

'Give that to me, Powell.'

Powell handed Copperton the receiver, and he unscrewed the damaged casing. Petey and Singh tried to peer inside as the crumpled bullet dropped to the ground. Inside the casing was a tangled mess of metal wires. More wire was tightly coiled around a bobbin, which appeared to still be attached to the wooden base, but the needle that normally skimmed along the top of the coil had snapped off. The lead crystal had also been dislodged from its metal and wood holder and was nowhere to be seen. The whiskery wire that usually communicated with the crystal was still suspended from a metal arm on a pivot.

'I dare say we could repair it with some improvisation,' declared Copperton. 'But for the present moment, we had better conceal it before we attract attention.'

Copperton had some difficulty fitting the battered trumpets back inside the case, adding several more dents to the speaking trumpet in the process. He concealed the receiver inside his chest once more. 'And the three of you deserve a rest. You should be off duty soon.'

'Perhaps we ought to put you in charge,' Petey grinned. 'You'd be a fairer officer than a lot of the ones we currently have. Half of them aren't worth their salt.'

'Guard your words, Petey. You never know who might be listening,' cautioned Powell.

'Do you disagree? You're always criticising the officers.'

'But I know when to conceal my opinions.'

'We shall reconvene in Petey's tent at the earliest opportunity,' said Copperton. 'I will consider how to best go about repairing the receiver. My masters gave me detailed instructions in the event that it should need repairing, although I don't think their instructions include what to do in the event of a bullet being fired at it.'

'We shall do as ordered, sir,' said Petey with a chuckle, as another shell came close to the battery.

As it turned out, there was not a convenient time for the four of them to reconvene for some days. The first battery had been completed on the Tuesday morning, and it wasn't until Friday evening that all four of the batteries were finished. The work during those three days and nights had been relentless, making it practically impossible for them to find any time to meet. The following morning, all four batteries fired in unison at the bastions and stone walls. The noise of gunfire was unceasing. Copperton had decided that he and the other three were to meet in Petey's tent around midday. The firing from the direction of the batteries could still be heard. He had spent the morning studying sheets of paper that had been hidden inside his chest panel along with the wireless receiver, folded into four so they would fit inside the compartment. These were instructions and drawings in Master Douglas's hand (with annotations from Master George) on how to connect this with that. In truth, Copperton had not been as confident that the receiver could be repaired as he had sounded. The mess of wires had been untangled and each wire placed in the correct position. Copperton had done his best to iron out the dents in the trumpets, but inside the receiver there were some parts in need of replacing.

'It should be straightforward enough to make do with things that are at hand,' Copperton declared.

'What will we require?' asked Singh.

'A pencil and a brooch pin.'

Singh felt at his pockets and produced a pencil stub. 'Will this do? It's not much.'

'It will suffice – only a small amount of lead will be necessary. I dare say I could even have used the bullet that struck the device, had the thought occurred to me. We cannot afford to waste any of our own bullets, however.' Copperton split open the wooden pencil to reveal the slither of lead inside. Snapping it in two, he placed the smaller of the pieces in the vacant holder.

'Well, that was remarkably straightforward. I expected there to be some tools involved,' said Petey before lodging his pipe between his teeth. He was struggling to light a match.

'This is only a temporary fix. As long as the receiver is not moved, it should work fine.' Copperton twisted his neck around. 'I will compensate you with a fresh pencil, Jatin.'

'It is fine, Copperton.'

Copperton gave Petey a meaningful stare. 'I know you have one of the required items.'

Removing the unlit pipe with one hand, Petey's other hand slowly slid into his trouser pocket, but when he drew out his fist, he simply stared at the locket brooch.

'I only need the pin, not the actual brooch.'

Petey held the brooch out to Copperton. The loose hinges betrayed the locket's secret and displayed the portrait concealed within.

'Your sweetheart?' Powell asked.

'No, my mother,' answered Petey, with only a tinge of sarcasm in his voice. He took possession of the brooch again once Copperton had snapped the pin off. Petey was to be disappointed about the lack of tools once again, for all Copperton needed to do was pull out the metal bar suspended above the gleaming copper coil, bend the fastener around it to form a loop with the ends of the wire twisted together, and replace the bar. The tip of the twisted pin just brushed the copper wire.

Copperton made sure that everything was connected and gave a satisfied nod. 'Now all that remains is to test it.'

Singh craned over Copperton's shoulder. 'So what do these parts do?'

'I couldn't explain the science of it to you, Jatin. I simply know how to assemble the various parts and connect them together.'

'Might I have a look at those instructions?' asked Powell.

'If you think you can make any sense of them.' Copperton passed the folded papers to him.

'Where does it get power from?' asked Singh.

'From the device at the other end, although the transmitter requires immensely powerful batteries to send a signal across continents.' As he uttered these words, the receiver crackled into life.

'Hello!' Copperton shouted into the speaking trumpet. There was no answer. 'I don't understand. The connection has been established. They should be able to hear us.'

'Are you certain?'

'Of course I am, Powell. The masters were explicit in their instructions regarding how to operate the device.' Copperton slid the brooch pin along the coil to make sure it was in the right spot. It was like tuning an instrument.

'Try speaking again,' said Singh. 'They might not have heard you the first time.'

'Hello! Master George! Master Douglas! We are here! Can you hear us?'

'Perhaps no one is there,' said Petey when they received no response.

'But they must be, or how else could our device have its power?' Singh pointed out.

'Wait. I think I hear something,' said Copperton.

The voice was distorted by the crackling at first, but Copperton soon realised that it was Master Douglas.

'Soldier! Soldier! Is that you?' Master Douglas shouted.

'Indeed it is!'

'Thank God! We thought you might have run into trouble.'

'We did, but there should be no risk of that this time.'

'Listen, soldier, we think we know what General Quincy is planning. He's going to deploy a bomb that contains a very powerful anaesthetic – possibly a high enough concentration to prove fatal if inhaled.'

'The mist!' cried Singh. 'The mist you saw, Copperton! He must have been testing the anaesthetic.' His tongue stumbled a little on the last word.

Copperton nodded his assent, the same thought having occurred to him at probably the same moment it struck Singh.

'There could be as many as nine bombs if our information is correct, or possibly one or more larger bombs,' Master Douglas continued. 'And it's likely that General Quincy will wait for an appropriate opportunity to use them – a decisive strike.'

'I think I might know the precise moment he'll choose, Master. There is a plan for a siege on the city of Delhi in two days' time. Its chances of success are unclear, but if we are victorious, it will be a significant gain.'

'That sounds like a prime opportunity. That's not all we found out either. Quincy is not acting alone. There's another man involved too – a Brigadier-General Fowler.'

'General Fowler? We know nothing to suggest that he is part of this.' General Fowler, to Copperton's knowledge, had been in hospital for weeks after he was shot in the back. At one stage, when his wound became infected, it seemed unlikely that he would recover.

'We – or George, rather – found evidence of a correspondence between General Quincy and his cousin, the man who made the anaesthetic. It mentioned Brigadier-General Fowler. We also have proof that a similar weapon was tested successfully on Fowler's estate. The remains of the bomb are in our workshop.'

Copperton wondered if General Fowler was the one who'd sent the encrypted note to General Quincy. 'I will take your word for it, Master Douglas. How do we stop this weapon?'

'If the bombs the generals are planning on using are anything like the one George and I found, there will be a pocket watch on each one that controls when the gas will be released. Get to the bombs before Quincy and Fowler deploy them, and remove the watches. If that proves difficult, removing just the hour hand should be enough. Once the anaesthetic is mixed into the air, it'll be too late. We cannot help you to determine the bombs' location, I'm afraid. That's up to you.'

'I understand. Thank you, Master Douglas.'

'We'll get in touch again if we learn anything else. Good luck!'

The line was severed. The receiver's hum abruptly stopped as the power died, and Copperton disconnected the device's wires. Anaesthetic gas utilised in the form of a bomb? This was unlike any weapon that Copperton had encountered in his studies of military history. In terms of range and effectiveness, it was advantageous from a purely strategic perspective. Yet what a monstrous method of death – creeping over a man and suffocating him. There was something distasteful about it to Copperton's mind – like those stories of diseased birds being launched into enemy cities to start a plague. What was more disturbing, however, was Quincy and Fowler's willingness to resort to such a weapon. What did they hope to achieve by using it? This had clearly been developed before the mutiny erupted. Something else was going on here. Copperton could not entirely believe it of General Fowler, a man so upright and honourable. And if the best of the British officers was engaged in illicit chemical warfare, just as there were rumours suggesting General Nicholson was a vicious, bloodthirsty brute without mercy where Indians were concerned, then…perhaps he was wrong to follow their orders. Such a cataclysmic revelation actually caused pressure to build inside Copperton's boiler. Once it subsided, he turned around to face his three friends.

'So, Copperton,' said Powell. 'What do you propose we do now?'

'We must stop the generals from deploying this weapon. This could be an indiscriminate attack on civilians as well as the rebels. And who is to say that the European soldiers and loyal sepoys will not be casualties in the confusion of battle? We do not even know for certain where Quincy and Fowler's loyalties are.'

'You would really do such a thing?'

'You were not entirely wrong, Powell – not all of the generals can be blindly trusted. I see that now. It's true that I'm bound to follow direct orders, but I can question authority when it conflicts with what is morally right, and act on my own initiative. And that is precisely what I intend to do now. I will find where these bombs are to be deployed and, if the two generals are plotting something diabolical, bring them before General Wilson. Please take heed of what I am about to say, however – if you choose to stand by me, then you will be traitors to the army. I cannot force you to join me.'

No one spoke immediately. Petey lit his pipe.

Singh eventually stepped forward. 'We have come this far. We will stay with you until the end.'

'I suppose I can forget about my army pension.' Petey blew smoke through his mouth.

'And me,' added Powell wryly. 'It's not as if I'm abandoning a glittering military career, anyway. We'll follow your orders from here on out, Copperton.'

'No.' Petey smiled at him. '*Colonel* Copperton. I think you deserve a rank after all, and you can't be a private if you're going to lead us. It does have a nice ring to it, don't you agree, chaps?'

'I do – it's pleasingly alliterative,' Singh nodded.

'I'd have thought "Corporal" was the more natural choice, but have it your way,' Powell shrugged.

'If it pleases you, you can address me as such. Oh, I've just remembered – I found this inside Quincy's tent. Someone – one of the other officers, I mean – most likely dropped it while coming to see him. It probably means nothing.' The newly appointed Colonel Copperton placed the sowar figurine on his charpoy.

'He's a nicely carved little fellow.' Petey peered at the creamy ivory figurine. 'Better than my effigy of you, Cop.'

'Where did you say you found it?' asked Powell, his dark brows knitted together as he regarded the figurine.

'Just inside Quincy's tent. It looked like someone had dropped it outside and it rolled away until it got caught under the canvas. I can't entirely say why I picked it up. As I said, it's probably meaningless.'

'*Lucy Locket lost her pocket, Kitty Fisher found it,*' Petey sang under his breath.

Powell picked up the little sowar. 'He is a knight.'

186

'No, he's a sowar – a cavalryman,' said Singh puzzledly. 'Although a warrior all the same.'

'But he is also a knight – the sort that does battle on a chessboard. He's very similar to the ones in my father's chess set from when I was a child. He was probably made in Berhampur, which is known for its ivory carving.'

'But it's not the exact same knight, do you think, Powell?' asked Singh. 'I know you kept a piece from your father's set when he tried to sell it along with his other treasures.'

'I did, much to his annoyance when he discovered his buyer was to have an incomplete set. But there must be hundreds of John Company chess sets like the one this knight is from – they've been making them for decades. And my piece has a white base. Here.' He reached into his trouser pocket and pulled out an object. The knight on his palm was identical to Copperton's, save for its ivory white base.

'Curious,' remarked Copperton thoughtfully, as the two pieces were placed beside one another on top of Petey's trunk. 'Did you say there are hundreds like these?'

'Yes.' Powell's voice was tinged with annoyance at having to repeat himself. 'Why? What are you thinking, Copperton?'

'I'm not sure. A chess piece is an unusual thing to be carrying in one's pocket, isn't it? I have a peculiar impression that it has some greater significance.'

'Such as?' Petey prompted.

'Perhaps it is a token or a signal of some sort. Like the mysterious appearances of the chapattis, which were passed around sepoy barracks just before the mutiny broke out.'

'A message,' muttered Powell, 'to warn that something is coming.'

'Like this new bomb?' said Petey.

Copperton nodded. 'It could be something along those lines. The fact the figurine depicts a sowar might hold some meaning – a call to attack.'

'Or what if…?' Singh shook his head, but the others stared at him enquiringly until he was compelled to voice his thought. 'I thought that maybe we are making something more sinister than it really is. If Powell has a chess piece to remember his boyhood days by, then why cannot another soldier or officer have a piece, as a token of something or someone now lost to them?'

'I agree,' said Petey. 'Some careless chap will have let it drop out of his coat pocket. Might have believed it brought him good luck and kept it with him all the time. Copperton can keep it safe for him in the meantime, can't you?'

'I suppose I'll have to. I feel it would be wise to keep it to ourselves, since it would be difficult to explain how I came by it.'

But something about the little ivory figure troubled him greatly. He couldn't escape the impression that it was connected to this anaesthetic bomb business. The sowar's unseeing eyes refused to tell its secrets.

Chapter Twenty-One

With the installation of the greenhouses' glass complete, Molly's new laboratory became the focus of attention. The laying of the foundations was going well, until three days of persistent rainfall halted work. Parts of the woodland resembled a swamp, with some trees being half-submerged in water. Molly observed the downpour from her bedroom window. On a positive note, the rain gave her an excuse to spend the day in her current laboratory – which was at least a proper room rather than four bare, knee-high stone walls languishing in mud. Every spare moment she could spend in her lab before she had to depart for Oxford was treasured. Most of her preparatory reading was done, even though she had a month or so left before the start of the new term. She could reread some of the books closer to the time. In truth, she'd found most of the books rather boring, apart from the ones on botany. Inorganic chemistry and experimental physics were not her forte. George was still giving her physics lessons. He didn't mind her asking him, as far as she could tell, and it kept him occupied for a short while. She wished she had just been allowed to attend lectures rather than be required to take the entire course, but it was too late to be having doubts about going now. Besides, she could always leave after the first term if she disliked it that much.

Molly had only been in her lab an hour or so when the wireless receiver on the wall beside her worktable began buzzing. Her brothers had recently installed it so she wouldn't be disturbed by anyone while she was working. (They really needed to get a patent for it at some point.) Molly reached for the speaking tube.

'Miss Molly?' The butler's voice came through the hessian circle in the middle of the receiver, which looked like an open mouth. Parsons was a soft-spoken man of around thirty, with impeccable manners. He didn't shout down the speaking tube in the north hall like Mrs Baxter did.

'What is it, Parsons?'

'I'm sorry to interrupt you, miss, but Mr Arthur Greenwood is here to see you.'

'*What?* I told him not to come because of the weather.'

There was a muffled exchange at the other end of the line.

'He says he did not receive any word of this, Miss Molly.'

Molly clawed at her hair and pursed her lips together to stop herself swearing down the speaking tube. 'Never mind, Parsons. Tell him I'll come to meet him.'

'Very good, miss.'

Thrusting the speaking tube onto its stand, she removed her gloves and left her desk. Why is it that Arthur never arrives when he's actually needed, she asked herself as she marched out of the lab. She'd expected Parsons to have shown Arthur into a reception room, but he was standing all alone in the north hall. He held a thick book under one arm. Parsons must have removed his mackintosh and umbrella, since there was water on the floor but Arthur was completely dry.

'I sent you a wire saying not to come because the weather was poor and there was no point surveying the work in the woodland,' was how Molly greeted him.

'I wasn't at my residence in Watford, so I never received your message,' he said defensively. 'I was in Newbury.'

'Your father summoned you home again?'

'My mother this time.'

'Can you not simply tell them that you have other business?'

'She was ill. I couldn't refuse her.'

Molly sighed, finding her determination to be angry with him melting.

They'd had such a blazing row about the garden the last time he was here that she was surprised he'd come back at all. 'Well, seeing as you're here, we might as well wait and see if the rain stops.'

'I had a bit of a journey getting here. Parts of the road were impassable after all this rain,' he persisted, apparently not willing to make peace just yet.

'I understand your point, Arthur. I'm prepared to be hospitable, seeing as I sent the message to the wrong location and you had such a difficult journey.' Molly was unsure how long ago they had entirely dropped the 'Mr' and 'Miss' when addressing each other.

Arthur took a step closer to her. 'I half-expected you to turn me out of doors when I saw your expression a few moments ago.' He looked set to say more, but flinched violently as the dogs on the newel posts growled at him. They held the lamps in their paws like spears.

'Ignore them. One of my brothers did that as a joke to try and frighten the other one. Douglas decided to keep them that way, as the reactions they get from visitors are priceless.'

'Ah.' Arthur watched as the dogs resumed their original positions at a whistle from Molly. He heard the ticking clockwork inside each dog. 'It's certainly effective, I'll give you that.'

'They're awoken when you step on a loose floor tile.' She lightly tapped the tile near the foot of the stairs that Arthur was standing on. He swiftly relocated his foot to another tile, half-expecting an axe to swing at him or something.

'We can discuss your idea for the orchard walk since you're here. I'll show you to the drawing room, unless...' Molly bit her lip. 'I could show you my laboratory? I think you might find it interesting. We won't be disturbed there.'

Arthur was half-distracted by the little clockwork mouse that had suddenly scuttered out of its hole, but his face brightened at Molly's suggestion. 'You'd really allow me to see your laboratory?'

'Yes, to prove I'm willing to be friends.'

'I'd like that very much. I might not be able to stay for long, though, if this weather doesn't improve.' He glanced towards the window. Raindrops pelted the glass on the other side.

'If getting back to the train station is a problem, I'll fly you there in the airship personally.' She saw Arthur's puzzled expression. 'My brother Douglas's favourite toy,' she explained. 'Although if you're not fond of heights, then you might not like travelling by air. Anyway, follow me.'

The laboratory, formerly a small parlour, was to the rear of the house on the ground floor. The old dark blue wallpaper and faded sage-green sofa remained, but Molly had brought in her worktable and chemistry equipment. Arthur marvelled at the vials and beakers of different coloured liquids, her collection of preserved specimens and the meticulously labelled glass containers. The laboratory led to a small conservatory filled with exotic plants. The rain sounded like bullets striking the conservatory roof as Molly and Arthur entered. Arthur was greatly intrigued by all he saw and asked endless questions about how she did this and that. He was slightly unnerved by the fact that he would catch some of the plants moving out of the corner of his eye every now and then. Some of the larger ones with teeth looked like they might try to eat him when his back was turned. The sweet aromas mingling in the fuggy air were invitingly intoxicating.

'Look here.' Molly tugged his sleeve and guided him to a row of flowerpots on a small, white table. Each flowerpot contained small flowers of different pastel colours. Molly turned the pots so that their labels were facing away from Arthur. 'Let's have a taste test.'

'A what?'

Molly plucked two little orange flowers from one of the pots. She slipped one into her mouth and handed the other to Arthur. 'What does it taste of?'

Arthur hesitantly placed the flower on his tongue and then chewed it. The taste was familiar, but it took him a moment to place it. 'Gingerbread?'

'Correct!' Molly giggled as she turned the pot around so he could see the label. She plucked a yellow flower from another of the flowerpots. 'And this one?'

Arthur didn't hesitate this time and put it straight into his mouth. 'Custard tart,' he declared.

'Yes! Let's try one more. Ah! This one took me ages to get right.' She presented him with a purple flower.

Arthur rolled it around on his tongue before he was confident of his answer. 'Plum pudding...and maybe mulled wine?'

'I'm glad you think so – that's exactly what I was aiming for!' She turned the flowerpot around; its label read '*Christmas*'. Molly pinched another flower and swallowed it, grinning all the while.

Arthur smiled. 'That was rather fun.'

Molly wove a pink flower that had fallen from another plant into her hair. 'But maybe you require something slightly more substantial than flowers. Come back to the laboratory and we'll have tea. You weren't offered any refreshment on arrival.'

'No, I wasn't. How negligent a hostess you are,' he teased.

Molly retrieved her private tea things that she kept in the lab. (It saved Parsons, Martha or Betsey the trouble of bringing a tray to her when they had enough to do already.) As the water boiled, Arthur noticed a rack of small bottles with silver stoppers on Molly's worktable. He picked up one that was filled with a pale pink liquid. 'What is this?'

'A love potion,' Moly answered from the sofa, where she was spooning tea into the teapot.

He raised his eyebrows at her. 'Really?'

'Good grief, you're gullible! Of course not.'

'It wouldn't be that inconceivable, considering what else you're able to do.'

'I theoretically could make a very strong aphrodisiac. Mrs Dempsey, the gypsy woman who mentored me, even gave me a recipe for one. But just imagine the mischief it would cause.'

'Hm, I suppose so. What is this, then?' He removed the stopper and a sweet scent escaped the bottle. 'It smells strong, whatever it is.'

'Oh no!' Molly sprang up from the sofa and swiped the bottle from him, replacing the stopper. 'You didn't breathe it in, did you?'

'A little.'

'Why didn't you think before opening it?' she cried.

'I didn't think that you'd leave anything dangerous lying around!'

'Does your nose itch?'

'Yes.' Arthur was starting to feel slightly anxious.

'Does your skin feel like it's burning?'

'No, but I do feel a little warm.'

Molly looked nervous. 'That's not good. We need to do something or your skin might start to flake off.'

'*What?*'

'It's a side effect of this deadly' – she flicked drops off the stopper and Arthur leapt back instinctively – 'perfume,' Molly concluded, her alarmed expression now replaced by a smile.

It took Arthur a few seconds to comprehend the joke. 'It's just perfume?'

Molly nodded. 'Peony and rose.'

'You had me panicking that my skin was going to fall off!'

'I was teaching you a lesson: don't open strange bottles without asking.'

'You could have stopped me opening it.'

'But you wouldn't remember the lesson as well that way.'

Arthur still looked annoyed.

'This one is rather popular with the girls in town. I peddle my wares at the market some days. The townsfolk aren't entirely convinced by my medicines yet, but the perfume is popular. This one is an eau de cologne.' She handed him a bottle of orange-tinted liquid. 'Keep it if you like it, as an apology for frightening you.'

Arthur applied it experimentally to the back of his hand. It was spicy and musky without being too overpowering (but, fortunately, strong enough to mask the smell of the sickly peony perfume that had caught his coat). 'Very well, I accept your apology.' He tucked the bottle into his coat pocket.

'This one is quite popular with the older ladies in town.' Molly showed him another perfume bottle that was a darker pink. 'You mentioned that you were stuck for a birthday present for your mother. Perhaps she might like it?'

'Well remembered. I'd forgotten all about her present.' He smiled as he took the second bottle from her.

'You forgot about it? I thought you were a dutiful son!'

'There was still plenty of time to decide on a present. I would have remembered sooner or later.'

The whistle of the kettle silenced them both before they could tease each other about the matter any further. Molly and Arthur sat at opposite ends of the sofa as they took their tea.

'I brought this to show you.' Arthur held up the book he'd brought with him. It was a rather thick volume bound in brown leather and had been lying forgotten on the table since he'd put it there on entering the laboratory.

'Is that Carl Linnaeus's *Systema Naturae*?' Molly asked.

'It is.'

'Tenth edition?'

'Yes. It's my father's, but I thought you might be interested to see it.'

Arthur placed the book between him and Molly. It crackled as he opened it. The book had probably been rebound at some point as the pages were pale brown and smelt musty. It was probably a hundred years old.

'It's a little too dark to read in here. Wait a moment.' Molly clapped her hands once and the potted, leafy plant on her worktable instantly illuminated with a strong lime-green glow.

'That serves as your reading lamp?' asked Arthur incredulously.

'Yes. It responds to sudden movement. Doing something like clapping your hands or stamping your foot near it will make it glow. It's a crude means of defence to confuse anything trying to munch its leaves. Its light will eventually start to fade after a while.'

With the aid of the little plant's light, Arthur leafed through the book's pages until he came to the section on plants. Molly's eyes eagerly ran over the illustrations. The book was probably rather outdated in some of its classifications, but it was still astonishing in its depth. Carl Linnaeus was the taxonomist who had created the Linnaean system of classification, whereby living organisms were named by genus and species, which made the naming of plants less of a headache for botanists. Molly remembered how her father, in a rare paternal gesture, had once bought her a small book on botany when she was six. Her mother scolded him for 'encouraging the girl's obsession', but Molly had avidly studied its pages and memorised the name of every species. She still had the volume on a shelf in her bedroom.

Molly and Arthur studied Linnaeus's book with almost the same fascination. After they closed the book, they discussed the orchard they wanted to create in what was currently a field wild with nettles and brambles, but soon drifted into other subjects. Arthur told her about his experiences at university, then recounted tales of his authoritarian father and nervous mother. Molly told him about her own parents, then about the childhood exploits of her and her brothers, as well as their more recent adventures.

Arthur's eyes were wide. 'So you flew the airship across London to rescue Maestro after he was stolen?'

'I did.' Molly smiled proudly. She bit the biscuit that she'd been making fly through the air throughout that part of the story.

'I can't believe that part about your brothers' escape from Newgate.'

'I promise I didn't make it up.'

'I'm not accusing you of dishonesty, Molly, having seen all of this.' He gestured to the laboratory. 'I know you're capable of incredible things. It's simply a lot to take in, is all. Automata, airships, all your plants.'

'You're the first person beside my brothers to commend my work.'

'I admire your self-possession. You always know what you want and you don't let anyone try to hinder you.'

'Well, I admire your determination to pursue your ambitions despite your father's objections.'

A peaceful silence elapsed, but she could tell he was working himself up to speak.

'Molly?' Arthur began at last.

'Hm?'

'There is something that I have been meaning to ask you.'

'Which is?' She hated how he dithered about sometimes.

'Well, I'd like to make an illustrated book of your floral specimens – with your help, of course. I've seen some of your drawings and they're superior to mine.'

'But it'll be your name on the cover?'

'And yours. I am proposing this as a joint enterprise. We could use the same publisher recommended to me by my friend who I am working on the fern encyclopaedia with.'

'I doubt the addition of my name would help you sell copies.'

'It's not about that. It's about recognising your achievements and preserving them for the future. It doesn't matter if we only sell a handful of copies.'

Molly could hear the passion in his voice. She didn't crave acclaim, although she would have liked to be taken seriously. She was content as long as her creations benefited people. But if they did make this book, she wanted to sell more than a handful of copies, as she was hoping to make a bit of money through this project. She still liked to earn her own pocket money by selling medicines and vegetables, but it wasn't the same as back in Soho, since the townsfolk here were more set in their ways and distrustful of her innovations. (Only Martha and Betsey had faith in Molly's medicines, and they did their best to persuade their family or friends to try them.) Molly was glad that she'd thought of making the perfume and eau de cologne.

'Do you honestly think there is a chance that it could sell?' she asked.

'There's every chance.'

'People will think it's a joke. They won't believe that half of the illustrations are not pure fancy but the result of a lot of experimentation and hard work.'

'The proof is right here.' Arthur pointed to the conservatory. 'And we can produce it at any time. And once those initial doubts are quelled, word of your achievements will spread and sales of the book will increase. I will cover the cost of having the book printed, but any money we make from this can be split equally. What do you say, Molly?'

Molly put her teacup on the table. 'Very well then.' She offered her hand to him.

'Excellent!' Arthur shook her hand heartily, as one would with a man, but then he tried to be more gentle. His hand felt firm and warm in hers; it was peculiarly pleasing. Molly realised that they were now sitting in the middle of the sofa, having gradually grown closer as they were talking, and she shuffled back a few inches once he'd released her hand. Sunlight suddenly flooded the room but neither of them seemed in a hurry to move, and they continued their conversation.

Chapter Twenty-Two

The infantry participating in the assault on Delhi was divided into five columns. Copperton and his three comrades formed part of the 1,000-strong first column that General Nicholson personally commanded. Their task was to enter the breach in the wall near the Kashmir Bastion, before proceeding to clear the ramparts and bastions as far as the Kabul Gate. The second column was to storm the breach in the Water Bastion before following Nicholson. The third column was tasked with blowing up the Kashmere Gate, by which means they were to penetrate the heart of the city. The remaining two columns were held as a reserve. General Fowler was leading a party in the second column under Brigadier Jones. General Quincy had been taken ill with fever shortly after the batteries had been completed, and was recuperating in his tent at camp. Copperton and his friends had been sceptical on hearing this news, especially after General Fowler had left the hospital tent only the day before, but they soon discovered that the report was genuine. This meant that General Fowler was the man to watch. At least they now had only one target to be concerned about.

'He'll wait for a moment of confusion, then bolt,' Copperton had said the night before the siege, when he and Petey were standing on the edge of the Ridge and surveying the city. Distant flashes showed that the heavy guns were still firing at the city walls.

'And you're to follow him?' Petey asked.

'Yes, if circumstances allow. I will keep an eye on him, so the three of you only have to worry about the enemy.'

'*Only?* That's no easy task.' Petey took a cigarette from his recently replenished case and lit it.

'You know that probably isn't good for you,' remarked Copperton.

'I've heard much to the contrary. Sal shares your opinion, after she overheard our local doctor telling her father about something he read in a medical journal which suggested smoking tobacco might be bad for you. Tell that to the old boys in the barroom who've smoked a pipe nearly all their lives and are still going strong in their seventies. But Sal says she'll make me give up tobacco after we're married.' The case snapped shut and Petey tucked it back into the breast of his khaki uniform coat. 'I just hope we succeed in taking the city. It'll be pure slaughter otherwise. Harford says Fowler came to see his friend on the day he left the hospital and that he was in a state of great agitation, which is unlike him. Seems he's no faith that the plan to retake Delhi will work. "The city is lost, Horatio. There's no hope of recovering it," Harford overheard him saying.'

From a tactician's perspective, Copperton knew the odds were against them, at least numerically. There were 40,000 rebels in the city and only 11,000 effective troops in the camp. Ideally, there should be three besiegers for every one rebel. But superior numbers were not a guarantee of victory; history had proven that time and time again. Skill, courage and sheer determination could – and would – tip the balance in the British's favour. And the soldiers in camp were not lacking in determination. As Copperton and Petey made their way back to their tent, he heard men in the other tents cleaning their guns and begging for stamps from friends for what might be their last letter to loved ones.

'I doubt I'll sleep tonight,' remarked Petey as he sat on his charpoy and took up his rifle to clean. 'It's almost like that feeling you get on Christmas Eve as a bairn, isn't it, Cop – oh, sorry, I suppose you wouldn't know, would you?'

'I wouldn't, having never been a child or experienced Christmas. I was only finished in early July of this year.'

'So that makes you…not even three months old. What an eventful life you've lived in that time! I suppose Christmas was a bad comparison anyway. Instead of presents, we might be waking up to death tomorrow. Although plenty of the boys here are excited to find one or two treasures to loot from the city – not that they'll get to keep them. The prize agents will gather everything in and see that every man gets his fair payout. Maybe I can keep the chess piece if no one claims it, since it's not really loot.'

'It'll hardly be worth anything on its own.'

'It might, seeing as it's ivory. Pawnshops aren't fussy. Or maybe I'll keep it as a souvenir. Least he has a friend now.' A wooden sowar on horseback stood beside his ivory counterpart atop Petey's trunk. Petey had made as good a copy as he could and, despite his damning assessment of his work, Copperton thought it was a very close replica.

Petey put away his gun, stripped down to his cotton drawers and shirt, then lay supine on his bed. He took out the locket brooch and held it cupped in his fist over his heart. When he spoke, it was like the ramblings he came out with after he'd had several beers, although Copperton was certain he wasn't intoxicated now. 'Folk are the same wherever you go, really, aren't they? I see the same types of people in India as I did on the streets of Liverpool. I don't feel any sympathy for those buggers who have been shooting at us from the bastions all this time, but the ordinary people in the towns and cities are just going about their business the best they can. Some of the sepoys in the camp are like the blokes who drink at the inn Sal's father runs. Powell should get a promotion – he might be a cynical bugger, but he could easily become a general if given the opportunity. And Jatin is probably one of the cleverest blokes I've ever met. He should be at that Delhi College he keeps pointing out to us from the Ridge, or even in an English university, not out here. We've all the same virtues and vices, and the same desires, at the end of the day.' Petey concluded his meditations by snapping the locket shut. He'd apparently been addressing most of this speech to Miss Sally's photograph. 'Anyway, there's no use thinking these things now. You've got to see a thing through once you've started it, haven't you?'

'I suppose so. I've never thought of anything in that light. For me it's simply always been a case of carrying out orders. I simply *must* see a thing through,' replied Copperton.

'Saves a fellow a lot of bother when he doesn't have to think and just does as he's told,' replied Petey drolly. He stifled a yawn with his fist. 'You probably think us weak, don't you, Cop? Humans, I mean. We squish like insects and can't lift cannons single-handedly like you can.'

Copperton shook his head. 'It's true that I am physically stronger than you, but I do not think you weak. You charge into battle knowing that you cannot be easily repaired, not like I can be. I can even be resurrected, so to speak, if my body sustains heavy damage – as long as my core cylinder isn't damaged. Mankind possesses a courage and nobility that I will never know.'

'Shame Jatin isn't here – he'd get a poem out of that,' Petey chuckled.

Despite Petey's declaration that he couldn't sleep, Copperton soon heard a light snoring from his charpoy. In his mind, Copperton renewed his vow to protect his friend, although he knew all three of his friends were capable on the battlefield. Powell was a natural fighter, although Petey and Jatin were not. (He'd observed them fire their rifles in battle and during drills, and was certain it wasn't clumsiness or cowardice that caused them to fire above the enemy's head during a volley.) They mentally snuffed something out before entering battle, whereas something lit up Powell from the inside and glowed ferociously. Copperton had seen that same spark in many of the men and officers here, General Nicholson especially. Like Copperton, some men were built for combat, it seemed.

A shadow fell across the tent. Copperton didn't hesitate and shot outside, only to find that no one was there. When he looked at the grassy ground, he was even less assured that his senses hadn't taken leave of him. Copperton adjusted the lenses of his eyes, thinking there was something wrong with them. But no, he was seeing what he believed he'd seen: an ivory knight on an ivory horse, just like the other two. This one also had a black base. He picked it up and examined it, scraping away some of the dirt that was embedded in its grooves. Copperton had never played chess but he knew this: there were two knights of each colour in a set. But of course, that would be assuming the other two knights were from the same set, which was not the case. This strengthened his idea that the knights were some sort of symbol. He suspected they were being warned by the conspirators not to interfere with their plan. Perhaps it ran deeper than Quincy and Fowler. Where had this second black knight come from? He hid the knight in his chest cavity until he could show it to the others, but soon forgot about it as his thoughts returned to Delhi.

*

The siege began shortly after dawn, at around three o'clock in the morning. Under the inky darkness – punctured by the unceasing white flashes of shells – the first wave of men and officers left the camp, marching in columns of four. Everyone was silent. They marched to the Flagstaff Tower to retrieve those on picket duty, then made their way down the slope. Copperton looked across at Ludlow Castle, from where General Wilson was watching the assault. The general had issued an order seven days ago forbidding plundering (any loot the men obtained was to be handed in to the prize agents) and, more crucially, asking his men to spare any women and children they encountered during the siege. No quarter was to be given to the mutineers, but civilians would be shown mercy. This order went some way to restoring Copperton's faith in the general.

The advancing columns were sheltered by trees and blooming gardens. The guns in the breaching batteries still fired until the columns were in their appointed positions, and a foreboding silence ensued – the flash of shells had given way to the blood-red sky over the horizon as dawn broke. The change must have caught the rebels' attention. They'd know something was about to happen.

The order was given to advance. The 60th Rifles advanced first, followed by the first and second columns. Before them was a huge gap in the red stone wall, made impassable by a broad ditch that was about twenty feet deep. The men stood on the edge of the ditch until the scaling ladders could be put in place. Many of the ladder parties fell victim to the enemy's ferocious musket fire from the crowded wall above the breach, where the rebels thronged. In addition to firing bullets, they hurled blocks of masonry on the British troops. Grape and shells screamed and whistled from the bastions. Men were rapidly being struck down before they had even entered the city. Copperton leapt into the ditch to help raise the ladders against the escarp on the other side. All the while, the columns fired fiercely at the rebels. Bullets whizzed through the air in the direction of the breach. Finally, after three attempts, the ladders were in position, and the two columns rushed up through their respective gates with loud cheers and shouts. Most of the rebels – faced with this torrent of indomitable, gallant warriors – deserted the walls and bastions. The attacking forces chased them into the city. Those rebels who stood their ground were shot or bayoneted for their courage. The first two columns were now inside the walls. From there, they swept across the ramparts and bastions under unrelenting grape and musketry. Each captured gun was put to use helping to clear the city streets. Copperton was at the front of the charge along the parapet, disarming the gunners that they encountered at every bend. He continuously glanced to his left to see guns firing from housetops in the streets. He picked them off where he could by shooting the gunners in the arm, but found it difficult to halt even for a moment, as every man behind him rushed relentlessly, like stampeding bulls. General Nicholson appeared to have been left behind. The troops advanced as far as the Kabul Gate, but by this time their strength was sorely sapped. All around Copperton, men were being picked off by field guns and muskets. He'd lost sight of his friends, but never took his eye off General Fowler for very long. He was manfully fighting alongside his men at the base of the walls below. The columns' goal was now the Lahore Gate, but they encountered a barricade, backed by a gun firing grape – where a cluster of small, iron balls were fired in one shot. Upon seeing this obstacle, Copperton touched the medal on his chest. Now would be a useful time to play his ace, but he couldn't. He'd had no water since before they left the Ridge and now he was almost out of steam. His abilities were hampered; his speed was impaired and his reflexes not quite as sharp. He could still fight while running on clockwork alone, but it put him at a disadvantage. Nor was he the only one in such a predicament. The men were utterly exhausted. A change came over them once they stopped charging. They were visibly seized by terror, and many were trembling violently. One or two troops ignored their officers' orders to remain where they were, and tried to retreat rather than face an onslaught of rebel musket and cannon fire. Eventually all of the troops made for the Kabul Gate, and their officers were powerless to combat the tide of their own men, being swept up with them. But Copperton did not go with them. He had seen General Fowler dart into a street when the men started to retreat, and he was pursuing him as discreetly as possible. If Copperton had possessed the energy, he'd have sprung onto the rooftops and flitted from one house to the other. Instead he leapt from the rampart to the ground. He stalked his quarry through endless streets and narrow lanes until he came upon members of the third column engaged in fearsome street fighting. He assumed they were pursuing the rebels and turning any civilians out of their homes. But then Copperton heard the screams of women and children, overlaid by musket fire. Some of the slain men on the ground did not look like rebel troops either. Smoke from burning houses snaked into the air. Everywhere he looked, British soldiers were running into people's homes in search of loot and dragging their occupants out into the street. He was torn as to whether to intervene or continue his pursuit of General Fowler; then Colonel Kirk entered the scene, shouting at the street fighters.

'Where are your officers? Have you all gone mad? You are disobeying General Wilson's order!' he barked. They paid him no mind but someone else had noticed Colonel Kirk's arrival: a rebel sniper concealed in a nearby building.

Colonel Kirk toppled from his horse.

'Sir!' Copperton rushed through the fury of the fighting, overpowering all enemies in his path. He lost sight of Colonel Kirk amongst the soldiers and horses, until he finally found him sprawled on the ground. The rebels surrounding him looked set to cut the man to pieces with their swords, but Copperton deflected them. He practically tore the swords from the dumbfounded men's hands and flung them where they could not reach them. The sniper had shot Colonel Kirk in the neck, and blood pooled from the wound. The man looked oddly serene, although it took all his strength to utter three gargled words.

'We will win.' His trembling hand plucked one of the medals from his coat and he offered it to Copperton, who accepted it at once. Colonel Kirk nodded at him and his head slowly sank to the ground. Copperton had never seen death this close. Perhaps it was worse because he had respected the man. He suddenly looked up sharply, turning his head in every direction.

He'd lost General Fowler.

Chapter Twenty-Three

Losses had been severe, numbering more than 1,000 men and officers. The British had been repulsed but held a firm footing in the city. It seemed the rebels had a dogged determination to resist them. Copperton had to give them credit where it was due. They were not as cowardly as he had initially believed. Pandy could be as good a soldier as Tommy Atkins. Not to mention he'd witnessed the British soldiers go to pieces once their momentum was stalled.

Some of the British officers and men were visibly doubting their chances of success. General Nicholson had been shot, possibly mortally, during an attempt to take the Lahore Gate. After what Copperton had witnessed of the man during battle, he had started to think that the rumours of his viciousness and cruelty were grounded in fact. The general took no prisoners and was almost possessed by madness when facing the mutineers. At least he hadn't time to indulge in torturing the sepoys during the heat of the siege, as he had been known to do on previous occasions. And yet, Copperton understood that this merciless madman and tower of strength was precisely what the Field Force needed. His death would certainly be a crushing blow to morale.

They had heard no report to suggest that the bomb had been used. It was possible that General Fowler was amongst the missing men, lying dead or wounded in a garden or street, since he had not returned to the

British position. But, for some reason, Copperton didn't think this was the case. There had been a change of plan. Most likely he'd anticipated that they'd have pushed further into the city than they had. If so, he'd find a new location to deploy the weapon.

'But where?' asked Jatin once Copperton had explained this. Under the cover of midnight, the four of them stood outside St James's Church, which, along with Skinner's House in the Kashmere Gate, formed the centre of the British position in the city. The church had been ravaged when Delhi fell under the control of the mutineers four months ago. They'd even taken the bells.

'It'll be somewhere with a high concentration of rebel sepoys. General Fowler won't worry about having a grand stage any more, if that was his original intention – not now that a lot of mutineers have started fleeing the city – as long as he demonstrates the weapon's capability of wiping out a large number of men at once.'

'You are a good tactician, Colonel Copperton,' remarked Powell. He uttered the title Petey had jokingly bestowed on the android with a touch of irony. Nevertheless, all three of the men had started using it.

'I am familiar with the tactics of every great military leader in history,' Copperton replied.

'Including Hannibal?'

'Especially Hannibal.'

'But at the rate the natives are leaving the city, there might not be many Pandies left by this time tomorrow,' said Petey.

'There'll be some. The ones who believe in their cause and who will continue fighting until the bitter end.'

'So we follow the fight,' said Jatin, 'and hope Fowler comes to us.'

'That's our best option, Jatin. And we have to see to it that Wilson's order is maintained where we can. From what I saw in the streets today, it was clear it was being violated.'

'So not only are we fighting the rebels and searching for Fowler, but we also have to protect the citizens from our own men?'

'Exactly, Petey.'

'You realise how ridiculous this plan is, don't you, Colonel?'

'If you dislike it, Private, you can leave now.'

'I'm not going anywhere, except to bed. I'm dead beat.' He drew his hand across his eyes.

'Before you do, Petey, I want you all to have a look at this.' He showed them the knight with the black base. 'It is a different black knight. Mine is here.' He let his knight's ivory head poke out of his trouser pocket.

'Let me see that, Colonel.' Powell stretched out his hand and Copperton placed the knight into it. He watched the man frown at it as he prowled up and down like a tiger. He whipped his own knight out of his pocket to compare. 'The same design again,' he said, before returning the knight with the white base to its home. 'Looks like your theory about it being a calling card might be right, Copperton.'

'How many more are there? An entire army's worth?' asked Petey of no one in particular.

'I don't like this,' admitted Jatin. 'And no doubt a fourth one shall appear soon enough.'

'A white knight this time.' Petey stifled a yawn. 'Or maybe red or green. The Order of the Ivory Knights might vary things a bit.'

'I have a feeling that if we continue to pursue Fowler, it might appear,' said Powell. 'Anyway, we can't afford to worry about such a trifling thing at the moment.'

'You're right, Powell. I'm sorry to have detained you from your beds. Goodnight, gentlemen.'

The three men withdrew but Copperton remained outside the church, listening to the wind blowing through the nearby trees. The sound couldn't entirely drown the pain-filled cries and moans from the field hospital that had been established inside the church. He touched the medal on his chest that bore his maker's mark, and Colonel Kirk's Punjab medal beside it. The silver medal hung from a dark blue ribbon with yellow edges, adorned with a single silver bar. Dried blood stained the ribbon and was also engrained in the medal itself. One side showed the scene of Sir Walter Gilbert receiving the Sikh surrender, with the legend '*To the army of the Punjab*' embossed above. There was more blood on the other side displaying the diademed head of Queen Victoria. Copperton understood why Colonel Kirk had given him this as he lay dying: as a token of acknowledgement. He accepted him as a soldier. But Colonel Kirk also meant to entrust a duty to him, to continue fighting. Copperton wore the medal to honour the dead man and, perhaps, to feel that he wasn't just a weapon but a warrior. Yet it also served as a reminder to himself of the fragility of a soldier's life, no matter how decorated and respected they were. And many more might die yet, including his friends.

His fingers closed around the medal. 'I won't fail.'

Copperton's plan to locate the heart of the fighting was not as easy as he'd imagined it would be. The following day saw a disorder of street fighting, during which European soldiers found beer, wine and other kinds of drink in the city's stores. They proceeded to get tremendously drunk and became incapable of doing their duty. Most of the army were terribly disheartened. They had not expected to face such a strong resistance from the remaining rebels, who continued to repulse them. The British advance through the city was slow. Troops went from building to building, securing one house at a time, and erected parapets on rooftops from sandbags and doors. Ground was gained by inches at a time and their force was slowly chipped away as more men fell. But gradually their hold over the city strengthened. The magazine was captured on Wednesday. The following day, the Bank of Delhi on the Chandni Chawk was occupied. The Chandni Chawk, or 'Silver Bazaar', was the main street that ran from the Red Fort to the Lahore Gate, so named as it was lined with jewellers and cloth merchants. On Saturday the Burn Bastion was stormed. Six days had passed without any sign of General Fowler. By now most of the mutineers had fled the city.

Wilson's General Order, it was clear, was not being adhered to by some. The ecstasy of looting and slaughter continued. The beer was eventually poured away, but the men were still not sober. They were intoxicated in another way – drunk from bloodlust and greed. The half-crazed men made no distinction between rebels and civilians. They thirsted for revenge and were not particular about whose blood sated that thirst. Wives were made to watch as their husbands were murdered and their homes ransacked. Each night Copperton reflected on what had passed. The Europeans had shown themselves to be little better than their enemies. Both had committed unspeakable atrocities. Both had broken the rules of warfare by murdering helpless civilians. Nothing justified such slaughter. Revenge, he now understood, only perpetuated such acts of brutality. His remaining faith in the British cause gradually eroded as each day passed. Were the British race really so superior? Their revelry in causing pain and suffering suggested otherwise, although not all of the soldiers shared these feelings. There were those who were honest, valiant and willing to do what was right: to raise the sword only to defend. Three such men accompanied him.

On Sunday, shortly before dawn, Copperton's band of four left the British position. When he'd been surveying the city with his magnified vision the previous day, standing on the wall near the Burn Bastion, he'd spotted something to the north-east: a camp outside the city walls, near the Delhi Gate. For whatever reason, some of the rebels had gathered there, even though the Delhi Gate had already been taken. It was like a ripe plum waiting to be plucked. Copperton persuaded the others that it was worth investigating, on the chance that General Fowler chose to make a desperate show of strength there.

They walked along the walls, passing captured ramparts and recalling the terrible sights they'd witnessed on that first day of fighting, until they reached the Burn Bastion. The Lahore and Ajmir Gates were further ahead, but they had not been captured yet. Copperton decided not to risk a confrontation, although he thought there were very few rebels defending the gates. Storming them would be effortless for the rest of the army. Instead the four of them cut across the city, passing along the dusty Chandri Chawk. It was completely deserted, its shops ransacked and ruined.

'Be glad you can't smell, Copperton,' whispered Petey.

'Why?'

Petey indicated several dark shapes lying in the road.

'Are they horses?' asked Copperton.

'I hope so. They smell like they've been there some days, whatever they are.'

They did not linger in that quarter of the city.

They ran through the labyrinth of alleys, houses and courtyards. All was still from within the buildings. The British soldiers had already torn their way through this part of town. Copperton kept his eyes fixed ahead of him until their destination was in sight. The Delhi Gate was made of the same red sandstone as the city walls and other gates. To the left side of the gate loomed three towers, their domes encircled by parapets. The rust-coloured stone shone brightly as the low morning sun began to creep over the gate. Now it was daylight, Copperton could clearly see a horse tethered to a nearby tree, as well as a man in the gate's pointed arch. General Fowler. He was kneeling on the ground, and faced them in profile. He seemed unaware of their presence.

Tightening his grip on his sword, Copperton nodded to his men and entered the archway, finding himself swiftly swallowed by its weak shadow.

'General Fowler?'

Copperton's booming voice seized the man's attention. He scrambled to his feet and instinctively whipped out his sword. On the ground beside him was a canister, exactly as Master Douglas had described – about twelve inches high and filled with a clear liquid. There was a shiny silver pocket watch on its front.

General Fowler's stance was proud and his face calm as he spoke. 'What are you four doing?'

'We might ask you the same, General Fowler, sir,' said Copperton.

'This does not concern you. Return to the battlefield and do your duty.'

'Our duty is to protect the innocent.'

General Fowler frowned. 'As is mine.'

'And this is the best way to do it?' Copperton's gaze darted from the general to the canister and back. 'We know all about this plot you and General Quincy have concocted.'

'This will revolutionise warfare and give us a decided advantage. We won't have to lose as many soldiers in battle.'

'You've missed your chance. Most of the enemy have fled the city,' said Copperton.

'Not all. There is a large camp of them on the other side of this gate. Their deaths will set an example, and the weapon will be used in other parts of India that are still in the hands of the rebels. You've seen it out there – the street fighting. I've lost most of my own men already. I'm not prepared to lose any more.'

'But you were willing to sacrifice your own men to test the bomb in the midst of battle?' challenged Powell.

'Oh, I see,' said Petey. 'You didn't miss your chance – you lost your nerve. You couldn't kill so many men in cold blood, nor risk killing any civilians along with them in the street fighting.'

General Fowler only regarded Petey impassively. 'Every man in the camp was administered with an antidote in their drinking water. The gas won't affect them,' he said at length, his tone veering on impatience.

'How do you know this?'

'General Quincy made sure it was so. His cousin supplied him with the antidote.'

Petey snorted. 'Did you ever see this antidote?'

'I don't have to answer to you, Private.'

'Which means you didn't. All you have is Quincy's word, which isn't worth much.'

'You have no right to speak so of an officer.'

'The man's a coward and a liar. I'm a good judge of character, and I know he's nothing but a weasel.'

'You know nothing of his character.'

'I know he's in debt and only marrying his cousin for her dowry.'

General Fowler's eyes narrowed. 'How can you possibly know that?'

'His aide told me everything. All Quincy's papers pass through his hands, mostly intentionally.'

The mask of calm fell from the general's face. The pocket watch ticked ominously in the silence that followed, the sound echoing faintly off the archway's interior. Copperton glanced briefly at the watch. It was half past nine. The trigger was positioned below the numeral marking the tenth hour.

General Fowler sighed wearily and shook his head. 'Quincy is a scoundrel. The two of us were schoolfellows, and even back then he was the same. I hoped time might improve him, but he just continued to spend and borrow money. Thought he could climb his way through the ranks of the army by purchasing commissions and utilising his father's political connections. He does not deserve that young woman.' The bitterness in those last words choked his voice. 'But he would never lie to me about something so...' He faltered.

Copperton took a stride towards him. 'Is that a risk you are prepared to take?'

General Fowler refused to meet his eye.

'You know this isn't right, sir.'

General Fowler remained stock still; Copperton could almost believe that he had wound down. It seemed the fight had evaporated from him, and he slackly held his sword in one hand.

'Jatin, remove the watch,' ordered Copperton, without taking his eyes off General Fowler.

'Yes, Colonel Copperton.'

General Fowler made no move to stop Jatin, even though his sword hovered above his head once he was crouched beside the canister.

'I have to just remove the watch, Colonel?'

'Yes. Or the hour hand if the watch won't budge. That is what Master Douglas said.'

Jatin nodded and stretched his hand towards the pocket watch.

Powell took out his revolver and aimed it at Jatin.

'Kindly step away from there, Jat.'

Chapter Twenty-Four

Molly kept her head down and focused on her sketch. Arthur was sitting at the other end of the drawing room, arranging the completed pages of the book. She finished the pencil outline of the flower, copied from the one in the vase in front of her, and opened her tin of watercolours to give it its bloom. Arthur's rustling pricked her nerves. Having wet the paper first, she rattled her brush in the jar of water, wiped the excess water away on the rim, and then dabbed the bristles in the pink paint. Sunlight intermittently ebbed from the room, making it harder for her to trace the pencil lines as she applied the runny paint. She let the paint fade where the light was meant to shine on the flower, adding more water to the raw paper that was still exposed.

'How are you getting on?' asked Arthur, sounding perfectly cheerful.

'Fine.' She applied dabs of red to the centre of each petal and watched the paint bleed onto the paper, mingling with the pink.

'Would you mind coming over here to see if you approve of these pages?'

'When I've finished this. The paint will dry before I can blend the different colours otherwise.'

'I see,' said Arthur warily. Her tone had put him on his guard now. It had taken him long enough to realise that she was angry with him.

Three days. For three days she'd watched for his return. He'd promised to arrive on Wednesday and finally appeared on Saturday. He'd brushed the matter aside when he greeted her.

'Father again,' he'd said breezily. 'I would have written or sent a wire, but each day I was certain that I could get away, only for him to delay me with further excuses.'

The only reason that Molly had bottled her anger was that she wanted to finally get on with their work for the book. Now it raged inside her, refusing to wane. How much effort did it take to send a quick note to say he would be delayed? Either he was incredibly absent-minded or he didn't take their work very seriously. Considering how much the garden (and book) meant to both of them, she couldn't quite bring herself to believe it was the latter. When he was with her in the garden, he gave whatever project they were working on his full attention and was full of schemes and promises. Then as soon as he went away, everything seemed to evaporate and be forgotten. Occasionally he'd come back with quotes for some aspect of the garden or completed illustrations for the book. But very rarely. Not only that, he stalled progress with his indecisiveness. He was often hesitant and failed to fix on a course of action. He wanted to add more and more to the book, until Molly feared it would never be published, and she'd had to rein him in: they would only include flora – nothing else. When Arthur did resolutely fix on something, however, he pursued it tirelessly. He could shepherd the plans of others well enough, but not his own, it seemed.

Once the flower was complete, having deliberately taken her time over it, Molly went to see what Arthur wanted. There were large leaves of paper scattered around him on the sofa and table. They scraped against her skirts as she came to stand beside him.

'Do you think this order works?' he asked.

'I suppose so, although I think some of your sketches could be neater.'

He looked up in surprise. 'You think so?'

'And some of these classifications could be clearer.' It was petty, trying to goad him like this, but she allowed herself to succumb to temptation, a red mist blurring her reason. The last time he'd visited, they'd laughed as they skimmed through a Latin dictionary and invented names for some of her species of flower.

'I thought they were fine,' he replied flatly. 'You know I have prior experience of putting such a volume together.'

'I'll leave it to you to judge, then, since your knowledge is superior to mine.'

A puzzled frown crossed his face, then he returned to sorting through the sketches as calmly as he had before.

Molly had gained a reaction from him, but that small triumph had been insufficient, feeding rather than sating her demon. She was out for a fight, and she'd bloody well get one.

She sauntered to the other side of the table, stooping to sift through some of the drawings and reckoning to look over them.

'I've been thinking,' she began, casually picking a book off the floor and opening it, 'that we shouldn't bother building that hideaway in the meadow.'

His head jerked up like a startled hare. 'But you were all for it before.'

'Yes, but I've given it some thought and I don't think it's going to work.'

'For what reason?' he challenged.

'Too expensive.' She turned a page in her book, although she wasn't paying much attention to the words written there. 'And, on reflection, I don't think the design is feasible – not that I have seen anything beyond initial sketches. In all truth, I thought you'd forgotten about it, since you haven't mentioned it in several weeks.'

'Because I was trying to prioritise the completion of the greenhouses and the construction of the new laboratory,' he said crossly.

'The greenhouses would have been completed much sooner were it not for the succession of delays in carrying out the work.'

'The delays were mostly due to the weather.'

'I suggested covering the frames but you were slow to arrange it. Just like you were slow to order the glass panes. One of the greenhouses is still not entirely finished. At this rate some of my specimens will be dead by next month, when the cold weather arrives.'

Arthur slammed his pencil down on the table. He stalled, momentarily puzzled by how to proceed, before springing up from his seat with such energy that he sent several drawings tumbling to the floor. 'Believe it or not, Molly, I am actually competent at what I do and I am genuinely trying to help you.'

The book in her hand snapped shut. She stared at him with that stiff,

215

unnerving manner she reserved for when she was extremely serious or vexed. 'I don't doubt your credentials. But I do find fault with your character. You're arrogant, indecisive, unreliable, and sometimes outright patronising.'

'Well, you're not the easiest person to work with. You're obstinate, hot-tempered, and there's no pleasing you – I can never get through to you.'

'Maybe I've just had enough of people telling me what I should do. And you of all people said that you admired my self-possession.'

'You said you admired my determination, but you obviously think me a meddling fool.'

'I think it's apparent then that we can't see eye to eye.'

'I agree with you on that point. In which case there is no reason for me to continue on this project with you.' He snatched his hat and coat, then marched towards the door. 'I'll inform your brother that I resign from my post.' Putting on his hat at an odd angle, he walked swiftly out of the room. Molly was left trembling when he had gone and the sound of his footsteps had faded to nothing. She breathed deeply to steady herself and then composedly began clearing everything away. Thank God she was finally free of that man. As she lifted her sketchbook off the table, something fell to the floor. Arthur's pocketbook. Trust the idiot to forget it in his haste. She bundled it in her shawl and carried her sketchbook under the other arm. She stamped out her anger through her feet as she returned to her room, each step ringing out *idiot, idiot, idiot.* Molly flung everything on her bed and tried to absorb herself in a book. Sometimes she'd read an entire page without really absorbing the words' meaning, having to force herself to focus. Eventually growing cold from being stationary at her desk for too long, she retrieved her shawl from the bed and the pocketbook tumbled out. Molly picked it up and was tempted to look inside. It seemed wrong to do so. To hell with it; why should she care about displeasing him? It was his fault for forgetting it. As she opened the pocketbook, his scent uncurled from the pages. It sent a pang through her heart. She flicked through the sketches and scribbles. Designs for the greenhouses were followed by designs for the new laboratory and the meadow hideaway. Everything was recorded in fine detail: costs, measurements, timescales and where he could call in debts from acquaintances. Letters were wedged between the pages. He put dates on everything. Towards the back was a sketch of the orchard, exactly as she'd envisioned it. The dates on the orchard drawings corresponded with when he'd last been at his parents' house. Flicking back through the pocketbook, she found the same was true of each stage of the project. Every time he'd been away, he'd been working out the finer details of whichever element of the garden they were working on at the time. The pocketbook suddenly fell to the third page from the back of its own accord. Molly felt a stab of shock at what she saw. It was a sketch of her. He'd drawn her sitting on a fallen log gazing wistfully to her left, her hair fanning out behind her. This was dated to his last visit. He must have done it in rough when she was sitting on the sofa opposite him (he had obviously embellished the sofa and carpet into a log and grass), then added detail from memory when he was away. Molly closed the pocketbook and slammed it on the desk. She sank onto her bed and hugged her knees, feeling the sting of regret.

Late the following afternoon, Douglas was in his study repairing a little drummer boy who belonged to a banker's son. The child had flung him down the stairs – breaking his arm, smashing an eye and causing a lot of dents. Douglas had more or less completely replaced his casing. It seemed a waste of time repairing the drummer boy for such an ungrateful child, but their client had requested that they do so. Most of the damage had been repaired. Now all that was left to fix was the right foot, which was hanging on by a thread. Douglas raised the android's little foot and slotted the nut into place.

The drummer boy tapped him on the head with one of his drumsticks.

'Please stop doing that.'

He began tightening the ankle joint and the drummer boy hit him again.

'That was an order. Do it one more time and I'll take away your drum – and the sticks.'

The automaton put the drumstick down.

Douglas was somewhat short-tempered and had sounded fiercer than he'd intended to. That pterodactyl had been giving him problems all morning. His shirt sleeve was shredded where it had clawed him. (At least his yellow-brown check waistcoat with the red trim had survived unharmed – it was one of his favourites.) With the joint tightened, Douglas flexed the foot experimentally, and nodded with satisfaction as the drummer boy twitched it himself.

'You're all done. I suppose I had better wind you down so you don't go causing mischief.' As he reached out his hand to the drummer boy, the android scrambled away from him and shook his head. 'Oh, very well. But if your banging on that drum disturbs anyone, you'll have to stop.'

Douglas left him in the study. The *rat-a-tat-tat* of the drum coming through the door was not as loud as he'd feared it would be. From his study, he made his way to his bedroom to write to the banker, informing him that the repairs were completed and that they would return the automaton whenever it was convenient. (They'd discovered the auto-carriage was useful for dispatching orders to clients who were not ridiculously far away from the Hall.)

Douglas's room could be best described as autumnal. Almost everything was a shade of red, orange or yellow. The patterned wallpaper, possibly once yellow, was now the brown of old book pages. The floor was carpeted in red and black, looking orange from a distance. Scarlet curtains screened the large window that looked onto the drive. The furniture was modern, save for the four-poster bed. Drawings and blueprints for his private projects were pinned to the wall above the cluttered writing desk. Douglas had to clear a space before he could sit down to write. Maestro's latest letter fell on the floor. Douglas wished he could travel like Maestro was doing, but he couldn't spare the time or money as things stood. One day he'd build an airship that could fly around the world. One day.

Douglas often found his mind drifting as he wrote, with fragments of ideas for inventions flashing in his head like fireworks. He understood why George couldn't tolerate his own thoughts to the point that he wanted to drink himself into oblivion, although he'd never felt the need to do such a thing (perhaps it was like comparing fireworks exploding to barrels of gunpowder igniting). Douglas had his private aviation experiments that he could turn to when he felt overwhelmed or was without something to do, and he did enjoy mixing with people. He'd suggested to George that he find a project to occupy himself with, and George seemed to have actually taken the suggestion seriously. Douglas never wanted to admit that he wasn't as good as his brother, but he secretly felt that it was true. Then again, he was not as…emotionally detached as George was. Perhaps that was the price

George paid for his exceptional genius: to be estranged from everyone. Even as a young child he'd been reticent, forbidding and dispassionate. It was like he'd been born frozen inside. Their mother and father hadn't petted them as some parents did their offspring, which probably hardened George's heart even more.

Douglas had the impression that George hated him for the first few years of his life. He'd regarded his little brother as an intrusion and an annoyance. This impression was rooted in Douglas's early memories, he was sure, but by now that chapter of his life was too faded and confused with dreams for him to recollect much clearly. But one memory stood out.

He was three years old. Their father had asked George to watch him while he stepped out of the shop for a few minutes, since the maid was busy doing laundry and their mother was paying a call to a friend. They were both sitting at the counter in the clockmaker's shop. George had ordered him to sit at the far end of the counter and remain silent while he tinkered with something. He wouldn't let Douglas see what it was. When he dared to ask him about it, George snapped at him to be quiet. Douglas rubbed his numb hands together, muffling them inside his overly long coat sleeves. It was snowing heavily outside and he wanted to play. Through the frosted shop window, he saw other children hurling lumps of snow at one another in the street outside. George would never play with him. Bored and restless, Douglas had picked up a broken pocket watch to examine. He'd observed his father repair watches and reckoned he knew how to fix it. He retrieved some tools and, after a lot of fumbling, succeeded in making the watch tick. He'd beamed with pride at his achievement, but stopped when he saw George standing over him.

'Give me that.'

Douglas placed the watch in his brother's palm. He watched George examine it with his sharp blue eyes. They were unnaturally keen for a six-year-old child.

'You fixed it?' he asked at last.

Douglas nodded, his thumb lodged in his mouth.

George opened a drawer under the counter and pulled out another broken pocket watch. 'Show me what you did.'

Douglas picked up his tools again. He often hesitated and made several attempts at certain actions, as he felt nervous under his brother's gaze, but he achieved his objective and got the watch ticking again.

'Did I do it right, brother?' he asked timidly as he offered George the watch.

George inspected it briefly then looked down at him. For once, he wasn't scowling. 'You did.' George returned to his chair. 'Bring your stool over here.'

Douglas looked at him in disbelief but promptly did as he was told. George showed him the clockwork mouse he was working on. He explained how it worked, and Douglas listened as if his brother was reciting the Gospel. Once the mouse was complete, George wound it and they watched it start to twitch. The mouse scurried across the counter and Douglas caught it as it neared the edge, laughing merrily as he did so. When their father re-entered the shop through the black door adjoining the house, his slate-blue eyes widened on seeing his two boys getting along. The door to the rear of the house creaked as their mother returned, and Mr Abernathy beckoned his wife with a whisper.

'Georgina, come see this small miracle.'

She'd joined her husband and shared in his wonder.

After that day, the two brothers were thick as thieves. George became his mentor, protector and, eventually, his rival. Throughout their childhood they'd never really had any friends besides one another. George didn't care. The other children were beneath him. 'They are not on the same level as us,' he'd say, leading Douglas away.

Douglas sometimes wished for other companions, but all the children their mother deemed to not be too 'common' or 'vulgar' to associate with them were frightened of George. Douglas had only made a couple of friends throughout his life. (He wondered what became of Dick Cullwick. He could still picture that wiry-haired boy soft with puppy fat, whom Douglas had befriended during his brief stay at Mr Meddlings' school, and who'd taught him to catch butterflies.) Not that it mattered really; he liked the fact that he and George were in a club of their own. And when Molly came along, he had someone with whom he could give and receive affection.

But Douglas wondered: had he and Molly never been born, would George's heart still have gradually thawed?

With his letter complete, Douglas took it downstairs for the evening postbag. He walked slowly and gazed at the house's splendid interior, with the sound of the tower's clock booming from above. He didn't quite feel like the lord of the manor. In himself, he didn't feel different at all really. He still wore the same old clothes as he had in Soho, still spoke the same, and still felt no inclination to treat his servants like they were…well, he couldn't say automata. Douglas was glad of his decision to hire servants from the town. His reason for doing so was to provide employment for some of the girls, and the odd man or two who was out of work, although Parsons came from an agency. George had called him sentimental and told him that he was wasting money when they could build devices to help deal with the house's domestic affairs, but he'd let Douglas have his way. The gratitude Martha's father had expressed when he'd helped Douglas retrieve George convinced him that he'd done the right thing, as did seeing Mrs Baxter comfortable (idle and cunning as she was). Betsey and Molly had become quite good friends too, even though they were servant and mistress.

He deposited the letter on the table in the south hall for one of the servants to find. Any other master would have rung the bell in his room and had the letter whisked away on a salver. It wasn't like he was pressed for time. Douglas wandered into the kitchen and, without a great deal of surprise, found his sister to be the only one there. She was gazing out of the window that faced the garden, while the kettle was whistling from the stove.

'Where are the servants?'

Molly shrugged. 'Church. Visiting family. It's Sunday.'

'Oh, I forgot. It's hard to keep track of the days since we've been so busy recently. Are you making regular tea or your herbal stuff?'

'Regular. Is that you saying you want a cup?'

Douglas sat at the kitchen table. 'If you please.'

'I thought you'd be out for a drive, since it's a dry, quiet evening.'

'I've just finished repairing the drummer boy, and I'm still waiting for the auto-carriage's batteries to charge. Perhaps I'll go for a drive later if the rain keeps at bay. You know, I've managed to get the auto-carriage up to eighty-seven miles per hour. I don't know why, but she's suddenly started picking up speed on the last few drives. I was flying along the road last time.'

Molly heaved the kettle off the stove and poured the water into the teapot. 'Maybe it's the stripes you painted on her,' she said drily.

'Stripes make you go faster, aye? There's a curious idea. I'm yet to finish the new motor, so it can't be that. I'm hoping to reach one hundred miles per hour once it's done.'

After adding a generous splash of milk and stirring in a heaped teaspoon of sugar, Molly placed his cup before him, without managing to spill any of its contents.

'I can tell something has you in a temper,' said Douglas.

Molly sat down beside him but didn't meet his eye.

'I take it you and Mr Arthur had a…disagreement yesterday? I heard you both two floors away.'

She frowned deeply. 'That's none of your concern.' She sipped her tea, even though it was not quite cool enough to drink. 'He quit his post.'

'So you finally managed to get rid of him?' Douglas asked half-teasingly.

'Eventually.' Molly ran the scalded tip of her tongue over the roof of her mouth.

'Are you certain that you really disliked him so much?'

'He drove me insane at times. He could be so pig-headed and arrogant. We found it impossible to agree on anything.'

Douglas tried his tea. Molly always made it exactly how he liked it. 'It seems to me that, despite your differences of opinion, you were quite similar really: both strong-willed and passionate about the same thing – even if your ideas about the garden differed. Would you say that's a fair assessment?'

'Possibly,' she muttered.

'Any two strong-minded people will clash in such a scenario. You only have to look at George and me to see that.'

'Now that's certainly true,' she said laughingly. He'd finally got a smile out of her, although it was short-lived. She let him glimpse the true nature of her feelings. 'I couldn't walk through the garden earlier without being reminded of him everywhere and feeling angry. Some parts of the garden are better for his input, but it'll take a while before I can forget about all his failed efforts. The laboratory still needs completing as well. I'll have to see to that.'

Douglas knew that what Molly really meant, whether she realised it or not, was that it would be a while before she would be able to forget Mr Arthur himself.

'Well, you'll be off to Oxford shortly, so you'll have plenty to occupy your mind.'

'I'll be coming back here as often as I can. It's only a short journey in the airship.'

'Don't think Spuggy will be at your beck and call all of the time. It's still a considerable distance from here to Oxford. Do try to mix with your fellow students too,' he added lightly.

'Oh, I will, if they give me half a chance. I don't want to be too far away from my garden either.'

'Never mind seeing your dear old brothers.' Douglas ruffled her hair. He didn't want to think about Molly leaving, in all truth. He'd certainly feel his little sister's absence.

She smiled reluctantly as she caught his hand. 'You know I'll miss you both.'

'If one can miss George.'

'You'll have to watch him, you know. Make sure he doesn't start drinking spirits again.'

'Like I haven't been doing so this whole time?'

'You know what I mean.'

'He'll be fine. Don't worry.' Douglas squeezed her hand.

A sudden rush of feeling came over her. She shuffled her chair closer to Douglas's and leant her head on his shoulder. He seemed to understand, and enclosed his arms around her. 'It'll be all right, Mol. You'll see.'

'I know,' she said in a mumbled mutter, her cheek against his collar. She felt like she was a little girl again, receiving affection from the only source she had ever found it at home. What was the cause of this undignified show? Surely she wasn't that afraid of going away? She would miss her family but she was more than prepared to live on her own; part of her even craved it. Or maybe it was the guilt at having driven Arthur away.

Chapter Twenty-Five

Copperton couldn't believe what he was seeing. 'Powell, what are you doing?'

Powell ignored him, cocking the barrel of the revolver. 'Step away from there, Jat. Now.'

Jatin looked stunned but did as he was ordered.

'Powell!' Copperton bellowed. 'Explain yourself this instant.'

'Gladly, Colonel.' He took Jatin's place and stood over the canister. When General Fowler opened his mouth to speak, Powell turned the gun on him. 'Pray be quiet, brother. I shall deal with you shortly.'

General Fowler appeared as astonished as the rest of them.

'Brother?' Copperton echoed.

'Don't you remember what I told you, Colonel? That I had an older brother who was sent to live with wealthy relations in England and who took his uncle's name? My aunt's husband was named Fowler.'

Now the two men were beside one another, Copperton could see there was a resemblance between them. He finally understood what had always pestered him about Powell's countenance.

'Henry?' cried General Fowler. 'Surely it cannot be!'

'I said be quiet, Fredrick. But I confess, Colonel, that I wasn't entirely honest with you. I neglected to mention that when my father died eighteen months ago, he left me a modest legacy. I didn't foolishly spend it all at once as some men would have, although I did purchase one or two little treats, including this Adams. It was only about a year ago, when I overheard Quincy mention his cousin's scientific pursuits to another officer, that I had an idea of how to best make use of my inheritance. I saw how Dr Quincy's anaesthetic gas could be utilised as a weapon. I was fond of reading about military campaigns as a child. Hannibal was my hero. It's an interest that has never really died. I'd heard how, during the conquest of Algeria, French troops forced around a thousand members of a Berber tribe into a cave and then used smoke to kill them all. I suppose that's what gave me the idea. I shared my idea with Quincy and offered to fund the project, since I knew he was badly in debt. Quincy was desperate for any means of making money quickly, so he didn't need much persuading. He put the scheme to Fowler, who had the means to construct such a weapon. I asked Quincy not to tell him of my involvement. I think Quincy suspected who I was, since he knew my brother's history. We planned to pin the blame on Fowler if things went badly when the army found out about the bombs. But it wasn't about revolutionising warfare and reducing casualties – that was just how Quincy knew he could sell you the idea, Fredrick. We intended to sell the new bombs to the highest bidder.'

Copperton scowled at him. 'You wretched traitor!'

Powell shrugged. 'Call me what you please, Colonel. It doesn't change a thing. It's simply good business. There are plenty of peoples oppressed by British rule who'd be all too glad of a quick means of disposing of their masters. Every empire falls. You should know that, Copperton, since you've studied military history. But commerce endures.' He pulled a folded wad of paper out of his pocket. 'The instructions you gave me for the wireless telegraph might prove useful – I thank you for them. It would be an advantage to be able to remotely deploy the bombs without relying on a timer.'

He replaced the papers in his pocket and then thrust his revolver at General Fowler's head. 'Tell the android that he is to obey my orders. He can't refuse if you tell him to, since you're an officer.'

General Fowler studied the gun and then met his brother's eye. 'I won't do it. You can shoot me if you like, but I won't leave him in the hands of a blackguard like you, Henry. I knew you had that weak side to you, even as a boy. Always wanting people to take notice of you.'

'Can you blame me? After I've been shunned and belittled all my life while you had everything? All because you are fair and I am not.'

'It was not as simple as that. You had a great deal of malice and vanity. You revelled in the gore and brutality of those wars you read about. Whenever we enacted them together, you always had to be the glorious general or emperor smiting his enemies. You admired Hannibal, but did not understand as he did the necessity of restraint. Remember the pets mother gave you and how you tortured them, pretending they were your prisoners – sometimes to death? I buried the monkey before mother saw what you did to it with your penknife. Father considered taking you to England with him and placing you in a boarding school where your behaviour might be corrected, but mother's relations wouldn't allow it. You were too wild for aunt's nerves, so placing you with her was out of the question. I see now that father should have taken greater care with you.'

'So the naughty child gets left to rot on some farm in the middle of nowhere?'

'Father hoped it might humble you.'

'Well, it appears that he was mistaken.'

'I searched for you when I returned to India, but mother's family said you had run away.'

'Well, you obviously didn't look that bloody hard, considering I've been right under your nose for some time now.' He screwed the gun into his brother's temple. 'Do what I say or I'll blow your brains out.'

General Fowler's stoic expression did not alter.

'Then how about I paint the wall with Private Peterson's blood instead?' Powell pointed the revolver at Petey. 'His blood will be on your hands, Fredrick.'

'I always thought there was something suspicious about you, Powell,' said Petey, with thinly disguised contempt behind his smile. 'And I'm never wrong about these things.'

'Too bad you didn't act on your feelings. I was surprised how easily you all trusted me.' Powell aimed his gaze at his brother. 'Give the order, Fredrick, or you can watch an innocent man die. How will your principled, noble consciousness bear that?'

General Fowler glared at him. 'Very well. I can see you're just as stubborn as you always were.' He turned to Copperton. 'Soldier, you are to obey my brother's orders.'

Powell gave a satisfied grin, that same flinty smile he always wore. It was his eyes that had changed; there was a glint of menace in them. 'And for my first order, I want you to shoot Private Peterson.'

Copperton blinked. 'What?'

'As a test of your loyalty, I want you to shoot your best friend.'

Copperton stared helplessly at his target. Petey smiled and pointed at his heart.

Understanding, Copperton aimed his hand at where he was pointing, and fired. Petey was flung against the wall and then slumped to the ground.

'No!' Jatin rushed to Petey's side and put his hand over where the bullet had struck his friend's khaki coat. He looked at Copperton aghast. 'What have you done?'

'You can't do anything for him, Jat. The colonel shot him in the heart,' said Powell. He patted Copperton's shoulder. 'Nicely done. You will make an excellent bodyguard. That was my whole reason for bringing you along—'

Copperton watched Powell's smile collapse as the unmistakable sound of Petey's roaring laugh reverberated around them. Powell looked at the laughing man as if he were a demon.

Petey managed to stop laughing. 'You should have chosen your words more carefully, Powell.'

Powell narrowed his eyes at him. 'How are you still alive?'

Petey dipped his hand into his breast and pulled out his cigarette case. There was a hole in the lid so that tobacco was spilling onto his coat. 'You didn't say where to shoot me.'

Powell stared sharply at Copperton. 'But you obeyed my order to shoot him.'

'You ordered me to *shoot* him, not to *kill* him. But even if you had, I wouldn't have done, as it is impossible for me to kill intentionally. My makers made it so.'

General Fowler frowned. 'General Brassington never said that.'

Copperton shrugged. 'He never knew. You all simply assumed that it was otherwise. Think about it, Powell. Have I ever actually inflicted a mortal wound on an enemy?'

Powell's incredulous expression matched his brother's. It was curious how alike they looked at that moment. Copperton took hold of Powell's wrist and the revolver fell from his hand. Jatin grabbed it and aimed it at his former friend, struggling to hide his anger and sorrow as his bottom lip quivered. Copperton thrust his other hand into Powell's pocket and retrieved the wireless receiver instructions.

'I will be sure to mind who I trust in future. Thank you for teaching me that lesson, Powell.' Copperton sharply struck Powell on the back of the neck and watched him crumple.

Jatin was staring at him open-mouthed. 'Did you just—?'

'Of course not. I merely put him out of his senses so he'll be less trouble to us, although he should regain consciousness soon enough.'

Something clicked.

Copperton caught sight of General Fowler kneeling beside the canister. He couldn't see what he was doing, as his back was to him. Was he triggering the mechanism? But when the general straightened himself, Copperton saw he was holding the silver pocket watch. General Fowler stared at the watch a moment, before planting it in Copperton's hand. The dial was face down so Copperton could see the hallmark on the back of the watch. He read the letters *AB.s*.

'I used your makers' watches for the timers. It was an afterthought, after General Brassington told me about their automata. I thought it might throw the authorities off our trail for a short while, making them falsely believe that there was a connection between the bombs and their inventions.'

'Are there any more of these canisters?'

'Seven. One is with my horse – a precaution I took should I have had to administer a second dose for the gas to be fatal. Dr Quincy made the mixture in two batches, and it appears one is stronger than the other. The remaining six canisters are hidden in Ludlow Castle. I had a spy take them from my tent and hide them there on the night the castle was taken.'

'I will take possession of this one here, General. We shall address the remaining seven at the first opportunity.'

'I will recover those. We will win against the mutineers without them. I see now that the bombs would cause more harm than they are worth.' General Fowler took hold of the unconscious Powell. 'And I will see to my brother. He is my responsibility, after all. I'll make sure he's answerable for what he has done, and I'll explain my part in this affair.'

Copperton nodded. 'Thank you, sir. Oh yes – am I correct in thinking that this belongs to you?' Copperton held out the knight with the black base.

'Yes.' General Fowler took it from him with a look of surprise. 'I thought I'd lost it at Najafgarh. But what made you think it was mine?'

'Your brother wished me to believe that the knight had some significant meaning, like a calling card for the plotters of a conspiracy. It was only moments ago that I realised he was trying to prevent me from making the connection between the knight and you, in case I realised that there were only two knights and that they were, in fact, from the same set.'

'They were from a set that had sentimental value to us in our youth, which my father sold to pay debts. I stole two of the knights and gave one to my brother, promising I'd return to India one day to find him and bring him to England. I always carried my piece with me as a sort of talisman, hoping it might lead me to him.'

'It seems it has worked.'

'Indeed.' He cast a troubled look at his unconscious brother on his arm, who'd threatened to blow his brains out only minutes ago.

And yet Powell always kept his chess piece with him too, Copperton mused. In the distance to the south came the sound of a catastrophic explosion. The attempt to take the palace had begun.

'Now, if you'll excuse us, sir, there is a battle raging and I think it is only right that we join the fight once more.'

But when they emerged from the Delhi Gate, it was all over. The remaining gates, the Jama Masjid and the mighty Red Fort had all been taken by the British. The last supporters of the king had either been killed or escaped. Now there was only a frenzy of looting. The palace was soon picked clean of everything of value by the victorious soldiers, like ravenous birds stripping a bullock carcass. Instead of indulging in the sport of plundering, Copperton, Jatin and Petey decided to help the remaining citizens gain safe passage from Delhi through the Ajmeri Gate on the other side of the city. They methodically searched the narrow streets near the Delhi Gate, close to the palace. Practically all the buildings were square or rectangular, depending on whether they had one or more floors. What a contrast to the opulent, splendid mosques and palace buildings, with their elegant curves and lofty domes. But the British troops were one step ahead of Copperton's trio. Not satisfied with reducing the city to a hollow husk, they seemed intent on massacring all of the remaining citizens. The three of them found not a soul who was left alive. Every house had already been ransacked – blood and debris were strewn across the streets. A stray bullock came plodding past them, aimlessly dragging an empty cart behind it, which struck Copperton as an absurdly comical sight. The only relief to the death-like stillness in the streets was the sound of gunfire some distance away. It was coming from one of the splendid havelis, and soon reduced to a sputter before dying away. They couldn't have got there in time to intervene, and Copperton cursed his own powerlessness.

They happened upon a few of their own men, both Indian and European, celebrating in one street, brandishing their spoils: some clothes, cooking utensils and a book. One of the men caught the three of them staring at him.

'Why so glum-looking, fellows? The city has been taken!' He waved the women's clothes in the air like a flag.

'Where did you obtain those things?' asked Copperton.

'A nobleman's house.'

'He just gave you them, did he, Ensign?' asked Petey.

'I ran my bayonet through him without asking him first,' the ensign chuckled. 'And we made short work of his family and servants.'

'You mean you killed them? Including any womenfolk?' asked Copperton.

'They deserved it. They were little better than beasts.'

Petey spat on the ground. 'You're a disgrace.'

'I avenged our womenfolk and children at Cawnpore!'

'Let's move on,' ordered Copperton.

The ensign shouted after them as they turned the corner.

A drunken grenadier was cavorting in the next street. Another was rummaging through the clothes of the fallen men on the ground, checking for anything of value. The scavenger scarpered like a rat on seeing Copperton.

'We'll check each house for survivors. Some of these men might be only wounded. I'm sure I can hear several heartbeats.'

Copperton suddenly heard something much louder than a heartbeat –
a shrill scream from the next street.

'Petey, you sweep the houses on this side. Jatin, follow me.'

The two of them raced around the corner. A screaming woman was
sprawled on the ground as a European soldier held her by her hair. Two
bawling children clung to her dress. Two more soldiers had hold of her
husband, and were loudly demanding money. Copperton swung his arm and
knocked the man who was terrorising the woman to the floor. Jatin aimed
his rifle at the other two, and the cowards fled.

Everything became still for a moment. The husband, finding himself
free, ran to his wife. Her screams were succeeded by sobs. Her husband
suddenly became aware of Jatin standing nearby and poured heartfelt thanks
onto him. Copperton did not have to know his language to understand that.
Jatin gently addressed the bewildered woman. She had an arm around each
of her children, and tears streaked her face.

'Tell them to gather their possessions and that you'll escort them to the
Ajmeri Gate,' Copperton instructed.

Jatin said something to both husband and wife. The woman shook her
head fiercely.

'She says they have nowhere to go.'

'Tell her if she stays here, she and her children will be killed for certain.
At least if they leave the city, they will be alive another day and have a chance
to find refuge.'

Jatin looked hard at Copperton, his lips pressed firmly together. At
length he sighed, and delivered the message. Copperton watched a wave of
shock roll over the woman's face. Her husband took her by the shoulders
and entreated her to do as she was told. Tears squeezed from her eyes, and at
last she nodded. As the family disappeared inside the house to gather their
things, a powerful explosion shook the ground. Copperton saw a house in
the neighbouring street collapse in a cloud of dust.

Petey.

'Jatin, stay with them until they reach the gate. I'll see to this.'

When Copperton retraced his steps, he found the drunken grenadier on
the ground beside the fallen house, laughing manically. Copperton grabbed
him by his shirt.

'Did you do this?' he demanded.

The man laughed in his face. 'Had some powder on me. Thought it'd be a lark,' he slurred.

'Was anyone inside?'

'Might have been. Can't say.'

'Did you see a fair-haired young man about?'

'Don't know.' He resumed his horrid laughter.

Copperton thrust him to the ground, not wishing to waste any more time on him. He would have to see for himself. The top floor of the house was gone. Chunks of masonry were scattered across the street – even a complete section of wall with a window in the centre. Debris filled the inside of the ground floor. Copperton hastily began tearing through the remains of the building, shifting huge pieces of stone and roof tiles. Under the remains of a wall, he caught a glimpse of a white, bloody hand.

'Petey!'

It didn't take too much force for him to heave the stone masonry off the man, who was lying face down. He was certain that it was Petey, although he was covered in blood and dust. The man screwed up his face and shielded his eyes with his free hand.

'Private Peterson?' Copperton saw the recognition in the man's face on hearing the name. It was Petey. His other hand was still trapped under a heavy beam that was wedged beneath another chunk of wall. It was too heavy for Copperton to lift.

'Do not attempt to move.' Copperton discarded the chunk of stone he was holding and drew his sword. 'I'm forbidden to kill a human, but you may force me to do something I do not wish to do.' Copperton wasn't confident that he could cut the beam without severing Petey's hand, since he didn't know where it lay. But he was rapidly running out of steam again, and had used most of his energy to lift the wall off Petey.

He sliced through the beam. The wood fell away, but there was no splurge of crimson as there would have been if he had cut through Petey's flesh. Copperton wrestled the rest of the beam from the debris and flung it away, freeing Petey's hand.

'Christ, I thought you were going to kill me!' exclaimed Petey as he raised himself on his elbows. His voice sounded hoarse.

'Don't be ridiculous, Private!' He examined his friend. 'Petey, I'm going to give you an order, and I want you to follow it without question.'

'What's the order?'

'Don't look at your legs.' It was obvious they were broken in several places. Petey moved as if to twist his head over his shoulder, but suddenly recalled Copperton's order and stopped. 'Are you in pain?' Copperton asked.

'What do you think?' said Petey, still managing to sound light-hearted. But then his smile contracted and a shadow was cast over his face. 'You might as well leave me, Cop. What use am I now? I'm little better than a cripple.'

'Poppycock! I am not leaving one of my men behind.'

'But I can't walk.'

'Some of your injuries might not be as bad as they first appear.' Copperton knew this was unlikely. At least, he didn't think Petey's legs could be repaired. The bones couldn't be welded together like his metal legs could, but there was a chance that they could heal in time to some degree, if infection could be kept at bay. 'I'll get you to a surgeon at once.'

'Then I *will* be dead for certain. Leave me, Copperton. Or, if you want to do me a kindness, stick a bullet through my head.'

Copperton ignored him and hauled him over his shoulder. He saw Petey wince when his legs were disturbed.

Copperton waded out of the house. 'You mistake me for one who breaks his word. I swore to defend you and return you to your Sally.'

'I can't expect her to marry me now.'

'You still have use of your hands, don't you?'

'I think the bones in one of my hands are crushed. Fat lot of good I am with one working hand.'

'Stop feeling sorry for yourself and stay alert. We could still come under fire from a stray Pandy.' This was not an entirely kind thing to say, but he could not have Petey in this despondent state at a time of crisis. Not to mention that seeing him not joking and laughing as usual was unsettling. 'Didn't Jatin give you Powell's revolver earlier?'

'Yes.'

'Good. You can still shoot then.'

'Where is Jatin?'

'Aiding some of the locals.'

Petey cursed sharply and instinctively felt for his leg. Copperton must have caught it. As Petey was evidently in a lot of pain, Copperton made a decision. 'I cannot carry you without hurting you. I remember seeing an abandoned buggy a little way up the street. I'll quickly retrieve it – it won't take a minute. If that grenadier rascal gives you any trouble, shoot him.'

He set Petey on a table that had been lying tipped on its side in the street, and ran back in the direction of the palace. Copperton had a feeling that he was being watched, but hadn't time to determine if this was a delusion or not. Perhaps his lack of water was impairing his reason. The buggy was still in the courtyard where he had seen it. As he started to drag it along, Copperton saw an Indian boy of around nine or ten crouched behind the remains of a wall, hiding from the two British soldiers on the opposite side. One of them spied him and hauled him into the open street.

'Filthy wretch!' the soldier barked. He struck the boy in the stomach with the butt of his rifle, causing him to fall backwards, then he rotated the rifle so the barrel faced the child. The boy looked bewildered and terrified.

Copperton shot out his arm and confiscated the weapon. 'You think it is honourable to maim a child, sir?' he asked the soldier, who stared in Copperton's direction with an expression of confusion mingled with fury. Copperton lifted a large stone off the ground and crushed it in his hand. 'It would be a lot easier to crush your skull.' He tried to sound as menacing as he could.

'It's gone mad!' the soldier's companion cried. 'We need to tell the officers! Come, before it kills us.'

He didn't wait for him to heed his advice, however, and fled. The other man was fast on his feet and soon chased after him. Copperton discarded the rifle, having broken the barrel over his knee first, and returned his attention to the terrified boy crouched on the ground. The child scrambled away when he knelt down close to him.

'It's all right. I won't hurt you.' He tried speaking in Hindi as Jatin had taught him, although he remembered little from his lessons. Gradually the child seemed to understand that the golden man wasn't a threat – either by instinct or as a result of Copperton's crude attempt at communication. Copperton tried asking the boy where his parents were, but he only stared at him. The boy rode on Copperton's back as he made his way back to Petey's position, while Copperton dragged the buggy behind him with one hand, wondering why the child didn't prefer to sit in the vehicle. When he reached the end of the street where the collapsed building was, he came to a stop. The boy strained to look over his shoulder.

An Indian man wearing dirty white pyjama breeches, a grey coat missing all of its gold buttons, and a pugree was standing over Petey. A rebel sowar. Copperton saw the man's tulwar was raised, its curved blade winking in the sunlight. As Copperton was about to disarm him, the man lowered his weapon. He nodded at Petey and walked away. It took Copperton a moment to realise what he had just witnessed. The sowar had spared Petey because he was wounded.

Chapter Twenty-Six

The boy walked alongside Copperton while Petey was pulled in the buggy. Petey made jokes about being a lord and pretended to whip Copperton like a horse, much to the boy's amusement. Copperton had dared to slip Petey some of the anaesthetic to ease his pain. The canister was stored in Copperton's chest and had, thankfully, not absorbed too much heat from his boiler. He'd broken the canister's metal seal, twisting it slowly to gradually release the pressure and allowing only a small amount of gas to be emitted, despite knowing that even a full canister had not been enough to kill those men on the bridge at Najafgarh. It seemed to have done the trick, even if Petey was more talkative than usual. Copperton wondered if he had given him too much. They soon found Jatin and briefly explained what had happened. The family had been escorted to the Ajmeri Gate to join the other evacuees.

Jatin was able to converse fluently with the boy. He discovered that the boy's name was Badshah Ali Khan and his family had most likely been killed by Sikh soldiers in the British ranks. His mother told him to run just before the British arrived, probably knowing that Sikh soldiers were targeting Muslim youths. He'd returned to his house to see if his family had survived, but found no one there. Ali told them about when the mutineers – or Tilangas, as he called them (which Jatin said essentially meant a sepoy) – had first arrived at Delhi all those months ago. How they'd plundered the city with as much enthusiasm as the now victorious British soldiers. They'd hunted down the Christians and spared none they came across. But lots of people, even Muslims, had been frightened by the rowdy mobs of rebel sepoys, and the city's badmashes (scoundrels) who joined them, and had hidden in their homes. They realised that the Tilangas weren't just raiding the homes of Christians but those of rich native families too. There was lots of shouting and screaming. Many streets had been on fire. It was tumultuous chaos, and it eventually reached the doors of the Red Fort. The sepoys had stormed the palace and demanded to see the emperor. The emperor had given them his blessing, and after that nothing could stop them. They rode up and down the streets, shouting and taking the best of everything for themselves – including all of the sweets. They apparently expected to be treated almost as well as the emperor. They got angry when they were not. They robbed shops and houses, and took what little food there was.

Copperton decided to take the boy with them and ask that he be given sanctuary, but was not entirely hopeful that this request would be granted. Everything around them seemed eerily desolate as they walked back down the deserted Chandni Chawk. Copperton wondered what would become of the rebel sowar who'd left Petey unharmed. If he had any sense, he'd disguise himself as a civilian and make his way to the Ajmeri Gate, otherwise the British would kill him on sight.

'I still cannot believe Powell betrayed us.' Jatin shook his head, having voiced the thought that had been rankling in the back of Copperton's mind for some time. No doubt Jatin felt the sting of betrayal the greatest, since he'd known Powell the longest. Even so, despite Powell's blunt, cynical manner, Copperton had taken him into his confidence and thoroughly believed him to be one of them. And then Powell had made Fowler order him to shoot Petey dead just to prove a point. Judas.

'I can't say I'm surprised,' remarked Petey, who was becoming more lucid. 'I never trusted him – not really. I can't say I suspected him of being involved in this, but I suppose it makes sense, seeing as he had no loyalty to any particular race or religion. He belonged to both and neither.'

Copperton shook his head. 'For Powell, this was about power and revenge, Petey. He's been shunned and overlooked since he was a child, while his brother had everything, and he nursed that feeling of injustice as he grew to adulthood. Even in the army, as a sepoy, he was unable to gain the recognition he craved, despite his intelligence and skill as a soldier. Powell wanted to feel important and for someone to take notice of him.'

'And to make a great deal of money while he was at it. Greed knows no bounds.'

Ali tugged at Jatin's coat sleeve and asked him a question. Jatin's answer seemed to satisfy him.

'What did he just ask you?' said Copperton.

'What we were talking about. I explained to him the best I could.' After a moment Jatin added, 'What did you mean when you said there were only two knights, Copperton? We saw all three together.'

'Not quite, Jatin. Recall what you saw: Powell took a white figurine with a white base out of his pocket, but only briefly and in the darkness of night. Had I magnified my vision, I would have seen the obvious – it was Petey's wooden knight, painted white.'

'Of course!' Petey laughed. 'I thought I'd misplaced it.'

'But why would…? I see!' Jatin exclaimed.

'The second black knight was in fact Powell's white knight. The base had been stained with charcoal or something. Note that he took possession of it immediately after I showed him it.'

'Crafty devil,' said Petey.

'But perhaps not as crafty as me.' Copperton held up the wooden figurine that he'd swiped from Powell as he'd knocked him unconscious. 'Powell wasn't too concerned that I'd witnessed Quincy testing the bomb, thinking the plot was still safe from detection. And even if I did find his note while searching Quincy's tent, he didn't think I'd be able to decipher it. But when I did, and happened across General Fowler's lost chess piece too, it put the wind up him. I think paranoia set in. He didn't discourage my idea that the knight was a warning, and desperately tried to encourage this belief.' Copperton tossed the knight to Petey, who just managed to catch it. He generously donated it to Ali after he expressed interest in it.

They walked down the narrow street adjacent to the Banking-house that brought them onto Canal Street. The canal ran down the middle of the street and Copperton was finally able to replenish his water supply. Crossing the canal, they turned into the street leading to St James's Church.

'What do you think they'll say when we tell them everything? You think they'll believe us?' Jatin asked Copperton.

'I couldn't say. At least we have the proof, even if we did use part of it on Petey. Everything depends on whether General Fowler keeps his word.'

Outside Skinner's House, they were greeted by a close order line of infantry, with their rifles pointed at Copperton, and mounted officers behind them. He spied the traitor Quincy amongst them – apparently recovered from his illness. Copperton also spied several snipers at the windows of the surrounding buildings.

'Stay where you are, soldier,' warned Quincy.

'Excuse me, gentlemen, but we are not the enemy. The siege is over – should we not be celebrating?' asked Petey from the buggy.

A dark-haired major whom Copperton did not recognise rode forward. 'Major-General Quincy told us about Henry Powell's plan and your involvement in it as his accomplices. He says that the automaton disobeyed orders and shot Brigadier-General Fowler dead several days ago, after he learnt about your plot.'

'That's a lie!' cried Jatin. 'Quincy is the traitor, along with Powell—'

'We also have a witness who says the automaton threatened to crush the skulls of two men.'

Copperton saw that wretch, Private Evans, lurking behind the officer's horse.

'It has been decided that the mechanical soldier is to be destroyed,' continued the major.

Petey snorted. 'Executed by firing squad? You do realise that bullets are useless against him?'

'If that fails, we have a contingency plan.'

As the officer spoke, a cannon was wheeled towards them.

'I'm sure even you, soldier, could not withstand the blast from a cannon,' General Quincy smirked.

Copperton studied the men's faces and then the cannon. Faced against an opponent such as this, he would have to play his ace. He had only used it once at the masters' house, and only they knew about it.

Discretion is your greatest ally. Don't let them know all of your secrets. He'd thought Master Douglas was referring to the mutineers, when really,

Copperton now realised, he had meant the British officers.

Copperton thumped the hallmarked medal on his chest. 'Steamknight!'

He was instantly enveloped in a shroud of steam. All that was visible from the outside were shifting shadows within the dense vapour. When the steam disappeared, the figure that emerged caused many of the foot soldiers to gasp and retreat several paces.

In the place of Copperton's slender form was a seven-foot-high steel juggernaut, clad in thick, armoured plating. His red eyes glowed from deep within his helmet. A cape bearing the union flag billowed out behind him. He drew his sword from its scabbard, the weapon now seeming petty and spindly in his gauntlet of a hand. But upon pressing a button on the pommel, and with a movement of his wrist too fast for the human eye, it transformed into a gleaming silver longsword.

Petey, Jatin and Ali looked amazed.

The curls of steam emitting from Copperton's joints faded to nothing and he straightened to his full height.

'Now...' His voice sounded deeper from inside the bevor. 'Which of you is man enough to strike me first?'

The wind suddenly changed direction and the cape flung itself over his head. He grasped it and there was a sound like a bedsheet tearing as he ripped it clean away, tossing it to the ground.

The officers looked at one another quizzically.

'Come on, you dogs!' cried Petey. 'You shot women and children – you can take a shot at him!'

General Quincy's horse stepped forward and its rider shakily aimed his Colt at Petey. 'You be quiet.'

'How typical of you, Quincy, going for the weakling.'

'Hold your tongue, Private, or I'll maim your arms as well as your legs.'

Copperton strode over to where his friend lay and placed himself before him. He looked down at General Quincy. 'I dare you to try.'

General Quincy stared at him with wild eyes. The revolver shook in his hand and then discharged. The bullet rebounded off the gleaming silver armour and struck the officer in the shoulder. He clutched the wound and gritted his teeth.

'Enough!' boomed a familiar voice.

General Brassington's horse galloped into the middle of the scene.

'Well, you are certainly full of surprises. Your makers failed to mention any of *this*.' He waved his sword at Copperton. His attention was captured by the groaning Quincy. 'You *shot* a commanding officer?'

'Technically, he shot himself, General,' replied Copperton.

'General Quincy shot at Copperton first, sir,' added Petey.

General Brassington scowled at Petey. '*You* should be shot for treason. I received word that the android and three men had disappeared, so I rode here personally, risking exposure to cholera, to see if the report was false. Don't think I have come to defend you.' He looked sternly at Copperton. 'Soldier, remain where you are. You are not to try and escape.'

'I have no intention of fleeing, sir. I am no coward. I only ask that you spare my friends and the boy.'

'Oh, your friends will get what they deserve,' said the grave-faced major. Two soldiers took hold of Jatin's arms and forced him to kneel, while a third trained his rifle on him. Another four surrounded Petey's buggy. Ali struggled fiercely as an enormous, red-faced captain clamped his arms around him.

'*Mujhe jaane do!*' shouted the boy. He became still when his captor whipped out his gun. Ali scowled at him, and Copperton admired his courage.

'If you try to disobey General Brassington's order not to flee, then we will shoot your friends. We cannot take you at your word – we have already learnt that much. Prepare the cannon!' ordered the major.

The men retreated away from Copperton, dragging Petey, Jatin and Ali along with them. Copperton found himself staring at the mouth of the cannon as the fuse was lit. Copperton thought of several strategies, but they would all result in an explosion that would undoubtedly cause many fatalities. As he considered his options, a cannonball shot out with a puff of smoke and a loud bang. Copperton felt it slam into his chest. He found his feet were being dragged along the ground as the force of the shot sent him reeling back, but he did not fall. When he came to a stop, hearing many startled gasps from the men around him, he looked down at the cannonball nestled in his chest. He pulled it out, seeing that it had dented his plating. A couple of mechanisms had come loose inside him. No matter. He held the cannonball in his glittering hands and crushed it.

'Fire again!'

As the men hurried to reload the cannon, Copperton strolled towards them. Raising his sword above his head, he sliced straight through the cannon.

'Fire your guns!'

A storm of bullets engulfed Copperton. He stood there motionless, feeling the patter of the bullets as they rebounded off him. One or two of them became lodged in his plating, but he picked them off like scabs as he continued to be fired at. Eventually the hailstorm passed. It seemed they had run out of ammunition.

'Save your bullets for the mutineers,' he said. 'Now release my friends or I shall demonstrate my true strength. If I can crush a cannonball, I'm sure I can crush your skulls with as much effort as it would take any of you to squish a grape.'

'I have seen him do it!' cried Jatin, his acting proving superb.

Terror filled the eyes of many of the men. None of them dared to speak. Jatin, Ali and Petey were released, Petey grinning broadly as he addressed General Brassington.

'So how exactly do you intend to explain all this? I'm sure the commander-in-chief would be interested to hear about your and Quincy's secret plans. You'd both be severely punished, if not cashiered. Fowler would probably fare better, since he was only an accomplice. It was General Fowler's brother, Powell, who was behind the plan to use a new chemical bomb. But I'm assuming Quincy and Fowler told you all about that?'

General Brassington was dumb. He glared at General Quincy, whose face told plainly that he was guilty of Petey's accusation.

'I shall want to hear all about this later, Horatio,' he said, flinching away when his arm threatened to brush Quincy's bloodstained coat.

'How about this – you ship Copperton and me on a boat to England and let this whole embarrassing affair be forgotten?' offered Petey.

'And see to it that Private Peterson receives an invalid pension, considering he is gravely wounded,' added Copperton.

'You're in no position to be negotiating,' General Brassington growled.

'Sir, I think we should consider all options,' urged Quincy.

General Brassington ignored him. 'And what of General Fowler and his brother?'

'General Fowler will confess to his share in the bomb business. He's an

242

honourable man.' Petey stared meaningfully at General Quincy. 'And I'm sure you can testify to Powell's guilt.'

General Brassington's gaze travelled between Petey and Copperton. He appeared at a loss to know what to do.

'Well, General Brassington?' demanded Copperton. 'What will your decision be?'

Chapter Twenty-Seven

'There, that should do it.' Douglas rose to his feet with a spanner still in his hand. 'Not too tight, I hope?'

'Oh no – not that I can feel it, of course.' Petey smiled from the armchair, looking down at his gleaming metal calves. His trousers were rolled back as far as the stubs below his knees, which the artificial legs neatly slotted over.

'What do you reckon, Sal?' He craned his neck to face the blonde young woman standing directly behind the armchair. 'Do I look a sight?'

'Undoubtedly.' She gave him a tender smile as she put her gloved hand on his shoulder.

'What about you, Colonel? Think I could take you on in a foot race now?'

The android, who was standing a little to the young lady's left, replied, 'I think you should master walking first, Private. Then you can challenge me.'

'Well, these new legs are better than those matchsticks you walk on.'

'You might be able to take the colonel on in a race,' said Douglas. 'Those legs are made of the same compound as his body.'

'And freer of impurities,' added George, who was at the other end of the drawing room putting their tools away.

'Can I try walking with them?' asked Petey excitedly.

'By all means, Mr Peterson. In fact, we won't let you out of this room with them unless you can cross the length of the rug without much difficulty,' Douglas smiled.

With Sally holding his arm, Petey pushed himself onto his feet. He staggered a couple of steps forward like a child learning to walk. Both Sally and Copperton hovered close by and were ready to catch him at any moment. He had only covered a distance of around six yards when he looked about to fall forwards, but he caught hold of a chair arm and steadied himself. Thank goodness he'd fully recovered the use of his left hand. He managed to take larger and larger strides, eventually reaching the end of the rug. He beamed at his audience.

'How was that?' he asked.

'Not bad,' said Douglas. 'Try walking back again now.'

Petey managed the return journey in less time and with more confident strides.

'Well, I think we can risk letting you loose on them, although I'd caution you to take your time getting used to them.'

'I can guarantee, Master Douglas, that he will ignore the warning,' said Copperton.

'What about these?' George held up the wooden crutches that Petey had previously been using.

Petey grinned. 'I suppose you could use them for firewood.'

'You might find that you still need to rely on them for the foreseeable future if you struggle with the artificial legs,' George warned.

'I intend to get him a very smart cane as an early wedding gift.' Sally wrapped her arm around her fiancé's. Petey smiled at her affectionately as she gently forced him back into the armchair. She then perched on the chair's right arm.

'Very well.' George propped the crutches beside the fireplace. (He reminded himself to move the newly finished rosewood cane with the gold topper from his study worktable to somewhere hidden from view. He couldn't have Douglas seeing it before his birthday, which wasn't actually until the fourteenth of next month, George having reasoned it was better to complete his present when he'd actually found a spare moment in which to do so. He just hoped his brother would stop using that bloody gauntlet as a means of defence after he gave him the cane.)

The drawing room door swung inwards and the under-housemaid, Betsey, brought in the tea tray, thirty minutes after it had been requested. She was a hearty girl with a moon-shaped face, who looked older than her fifteen years. Her brows were knitted together in concentration as she set the tray on the table. Douglas had overheard Mrs Baxter scolding her for her sloppy manners and rudeness many times. But the girl worked hard when left to herself and she took everything in her stride. If she was unnerved by the automata, she didn't show it. She'd confessed to Molly that her grandmother had only reprised her role as housekeeper because she'd quarrelled with her daughter not long after she went to live with her, following Mr Baxter's death – which was not the result of a carthorse accident but a precarious heart. Rather than helping to care for her six grandchildren, Mrs Baxter sat in a chair inventing ailments and criticising the way Betsey's mother ran her house, until Mrs Bates couldn't stand it any more.

Betsey exited the room with the grace of a rhinoceros, causing the ornamental vases on the mantle to rattle. She failed to close the door properly, and left it ajar.

'So how long have you been back in England?' Douglas enquired.

'Four days,' answered Copperton. Sally handed him a cup of water and her betrothed a cup of tea. 'We docked at Southampton, where Miss Sally was waiting for us, and then caught a series of trains to Hertfordshire. There was only just time to write that we were on our way to you, in between jumping out of one train and into another, and the trains were so unusually punctual that we threatened to overtake the letter. The wireless receiver was beyond repair after I was struck in the chest by that cannonball.'

'We had quite the shock last night when we received your letter, that's certain! We believed you were over four thousand miles away in India. Now that you're repaired and Mr Peterson has his new legs, we'll have the rest of your story.'

'What became of Quincy and Fowler?' George asked as he sat on the sofa beside his brother.

'General Quincy was court-martialled for treason and cashiered. They dashed his medals on the ground, then ripped the braid, buttons and epaulettes off his coat. General Fowler more or less got off scot-free. No one believed an officer of such exemplary conduct could be involved in the plot – they even made him a major-general following Quincy's dismissal. They thought he was trying to protect his brother. There was no evidence to connect him to the affair, anyway,' said Copperton.

'But General Quincy's cousin has evidence against him. He could use it one day,' Douglas pointed out.

Copperton put down his cup of water. 'General Fowler intends to marry Miss Quincy.'

'Ah. So Dr Quincy has every reason to let the matter rest, if it means his sister becomes mistress of Spurwick Abbey. What became of your friend, Jatin Singh? And the boy Ali?'

'Ali's family in Delhi were almost certainly killed by the British, and so he was taken in by his uncle in Simla,' answered Petey. 'General Fowler got Jatin a post as secretary to his uncle's friend, who's a surgeon and trader for the Company. The man was quite taken with Jatin, and even bothers to help him improve his English. Maybe he will attend university in the near future, if his benefactor's generosity stretches that far. Of course, Jatin was offered the post in return for his silence, although he intends to write a poem about what happened – an "English epic", he says. He's going to call it *The Copper Chevalier*.' Petey grinned. 'Everything will come out in the papers a month or two from now. Well, most of it. No mention of Colonel Copperton or Powell's weapon, of course. Military secrets. They'll invent an alternative story – maybe that Quincy and Powell were selling arms to the rebels. How they'll explain the stories and letters home from all the soldiers who saw Copperton, I don't know. Apparently word of Copperton has reached Lord Palmerston himself, and he wants to keep it all hushed up. If Cop is lucky, he'll let him be and not send him off to war in future – or have him dismantled.'

'Most of the blame fell on Powell,' resumed Copperton. 'They would have hanged him had General Fowler not intervened and merely seen him dismissed like Quincy. General Fowler wished to take his brother to England and get him a position overseeing his engineering works.'

'Well, I suppose there's some justice in all that. Do you think the mutiny will be successful?' asked Douglas.

Copperton shook his head. 'The uprising lacked coordination from the very beginning. It was not a unified effort with clear leadership and organisation. Different parties wanted to achieve different things from it. Delhi's recapture by our men was no doubt a crushing blow to the rebels, although it is far from over. Several strongholds, such as Jhansi and Gwalior, are still holding.'

'Hm. I suppose we shall see,' remarked Douglas as he drank his tea.

There was a brief silence as their guests did likewise. Douglas eyed the empty decanter on the table, which sparkled in the cold winter sunlight crawling in from the windows. George had remained sober for four months now, although he was by no means cured of his dependence on spirits. Douglas was proud of his brother for showing such self-control thus far, even if he'd never dare tell him that.

There came the sound of glass smashing from another room. Martha screamed.

'Oh no, that'll be one of the automata causing trouble again,' Douglas sighed.

'Allow me, Master Douglas.' Copperton extended his left arm, which slithered through the open door and into the corridor. When Copperton reeled it in, he held his catch aloft in his gloved hand: the little drummer boy. (The banker had never sent for him, and so Douglas had made one or two modifications to the mechanical boy as a test.)

Copperton yanked the little automaton closer to his face, so he was made to look into his glowing red eyes. 'What do you have to say for yourself, little ruffian?'

'I'm sorry, Colonel Copperton,' the automaton lisped.

'Any more of your foolery and I'll lock you in the cellar.' He delivered this warning in a stern tone, although there wasn't much force behind his threat.

The drummer boy ran out of the room as soon as he was released.

Petey cleared his throat. 'Well, I suppose we had better not take up much more of your time. Our train will be leaving shortly.'

Douglas put down his cup. 'Our butler will show you out. My brother and I had better make sure the housemaid is fine, if you'll excuse us. George?'

George followed Douglas out of the room, allowing Copperton and Petey to say their private farewells.

Petey rose without much difficulty. (Copperton thought to himself how peculiar it still was to see him in civilian clothes and a cloth cap.) 'Well, it looks like I won't be seeing you for some time, so this will have to be farewell for now.'

Petey and Copperton shook hands.

'It's been an honour serving with you, Colonel Copperton.'

'Likewise, Petey. I wish you both the utmost happiness. I officially hand command of him over to you, Miss Sally.'

'I'll keep Simon in line, don't you fear, Colonel.' She winked. (How peculiar it also was to hear Petey referred to by his Christian name!)

'Oh, I almost forgot.' Petey reached into the carpetbag that his fiancée was holding open for him, and placed a brown paper-wrapped box on the table. 'A little present – from Sally and me. You'll need some sort of occupation now you're retired.'

He rejoined Sally, his strides now far more fluid, and took her arm. He turned to salute the colonel, then the couple left the room together. Copperton waited until their steps had faded before approaching the box on the table. Sitting down in the armchair, he carefully tore off the paper to reveal a cardboard box beneath. Inside were pieces of wood. He sifted through them and found a picture of HMS *Victory*, a list of instructions, a jar of a substance like thin honey, and a small paintbrush. All that was needed to make a model ship.

He softly began humming the tune to 'Cheer, Boys, Cheer', one of the songs the band played at the camp, and arranged the wooden pieces on the table.

Chapter Twenty-Eight

Molly spied the trio of natural sciences students walking the opposite way down the mineralogy gallery of the Ashmolean Museum. She stared straight ahead and tried to ignore them. Out of the corner of her eye she saw them pause expectantly as she approached.

'Mary, Mary, quite contrary, how does your garden grow?' they sang in hushed voices as she passed them by. The rest of the song chased after her across the echoing gallery as she marched on. Her grip tightened on the books in her arms until her knuckles whitened. She even felt her hair straining against its pins. (Miss Doddy might bemoan how unfashionable her hair was, but at least it was more respectable pinning it up than letting it hang naturally as she was accustomed to.) The three students tittered and chuckled as they went on their way. Stupid little schoolboys. Not worth her time. That was the third time a group of students had sung that song to her. It was a joke that one student, Professor Penrose's son, had started after she'd embarrassed him in class by answering a question he failed to. Again.

'I'll see to it that you're gone by the end of term, you bluestocking,' he'd hissed at the end of the lecture.

'You'll have to think of better names than that to call me if you want rid of me by Christmas,' she'd replied, smiling sweetly at him. Mr Blake Penrose had then discovered exactly who she was, presumably from his father, and found a number of ways to ridicule her based on this new intelligence. He apparently knew she was the granddaughter of a duke, as he'd bow to her and say 'my lady' whenever they met, and enquire if she'd recently dined with any members of the royal family.

Molly found herself at the museum's entrance and paused. She seemed to be alone. Feeling suddenly ridiculous, she picked the pins out of her hair and shook it free. To hell with respectability. What should she do with herself in the time she had before the next lecture began? She knew she should do her reading for experimental physics, but she was willing to put it off. Each time she returned home, she had a new set of questions on the subject to ask George. Sometimes, during her supplementary physics lessons, Douglas would wander past, scan his eyes over what they were doing and insist George had taught her it wrong. That wasn't how they taught it, that was too advanced, that sum was off by a fraction. Then they'd quarrel about it for five minutes or so. How she missed them both when she was away.

Since the laboratory in the Ashmolean's basement was not often used, she spent a lot of her time there between lectures. She was not bound by the strict rules and routines of Oxford life, since they did not consider her to be a true student. A lot of her fellow students, she thought, were just there to pass the time and drink excessively while appearing to be doing something. None of them were really expected to find a vocation at the end of their studies. No wonder they'd admitted her. Molly realised she'd been naive in assuming that all colleges and universities were of equal worth. Her tutor had spoken of the University College as a more liberal institution than Oxford, less grounded in religion and classics. She wondered if they'd be willing to teach a girl natural sciences. For all the new knowledge that she was learning at Oxford, she might as well have continued reading periodicals at home.

There was one student, Samuel Rose, who seemed to take his studies seriously. He was the son of a famous naturalist, and aspired to become a botanist. On catching his eye in the lecture theatre, Molly thought she recognised him. Samuel confessed he was the student who had flown away from her in the Royal Botanic Gardens at Kew during the summer.

'I saw you revive that palm and it unnerved me. I was quite terrified by your witch's powers.'

He was the only friend that she had at Oxford, although she feared that he might have feelings of an amorous nature for her. After the botany lecture that morning, she'd found a small card wedged between the pages of one of her books. A red rose was painted on the front of the card, and there was a long verse written inside that compared her to numerous flowers. (She would need to have stern words with Samuel.) From the rest of the students, she was met with contempt.

She'd found cheap lodgings near the college with Miss Doddy, an elderly spinster. The old lady must have hoped to have her as a companion, and could not comprehend that Molly had reading to do when she came back in the evening, thinking nothing of summoning her to the drawing room on a whim. It was too quiet at night, apart from Miss Doddy's crazy cockatoo squawking downstairs (Molly contemplated strangling that damn bird every night). She was used to noise: the old house creaking, clocks ticking, her brothers arguing. All the other students were probably at wine parties. Of course, she was never asked to these parties – not that she cared. It was bad enough being around her fellow students when they were sober. She couldn't wait for the end of the term when she would be able to go home for weeks at a time. The only three reasons she had for staying were the botany lectures, the Radcliffe Library, and her own pride.

Perhaps she'd go down to the laboratory and brew something. She didn't know what.

'Miss Abernathy?'

Molly froze, prickling at hearing herself addressed by a familiar voice. Behind her, with that usual stupid smile of his, was Arthur.

'What are you doing here?' she asked, side-stepping introductory pleasantries.

'I had a meeting with one of the professors here who's a potential client.' He advanced towards her a couple of steps. 'How are you finding it here?'

'Not easy, but I knew it would be challenging. Not so much the lessons but, you know, being a woman.' She gave a one-shouldered shrug, ashamed of how ridiculously fast her heart was beating.

'I wouldn't have thought you one to back down from a challenge,' he grinned.

'Who says I am? I'll see it through. You watch – I'll make them give me a degree.'

'I don't doubt you will.' There was a few seconds' silence. He was deliberating as usual. 'Do you have a lecture now?' he finally asked.

'No, not until later this afternoon.'

'I have no urgent business. Do you think we could walk through the campus's botanic gardens together, and have a conversation without insulting each other?'

Molly grinned. 'But where's the fun in that?'

She led the way outside. It was a cold, crisp day, and Molly wished she'd worn a thicker cloak. They were both silent as they made the short walk through the campus to the gardens. Molly wanted to ensure that she was fully calm before speaking again. 'I found your pocketbook,' she said as they passed through the stone gate that was the entrance to the gardens.

'Ah. I was wondering where that went.'

'I had a look through some of your sketches and notes. It seems you were kept busy while you were at your father's.'

'I couldn't help myself. I knew how keen you were to put things in motion.'

'It appears so. I underestimated you.' That was as close to an apology as he was going to get. She hated saying 'I'm sorry'. It sounded weak and empty. She preferred to let her actions speak for her.

'No. I was often preoccupied with other matters, or struggled to come to a decision regarding a particular part of the garden. Your accusations were justified.'

'You can have your pocketbook back, although you might have to wait until I next return home. It's on my desk.'

The botanic gardens were rather barren and bare now it was November. The wind toyed with the brown leaves littering the paths.

'Have you found another landscape gardener?' Arthur enquired.

'No. A different landscape gardener will come at it armed with a different vision. I think our plan is what I want.'

'*Our* plan?'

'Well, we often compromised on aspects of the design, didn't we?'

'True. But I'm no longer employed by your brother, so it's out of my hands. You'll have to convince my replacement of the old plan's superiority and hope he agrees.'

They sat down on a cold bench. The gardens were quite deserted;

apparently other people had more sense than to walk on a chilly afternoon in winter.

'Have you found a new project?' Molly asked as she placed her books down beside her.

'Not yet. I can convince hardly anyone to abandon marble urns and hedgerows. I'm too radical for them, thanks to you.'

Molly exhaled deeply, not believing what she was about to say. 'Would you care to return to your old one? If I can't convince my brothers of your worth, I'll pay your wages myself.'

He stared at her wide-eyed. 'But you can't possibly—'

'Do you know how much allowance I get a year?' She whispered the figure to him.

'Good God! That's nearly twice my yearly income!'

'It's my brothers' money really, although I'm thinking of investing some of it.' Molly wasn't stupid. It made little difference whether the money came from her pocket or her brothers', it was effectively the same. Besides, she was sure that she could persuade George and Douglas to let Arthur be her landscape gardener again, without risking bankrupting herself.

'You must value my expertise highly if you're willing to squander your fortune for me,' Arthur grinned.

'I plan on doing no such thing. Don't start thinking too highly of yourself, Mr Arthur.'

They smiled at each other. Arthur realised how much he'd missed that smile and those alluring green eyes. In truth, he hadn't been able to get Molly out of his mind these last two months. He'd only agreed to meet this Oxford professor on the chance that he'd run into her, knowing he was unlikely to get the commission. Yes, she was stubborn and often lost her temper with him, but he liked her all the more for it. As he looked into her eyes, he was overcome by a rush of tender warmth and happiness at having regained her friendship. It made him bold. Without thinking of what he was doing, he leant forward and kissed her.

Molly slapped him in the face.

The next minute, Arthur was sitting with a stooped posture and inclined away from her. His cheek still smarted.

'I'm sorry. I wasn't thinking clearly, or thinking at all really,' he said.

'Evidently.' He couldn't see her face for her hair, and her voice gave little clue as to what her mood was. Molly was trying to hide how deeply she was blushing. It had been shock rather than anger that had made her slap him. Although the fact he'd caught her off guard, and kissed her for the whole world to see, had angered her a little.

Arthur resumed speaking. 'It seems I made a grave mistake. I wrongly believed that your regard for me was the same as mine for you. But, in all fairness, you gave several indications that it was so.'

'What indications?'

'Well...' He hesitated. 'Certain things you said, your lack of formality with me, and how you never seemed to mind being in close proximity to me.'

Molly couldn't contradict him, as she had given him such indications without really realising it. 'I feel so at ease with you that I wasn't really thinking about what was proper or improper behaviour,' she confessed with a shrug. She realised that she'd started picking the dirt from her nails, and immediately stopped.

'Likewise,' said Arthur.

Molly shuffled along the bench so that she was closer to him, catching the scent of the eau de cologne she'd given him all that time ago.

'Perhaps I should give you a clearer indication of what my regard is for you.' She forcefully pressed her lips against his, readjusting the pressure as he repaid the kiss – with interest. Her inexperience showed itself, and each kiss felt rather mechanical to begin with. But she learnt quickly. Her initial self-consciousness melted away, and it felt like she was glowing inside. At some point Arthur lifted her onto his knee, but she didn't object. The roughness of his wool coat contrasted with the warm softness of his hair. They eventually retreated at almost exactly the same moment. Arthur smiled warmly at her and brushed back a lock of her wild hair that was sticking out at an odd angle. A look of mutual understanding passed between them.

'If you do choose to have me back as your landscape gardener, this might be a problem,' he said, although he didn't sound terribly concerned.

'I'm sure we can stop ourselves becoming too distracted.' Molly slid off his knee on hearing footsteps. The pair of them moved on as two elderly gentlemen appeared to claim the other end of the bench. Neither Molly nor Arthur paid much notice to the gardens as they strolled arm in arm down the path.

Author's Note

What is now commonly referred to by Indian and western historians as the First War of Indian Independence lasted between 1857 and 1858. This conflict has also been referred to by British historians as The Indian Mutiny or Sepoy Rebellion. I refer to the conflict as 'the mutiny' throughout *The Copper Chevalier* as this is a more contemporary reference for the period the novel is set in. I continue to use the term here for clarity and consistency. It is for a similar reason that place names mentioned in the novel are rendered as they were at the time, e.g. Calcutta (now Kolkata).

This book does not attempt to give a full history of the mutiny, as this was not possible within the scope of the story and, like Copperton, the reader is dropped into the midst of the conflict. To fully examine the causes, events and outcomes of the mutiny, I refer the reader to the Selected Bibliography below, in particular William Dalrymple's work, which paints a picture of life in Old Delhi under Company rule in the years immediately prior to the mutiny, before chronicling the siege of the city and its aftermath, showing events through the eyes of both Indians and Britons. Dalrymple highlights the topsy-turvy nature of the mutiny, which was neither entirely a coordinated nationalist uprising nor a religious war, but something harder to index. The causes of the mutiny are too complex to be discussed here, although two widely cited factors are the threat of imposed Christianisation on the sepoys and unaddressed grievances over pay and working conditions. The siege of Delhi was a turning point in the conflict, marking the beginning of the end for the rebellion.

Losses during the siege are estimated at 1,000 dead and 2,800 wounded on the British side and 5,000 to 10,000 dead or wounded on the rebels' side. This does not take into account the civilian death toll in Delhi during the British reprisals, for which no reliable figures exist. Many of those who escaped the city died from exposure, starvation or illness, while those who survived struggled to rebuild their lives. General Nicholson died as a result of his gunshot wound on 23 September 1857, three days after the end of the siege. The last Mughal emperor, Bahadur Shah Zafar II, after fleeing Delhi and taking refuge in Emperor Hamayun's tomb six miles away, was captured by the British, tried and exiled.

While the use of poison gas bombs during the siege is fictitious, natural and synthetic poisons have been utilised as weapons for over two millennia, with examples stretching as far back as ancient Greece. Using chlorine gas projectiles in warfare was discussed as early as the American Revolution in the 1860s. In the First World War, chemical weapons such as chlorine, phosgene, and mustard gas were responsible for 1.3 million casualties and approximately 90,000 deaths. Such weapons were subsequently banned under the 1925 Geneva Protocol.

One consequence of the mutiny's failure was that 'the East India Company was abolished and India came to be directly administered by the British Crown' (Lahiri, 2003: 36). Fremont-Barnes (2007) argues that another consequence was that the British mission to 'enlighten' and reform India along Western lines gave way to intense racial prejudice, with British settlers wanting as little to do with the native population as possible. India was finally granted independence from British rule in 1947, almost a hundred years after the mutiny.

While only a third of *The Copper Chevalier*'s action takes place in India, echoes of colonialism can be felt across the novel. While spices were initially the main commodity the Company exported to Britain, by the 1850s all manner of goods were being transported from India to England by merchants like the Fowlers. Tea, as Molly points out, was one such commodity, now being grown on Indian plantations. Other commodities included textiles, porcelain, salt – and opium. These luxuries came with a hidden cost.

Selected Bibliography:

Dalrymple, W. 2009. *The Last Mughal: The Fall of a Dynasty, Delhi, 1857* (London: Bloomsbury)

David, S. 2003. *The Indian Mutiny 1857* (London: Penguin)

Fremont-Barnes, G. 2007. *The Indian Mutiny 1857–58*. Essential Histories (Oxford: Osprey)

Islam, A. 2011. 'The Backlash in Delhi: British Treatment of the Mughal Royal Family following the Indian "Sepoy Mutiny" of 1857'. *Journal of Muslim Minority Affairs*. 31(2), pp. 197–215

Srivastava, P. K. 2018. 'Nationalism imagined? Hidden impacts of the uprising of 1857'. *South Asia Research*, 38(3), pp. 229–246

Tytler, Harriet. 1986. *An Englishwoman in India: The Memoirs of Harriet Tytler 1828–1858* (Oxford: Oxford University Press)

Young, K. [1902.] *Delhi – 1857; the siege, assault, and capture as given in the diary and correspondence of the late Colonel Keith Young* (Uckfield: The Naval & Military Press)

Lightning Source UK Ltd.
Milton Keynes UK
UKHW011345080322
399750UK00001B/85